NEVER TOO LATE

GLENDA POULTER

Affinity
Rainbow Publications

2025

Never Too Late
© 2025 by Glenda Poulter

Affinity E-Book Press NZ LTD
Canterbury, New Zealand

1st Edition

ISBN: 978-1-991357-12-0 (paperback)

All rights reserved.

This is a work of fiction. Names, characters, places, and incidents are the product of the author's imagination or are used fictitiously and any resemblance to actual persons living or dead, businesses, companies, events, or locales is entirely coincidental

Editor: A Koenig
Proof Editor: Lisa M
Cover Design: Irish Dragon Design
Production Design: Affinity Publication Services

ACKNOWLEDGMENTS

I have several people I would like to acknowledge for their encouragement and assistance.

Never Too Late is the result of a November writing challenge to write every day for thirty days. I'm grateful for the organizations that organize these challenges.

My beta readers, Cat Benson and Deb Irvin, and my final readers, Suzi Vilkman and Sarah Shaw, have been invaluable in helping me get this book ready for you, the readers, for whom I'm also grateful.

And last, but never least, I'd like to thank and acknowledge the hard workers at Affinity Press for helping me make *Never Too Late* the best it can be: Editor A Koenig, Proof Editor Lisa McDaniel, the Cover Designer – Irish Dragon Designs, and everyone at Affinity Publication Services. Thank you so much!

DEDICATION

I dedicate this book, like all of my books, to my long-suffering and loving partner, Lisa Beemon. All my love, now and always.

TABLE OF CONTENTS

CHAPTER ONE

Getting my hands in the soil helped calm the turmoil in my mind. The peaceful exercise of planting flowers along the edges of the sidewalk of my new house helped me feel somewhat normal. The cool breeze of approval had, as yet, not materialized.

When I heard the tires of a bicycle coming down the public walkway, I made sure I was out of the cyclist's way, but the sound stopped beside me, and I looked up. Instead of a bicycle, it was a tricycle ridden by a brown-eyed beauty staring at me from below her oversized helmet.

"Those are pretty salvia." The child smiled as she pushed the helmet off her face. "Red is my favorite color. Momma's, too."

"Thank you," I said, raising my eyebrows as I returned her smile. "You're pretty smart to know what these flowers are."

"Oh, that's because I help Daddy and Momma at the nursery all the time." She pointed at some of the other flowers in the bed. "Those red and yellow flowers are celosia, and those are impatiens. Hosta would look good under your tree."

I sat back and studied the child. She didn't look like she could be much over five years old, although she spoke with the certainty and maturity of a much older child. I looked around but didn't see anyone with her.

"Where do you live? Who are you staying with?"

Except as guests, children were not allowed in this over fifty-five neighborhood. Before she could answer, two women, one heavily pregnant, rounded the corner.

"Ocee, I told you to wait at the fire hydrant," the older woman said.

I stood up and wiped my dirty hands on my gardening apron, nerves on high alert.

"I planned to," Ocee said, "but when I saw her planting her flowers, I had to come say hello. Look how pretty they are."

"I'm sorry." The woman directed her attention towards me. Her piercing blue eyes caught me off-guard, and I was more tongue-tied than usual. "I hope she wasn't bothering you."

"Not at all," I managed to say without stammering. "She knows a lot about flowers and made a nice suggestion to help me out."

I glanced at the pregnant woman, who was bending slightly at what waist she had left.

"Would you like to sit down for a few minutes?" Despite the anxiety I felt when I was around strangers, I couldn't ignore someone in need. I gestured toward the slab of cement the housing developer called a porch, where I had put a couple of rocking chairs and a small table to make it look inviting.

"Thank you," she said. "I didn't know we would need to chase after my wayward child when we left Mom's house, and now I'm a bit tired."

The older woman took the younger woman's elbow and led her to a chair.

"Are you okay, Mae?" She squatted beside the chair.

Mae smiled, and the family resemblance between them shone through. I was curious about where Ocee's deep brown eyes and almost black hair came from since the two women had the bluest eyes I had ever seen, and Mae's hair was strawberry blonde. The other woman had a thick shock of silvery gray hair adorning her head.

"Let me get y'all something to drink," I said. "I have fresh-squeezed lemonade, water, and iced tea."

"Oh, no." The older woman stood up. "That's not necessary. By the way, I'm Tam Murphy. I live around the corner."

"I'm Janice Halston. My hands are kind of dirty, or I'd shake your hand. Please let me at least get Mae a glass of water. You're welcome to sit down, too."

"May I have some lemonade?" Ocee had left her trike and helmet at the edge of the sidewalk and followed us to the house.

"Ocee." Mae shook her head. "You've already pushed almost all of my buttons. Sit there and hush for a couple of minutes, please?"

I watched the child's eyes fill with tears as she plopped on the ground and leaned back against one of the porch columns, her arms folded across her chest.

3

"It's no trouble," I said. "She can be my guinea pig. It's the first time I made homemade lemonade instead of using a can."

Mae smiled, but it was a strained smile.

"That's sweet of you, Ms. Halston," she said. "You're kind to let me rest here a moment."

When I reached the kitchen, I inhaled deeply and wondered what I was doing as I washed my hands and took off my apron. It was out of character for the new me to invite people to visit, much less offer them refreshments.

I pulled a tray out of the cabinet and filled two glasses with water and one with lemonade. I put a few Oreos on a napkin for good measure. When I returned to the porch, Ocee was standing between her mother's knees with her hands on Mae's belly.

"Aaron, Mommy really needs you to come out of there," she said as I opened the screen door. She looked at me and smiled. "My baby brother is being stubborn. He needs to be born already."

"I'm sure he'll come when he's good and ready," I said. "Why don't you sit back down, and I'll give you your lemonade and a few cookies, if that's okay with your mother?"

I glanced at Mae as Ocee sat with a big grin on her face. Mae nodded, so I set the glass of lemonade and a napkin with two cookies on it in front of Ocee. I handed Mae and Tam each a glass of water.

"Your name sounds familiar, Ms. Halston," Mae said after taking a long drink of water. "May I ask what you do?"

"Mae, now look who's being rude," Tam said.

My heart was pounding as I considered answering Mae's question. For me, it was a loaded one, fraught with danger.

"Please, call me Janice," I said. "I've worn many hats over the years. Among other things, I'm an artist, a musician, and a writer. I used to teach at some of the local schools as well."

"Wow," Tam said. "That is a lot of hats. Have you hung them all up?"

"For the most part." I hoped it would be the end of the conversation.

"I like to draw." Ocee used the back of her hand to wipe her mouth. "And I want to learn to play the piano, but Daddy says we can't afford it. So, I'll just stick with the recorder Grams gave me for my birthday."

"Speaking of Daddy," Mae said, "he's supposed to pick us up pretty soon. We need to get back to Grams' house. Come help me up."

Ocee and Tam each took one of Mae's hands. I held the rocker still while she struggled to her feet. She winced, and Tam's face blanched.

"Sweetie, are you okay?" Tam leaned close to Mae.

"I'm fine, Mom. I promise. He's sitting low, and sometimes when I stand up, he rebels and pokes me."

I followed the small family to the sidewalk, where Ocee put her helmet on and climbed back on her tricycle.

"Thank you for the lemonade," she said. "May I come see your garden the next time we visit Grams?"

"You're welcome to come see it any time you want." The little girl didn't make me feel as threatened as most adults did. But neither did her mother or grandmother.

She grinned and took off toward the fire hydrant at high speed.

"Ocee, you wait right there," Tam yelled after her. "Don't get out of our sight again, or you won't be allowed to ride that thing anymore."

Ocee waved over her shoulder, and the other two women groaned in unison.

"Janice, thank you for your hospitality." Tam extended her hand. I only hesitated a moment before shaking it. The firm grip of her hand surprised me. She held my hand a moment longer than I expected, and I wondered if she sensed the same connection I had.

"You're more than welcome. Mae, good luck with the baby. I hope he comes soon. Y'all take care."

I watched as they slowly walked down the sidewalk to meet Ocee, who was doing donuts on her trike around the fire hydrant.

CHAPTER TWO

I occasionally thought of Ocee as I puttered around in the gardens during the following weeks. The flowers were blooming profusely, providing a carpet of color on either side of the sidewalk and along the front of the house. And the veggies I planted in the back garden—tomatoes, peppers, zucchini, cucumbers, and a few others—were producing for me.

"How do you like your new place?" my friend Allison asked me one day when we met for lunch. She was among the small number of people I knew I could rely on, even if she was an ass once in a while. "Are you all settled in?"

I nodded as I wiped my mouth with my napkin.

"It's nice. Kind of small, but I don't need much room. The best part is I've planted a little garden, and it's growing." I grinned at her. "I'm not the master gardener you and Beth are, but it looks like I'll have a few fresh tomatoes and peppers to show for my trouble. Y'all need to come visit."

Allison returned my grin as she raised her mug of coffee in salute.

"Congratulations," she said. "It sounds like we've lured you to the dark side."

"Not just you. I gardened with Mom when I was a kid, and Sandy and I dabbled in it in another lifetime."

"I forgot about that." Allison pushed her plate away from her and sat back. "Other than gardening, how are you doing? Honestly. Have you made any new friends?"

I sighed. Allison was well-meaning, but her questions still stung.

"I don't have any idea how I'm doing," I answered honestly. "Making friends is not something I plan to do. I just nod and smile at people and speak when spoken to. I helped one of my neighbors out several weeks ago, but I haven't seen her since. Look, Allison, I don't need or want any new friends. I'd rather not go through the trauma of explaining who I am and what actually happened."

"It's been almost three years since the shit hit the fan, Janice. People don't remember like you seem to believe they do." Allison leaned over the table and gave my hand a gentle squeeze. "And you won your case in court. That's why you could afford to buy your house. You have nothing to be ashamed of."

"You know that. Beth knows that. The courts know that. No one else seems to. All they remember when they hear my name are the accusations and bam, they're gone. So, I keep to myself."

"How can you be certain without speaking to people?" Allison tilted her head at me. "I'd be willing to bet ninety-nine percent of anyone you meet won't have any idea who you are, or why your name sounds familiar, or even care. It's time to release your paranoia."

I shook my head and said nothing. The anger left a metallic taste under my tongue. I was ready to lash out at my best friend, and I didn't want to do that. A cool breeze caressed my cheek, instantly taking away some of the ire.

"Come back to church, Janice. Everyone there knows you, and we all miss you and your music. It's not healthy to be alone all the time."

I shut my eyes for a minute. I had quit performing, quit showing my art, quit writing books when all hell broke loose, and I didn't plan on ever performing again. It was three years since it all began and almost a year since the court case concluded, but I believed people had longer memories than Allison assumed they did.

"Okay," Allison said as she squeezed my hand. "I won't push you. But at least come to dinner next week to celebrate Beth's birthday."

"How many people are going to be there, and who?" I already knew what I was going to do. Social gatherings were beyond my ability to handle safely or with any amount of confidence.

"Charles and Danny, and Melba and Carmen." Allison glanced at me. "People you know and love and who love you."

"I'll be a fifth wheel." I shook my head.

"You are a hard nut to crack." Allison checked her watch. "I told Beth I'd pick her up at three, so I need to get going. Please think about coming next week. If you don't come, Beth will be disappointed."

I rose when Allison did, and we shared a quick hug. I watched her leave before I returned to the booth and studied my unfinished lunch. My sparse appetite waned even more as I replayed our conversation, oblivious to what was going on around me. I jumped when someone touched me on the shoulder.

"Are you okay?" Tam asked. "When I said hello, you just sort of stared off into space."

"I…I'm sorry," I stammered. Allison and I had chosen an out-of-the-way diner so we wouldn't run into anyone we knew. "I guess I was off in another world. How are you and your family?"

"Do you mind if I join you?" Tam glanced at the empty booth bench across from me. "Or is your friend coming back?"

"I'm sorry," I said again, blushing at my lack of manners. "Please. Have a seat."

The waitress rushed over, cleared Allison's dishes from the table, and handed Tam a menu. She shook her head and handed it back.

"I already ate, thank you. But I'll have a glass of sweet tea, if you don't mind."

The two of us exchanged glances for a moment as the waitress scurried away. I was unsure of what to say, so I didn't say anything.

"Ocee asks me to drive by your house every time she comes to visit," Tam finally said. "Your flowers are beautiful."

"Thank you. How is Ocee and your daughter—uhm, I'm sorry, but I don't remember her name?" I blushed again.

"Her name is Mae. They're fine. Mae had the baby the day after we met you and he is precious, almost three months old now, and Ocee loves being a big sister." Tam's smile lit up her face. "They would love to see you again. We're having a 'gotcha' party for Ocee on Saturday afternoon. Why don't you drop by?"

"What kind of party?" I tried to figure out what she meant even as I began to sweat at the thought of meeting a house full of strangers.

Tam laughed. "We celebrate the anniversary of the day Ocee came to live with Mae and her husband, Duke, which also coincides with the day they finalized her adoption a couple of years ago. It's sort of like a birthday party with no presents since Ocee is our present, and we're hers."

"That explains her dark hair and brown eyes," I said, smiling. "I wondered about it since you and Mae both have blue eyes."

"And my hair was almost the same color as Mae's before I was blessed with wisdom hair." Tam ran her hand through her short hair.

"Wisdom hair. Hmm, I like that." I grinned at her. "My friend who was here calls my hair margarita salt and cayenne pepper hair."

Tam's laugh was contagious and full-bodied, and I laughed along with her.

"Does the cayenne pepper fit your personality? You seem more mellow than that."

"I have my moments," I admitted. "I am a lot more mellow since, uhm, well, since I grew older. Doesn't seem there's as much to go off about. Things don't bother me as much as they used to."

Tam was quiet for a moment while she studied my face.

"I have an admission to make." She looked away. "I googled your name the day we met you. You've had a full life. I believe if I were in your shoes, I'd be angry all the time, and yet you sit here looking as cool as a cucumber."

"Oh." I gulped. The newspaper articles and reports about me were anything but flattering. Since those articles had been published, my mental and physical health had suffered dramatically. I wondered when I would have to bolt from this conversation.

"I'm sorry. I didn't mean to embarrass you," she said, her brows furrowed. "It seems you came out on top and, hopefully, none the worse for wear."

"*None the worse for wear* is not how I would describe it. I'm not the person I was before. It was stupid to get fired over something as personal as my artwork and who I had sex with. But it was huge then. That's why I sued them, to show them how stupid it was. Winning the lawsuit and settlement surprised me, but it ruined my life."

I looked out the window, away from her.

Tam leaned on the table with her arms crossed in front of her.

"I'm sorry about that. From what I read, you were quite a success in the art world," she said. A strange look crossed her face. "Do you still have a website? I looked for the one mentioned in the articles, but I couldn't find it. I'm interested in seeing some of your work."

"The website is gone," I said with a slight croak in my voice. "I couldn't bear the ugliness sent by trolls and haters. A friend suggested I start a new site, but there isn't anything to put on it, and I doubt there will be."

"I don't know you." Tam reached across the table and took my hands. I'm not sure why, but I let her. She turned them over and studied my palms. "But I can tell from your gardens that you're a talented woman with a penchant for

color. You said you're a musician as well. Have you stopped
making music, too?"

I pulled my hands back and put them in my lap. Why was
this woman so curious about my life? And why was she
being so nice? The few people I had met socially since
everything happened were distant, cold, and rude. It was the
main reason I avoided meeting new people as much as
possible.

"I can see I've made you extremely uncomfortable."
Tam's eyes were bright, and I thought she was about to cry.
"That wasn't my intention. I believe you need friends who
are nonjudgmental and don't care about your past. What
happened to you before we met is none of my business
unless you decide it is, and I try hard not to judge people. If
you choose to trust someone again, here's my address and
phone number. You're welcome to come by or call anytime.
Ocee's party is at two on Saturday. I hope you'll try to
come."

Tam had pulled a pen and paper from her bag as she
spoke, and now she slid the paper across the table to me. I
looked at it but didn't pick it up. She gave my shoulder a
quick squeeze before walking away without another word. A
cool breeze rustled the paper and settled on the bench next to
me.

CHAPTER THREE

I argued with myself and Allison for the remainder of the week about attending Tam's party.

"Why not?" Allison asked for the umpteenth time. "So what if you don't know her? How will you get to know her if you don't go?"

"Allie, my heart is pounding so hard it hurts." The fear overwhelmed me—the fear of meeting new people, the fear my heart would stop from beating so fast—fear, plain, damaging fear.

"Take some deep breaths," she said. "Do you need me to come over?"

"No." I did as she said and took three deep breaths, and it helped calm me some. Something in me shifted as Sandy's cool breeze enveloped me, and I could almost sense her embrace. "I'm going to try, Allie. Can I call you if I get too overwhelmed?"

"You know you can." Allison's voice was gentle. "Beth and I will come and bring you home with us. I love you."

"I love you, too."

Saturday afternoon, I walked around the corner to Tam's house carrying a basket full of cut flowers and some early tomatoes and peppers. I stood and looked at the house, so similar to mine but decorated with streamers and balloons. Several parked cars lined Tam's driveway and the curb in front of the house. I could hear laughter coming from the backyard and the smoke from the outdoor cooker was filling the air with a delicious aroma.

I hesitated at the end of the sidewalk. It had been quite a while since I was at a social gathering, and even with Sandy with me in spirit, I wasn't sure I was ready to take the chance now. As I was about to turn to head back home, a small whirlwind flew out the front door and wrapped her arms around my legs.

"Hi, Miss Janice." Ocee grinned up at me. "Grams said you might come, but Mommy told me not to count on it, and look at this, here you are. Come say hello to everyone."

She grabbed my free hand and led me toward the house. Tam was standing on the porch, her arms crossed, trying to scowl but failing miserably. She grinned at me and took the basket before giving me a quick one-arm hug.

"I said no gifts." She held the door open for me to enter. Ocee had already run through the house and out the sliding door to the patio.

"I know." I smiled. "But I know how much Ocee likes my flowers, and I have an overabundance, so I wanted to share them with her. And you. There are tomatoes and peppers from my vegetable patch in the basket, too."

"Thank you." By then, we were in her kitchen. Dishes of food and desserts covered every counter and the small kitchen table.

"Should I have brought something to share?"

"Oh, no." Tam laughed as she pulled a couple of vases from a cabinet. "As you can see, we have more than enough. I might slice these beautiful tomatoes, though. They look scrumptious."

"Miss Janice, you have to come see my baby brother." Ocee banged through the kitchen door and grabbed me by the hand again. "He's out here in his bouncy chair."

I allowed her to lead me through the door and onto the patio. Mae sat in a lawn chair next to the baby's seat, keeping it moving with her foot. She smiled at me.

"Hi, Ms. Halston," she said. "I'm happy you were able to come today."

"Please, call me Janice." I bent over the baby. "Oh, my. Look at that red hair. He is as cute as a button. Remind me what his name is?"

"Aaron Duke Gallagher." Ocee squatted next to her brother. She took his hand and kissed it. The baby's face lit up, and he gave an adorable baby laugh. "Isn't he precious?"

"He definitely is precious." I grinned at her. "And it looks like he adores his big sister."

"Oh, he definitely does." Mae chuckled. "He grinned at her first, laughed at her first, and she can make him stop crying just by walking in the room."

She got up and looked down at her children.

"Ocee, stay here with Aaron while I introduce Miss Janice to Daddy and the others."

Ocee nodded as she leaned over and gave Aaron tummy raspberries, making the baby chortle in a way that elicited

16

grins from everyone in the vicinity. Mae led me to the cooker, where a tall, thin man with a head full of red curls similar to Aaron's was flipping hamburgers.

"Janice, this is my husband, Duke," she said as she slipped an arm around his waist. The look he gave her melted my heart. It had been quite a while since I last witnessed so much love between two people. "Duke, Janice has the most beautiful flower garden."

"And she brought some of those flowers to share." Tam joined us. "And a basket of tomatoes and peppers. I sliced the tomatoes and put them with the other sandwich makings."

"It's nice to meet you, Janice," Duke said. "I'd love to see your garden someday. Mae and I own a nursery here in town."

"I remember Ocee mentioning something about helping y'all at the nursery. I live around the corner. You're more than welcome to stop by anytime."

Duke and Mae laughed as they glanced over at Ocee playing with the baby.

"I guess you could call it help," Mae said. "She entertains our customers more than anything else."

Mae took me by the elbow, led me around the small yard and introduced me to the rest of the guests, most of them members of Duke's family. I was glad when she only used my first name in the introductions. It kept at bay the weird looks I usually got and helped me stay calm.

Tam brought me a glass of lemonade when Mae and I returned to the patio. As she opened her mouth to say something, Duke cleared his throat to get everyone's attention. Ocee stood in front of him, leaning back against

17

his legs, and he had a hand on each of her shoulders. She looked up at him with a sweet smile.

"Thank you all for coming today," he said. "It's a special day for our little family because it is the day this one came into our lives and made us a complete family. She was so tiny and so vulnerable, but look at her now, our little live wire."

Everyone laughed, including Ocee.

"It's also the day the courts officially made her our daughter, and we are so blessed," Duke said, a bit of a catch in his voice. He squatted beside her, and she threw her arms around his neck. "Ocala Marie Gallagher, you are my best girl, after Mommy, of course, and you always will be."

"Thank you for choosing me, Daddy." She dried a tear from his face.

I had to wipe my tears away, and from the sniffles I heard around me, I knew I wasn't the only one.

"Well, then." Duke stood up and cleared his throat again. "These burgers and hot dogs are ready when y'all are. Thanks again for coming today to help us celebrate."

It was a nice surprise to find I enjoyed visiting with Tam's guests. Everyone was welcoming and accepted me as though I was one of them. They included me in their conversations. Several filled me in on some of the inside jokes and about the antics of Ocee as she grew from infant to almost school age. Most of my fear stayed at bay.

As the day wound down, a few people left but almost everyone else, including me, pitched in and, by the time Duke and Mae tucked their children into their car seats, Tam's house barely looked as if anyone had visited, much less hosted a party. I turned to Tam to thank her for the invitation and hospitality and found her smiling at me, her head tilted to one side.

"I'm glad you came today," she said. "Why don't you come back inside? We can take a bit of time to get to know each other. I can get us some more lemonade, or something harder if you prefer."

"Uhm, well, I, well …" I stammered, trying to find a polite way to decline her invitation and race back to the safe sanctuary of my house and garden. She touched my arm.

"Come on, Janice," she said. "You're going to go home to your empty house, and I'd lay a bet you'll either veg in front of the TV or get lost on the computer or tablet or phone or whatever. I need to recover from the day, and I hate doing it alone. Stay for half-an-hour or so. Please?"

I couldn't keep from smiling when she nailed exactly how I planned to spend my evening—the TV droning in the background while I surfed the net or read a book. Sandy's cool breeze encouraged me to stay.

"When you put it that way, how can I say no?"

Tam opened the screen door and stood back so I could go inside. After the late afternoon and early evening heat, the coolness of her living room was a relief.

"I have to make a pit stop, but then I'll bring us some lemonade," she said. "Make yourself comfortable, and I'll be right back."

I watched as she headed to the back of the house and gave myself a mental shake when I realized I was admiring how well she filled out her blue jean shorts. There were a few other times that day—such as when she smiled at me or her cleavage became a bit deeper when she laughed—when I had reminded myself that I was not currently, nor for the foreseeable future, seeking a relationship with anyone.

Family photos covered one of the living room walls. On a small table set in the center of the wall, a folded flag in a display case had a place of honor. Next to it was a picture of a grinning young man in full military gear whose family resemblance to Mae and Tam was uncanny. A set of dog tags hung from the corner of the picture frame.

The pictures on the wall were of Tam with Mae and the young man from the time they were infants, through their teen years, and then young adulthood. A few included a man who was no doubt the kids' father, and more than a few were with a woman I assumed was Tam's sister or some other relative, as well as some of the kids and their friends. Senior school pictures of Mae and the young man, his formal Army portraits, Mae on her wedding day, and pictures of Mae and Duke holding Ocee as an infant graced the wall. Photos of the family with baby Aaron rounded out the pictures.

I turned when the door between the kitchen and living room swung open. Tam had a tray with fresh glasses of lemonade as well as some crackers and grapes. I took it from her, and our fingers brushed as the tray changed hands. The unusual feeling of connection flowed through me once again. Tam plopped into the comfortable-looking recliner as I set the tray on the table. I made myself at home on her couch and gestured at the wall of photographs.

"You have a beautiful family," I said. "Mae was a cutie pie as a child and has turned into a beautiful young woman. Do you mind if I ask who the young man is?"

A shadow crossed Tam's face before she smiled at the pictures of her family.

"That's my son, Aaron," she said. "We lost him in Afghanistan about eight years ago. He was a pretty special kid. He would be over the moon that Mae named the baby after him."

"I'm sorry." I did a mental face-palm at my huge faux pas and wondered if I would ever learn to keep my mouth shut. After sixty years, I was beginning to believe it was a lost cause. Another good reason not to leave home.

"No need to apologize." Tam reached over and patted my knee. "You have a right to be curious, and I'm proud of him and the man he became and the sacrifice he made. I love talking about the kids, so they're a dangerous subject because sometimes I can't stop once I get started. Do you have a family?"

"No. I never married, so no kids or spouse. Well, that's not technically true. I was in a long-term relationship, but she died in 2015. And you read in the news reports about how my last so-called relationship ended." I cocked my head toward her wall. "Even when I was growing up, I didn't have a family like yours. I envy you for that."

"Tell me about your partner. What was her name? What was she like? If you were in a long-term relationship, she must have been pretty special. Do you mind talking about her, or is it still too painful?"

"It will always be painful." I couldn't help but smile as memories of Sandy flowed over me, and her cool breeze settled beside me. "But, yes, she was pretty special. She worked hard to get me to fall in love with her, and once I did, there was no looking back."

"How long were y'all together before she passed?"

"Since college. Right at thirty years." I grinned as I remembered how Sandy and I met. "We were in the same gym class. She was in the class by choice, me, because it was a required course. The story she told people about why she fell in love with me was that I looked so lost and vulnerable in class that she had to rescue me and take care of me. She was athletic and loved playing in pick-up baseball or basketball games. I always watched and cheered from the sidelines."

"And you? Why did you fall in love with her?" Tam's smile was gentle and empathetic.

"Oh, I tried not to," I admitted. "I was a bit of a player, and I enjoyed having a string of women to choose from. But Sandy was always there to help me regain my balance when I stumbled or had a bit too much to drink. She made sure I cracked my books and stayed on track with the boring or the tough classes. I doubt I would have graduated without her pushing me."

I sipped my lemonade as I reflected on those days. How I tried to distance myself from Sandy after graduation, and how she chased me to keep me in her life. Tam sat in silence, watching me.

"I got a job teaching art and music in a private school while she worked on her master's in mathematics and computer science. She was so smart I couldn't figure out what she saw in me. But she was always there, regardless of what an ass I was, and soon not being with her was torture. I moved in with her within a year of graduation, and we were together until, well, until."

"What did y'all do for fun?" Tam leaned over, put some crackers and grapes on a napkin, and handed them to me. "Was it always something athletic?"

I laughed.

"She tried to get me interested in sports, but it didn't happen. I could play mini-golf, and I was a decent bowler.

And we both loved to hike and swim. We went camping on a regular basis."

"Do you still do any of those things?" Tam tilted her head at me. "I used to bowl a lot. Both kids were in junior bowling leagues. Aaron played every sport available to him, but Mae preferred to skate—not figure skating, though. She liked to go fast."

"That's where Ocee got it from," I said without thinking. When I realized what I said, I face-palmed myself.

Tam laughed.

"I've said the same thing. Despite being adopted, she has a lot of the same traits Mae had as a child. If a person can be reincarnated while they're still alive, Ocee is Mae."

"Ocee seems to be such a special kid. Smart as a whip." I smiled as I recollected some of the conversations I overheard her having with the adults at her party.

"Too damn smart." Tam groaned. "We were so scared she would be brain damaged considering what she lived through before she came to Mae and Duke. Her biological parents were both addicts, and she was addicted when she was born. The withdrawals the poor child suffered were horrendous and heart-wrenching. There were times we didn't know if she would survive. But she not only survived, she's thriving."

"Poor kid," I said, shaking my head. "Why did Mae name her Ocala?"

"Oh, Mae didn't. Ocala was her name when she came to them. Mae and Duke kept it, even though they could have changed it. They had a DNA test done. She is almost one hundred percent native people, and Ocala is a native people's name, so they kept it in homage to her heritage."

I looked around the living room, and my eye caught the clock on the desk on the far side of the room.

"Good grief. It's almost nine o'clock. I should get out of your hair. Thanks for having me and for letting me ramble. It's been quite a while since I talked so much."

We both rose and walked to the front door. After an awkward moment, Tam pulled me into a hug, which I tentatively returned.

"You should have a chance to open up more often," she said as she stepped back. "I've enjoyed getting better acquainted with you. Let's get together again sometime. Are you planning on going to the community center's midsummer celebration?"

I had avoided all the social activities the community put on. The closest I came to being social was when I swam laps at the pool and said hello or nodded when acknowledged by other women in the locker room. Even that took more out of me than was reasonable. I hated the idea of having to socialize with a bunch of people I'd never met, even though I'd survived her small party unscathed.

"Uhm, no. I hadn't even thought about it," I lied.

"I haven't been to one yet," she said. "I'd like to go, but going alone, well, I'm a bit socially shy, and doing activities without company is really difficult. Would you consider going with me?"

I hated to say no after she had been so hospitable to me. But I remembered something.

"I have to check the date. If I'm not mistaken, one of my friend's birthday dinner is on the same day. Let me look, and I'll let you know."

"That's fair. Well, I hope the mosquitos don't carry you away. Would you like something to put on your skin before you leave?"

I thanked her but shook my head. After a moment of silence while I wondered if there was something else I should do or say, I pushed through the front door and waved at her as I headed toward home, Sandy's cool breeze beside me.

CHAPTER FOUR

The following Saturday, I secluded myself in my cottage and avoided all contact with anyone in the world. I had no desire to go to either Beth's birthday dinner or the social at the community center. It was easier to hide out, to have nothing to do with anyone. The curtains on the living room windows stayed closed, and I only ventured out the backdoor because I had a privacy fence and no one could see me.

But my pushy friends had other plans for me. I jumped when the doorbell interrupted my reading mid-afternoon. I peeked through the peephole and groaned. Not only was Allison standing on the front porch, but also her partner, Beth, as well as the four other people she told me would be at Beth's party. Each of them held a dish of food or a bag in their hand, except for Allison, who held an armful of flowers she picked from my garden on her way to the door.

"I'm not home," I yelled through the door.

Allison laughed while everyone else grinned.

"In that case, we'll camp here on your front porch until you get home," she said.

Everyone disappeared from view as they moved toward the rocking chairs. I pulled the curtain back just enough to see what they were doing. Charles and Danny were heading back to their car. I hoped it meant they were leaving, but instead, they pulled camp chairs from the SUV and headed back to the porch. Soon, the motley crew had scattered across the porch and yard. Someone produced a bottle of wine and some wine glasses. Allison caught me watching and put her face against the window.

"Come on, Janny," she said. "Either open the door and let us in or come out here and join us. But we're not leaving until Beth blows out the candles on her cake at sundown."

I dropped the curtain so that she couldn't see me, and I couldn't see them.

"Goddamn it, Sandy," I whispered. "Why did you have to introduce me to these idiots?"

A cool breeze brushed the back of my neck, and I struggled to keep my tears at bay.

"Okay. This once. But then I'm done with them."

The breeze caressed my face and was gone.

I opened the door to the cheers of my friends. They gathered the food and the wine, and I stepped aside to let them in. They each planted a kiss on my cheek as they passed by. Allison was last, and she attempted to hug me, but I stiffened and shook my head.

"Unh-uh," I said. "I'm mad at you. I don't hug people I'm mad at."

"Even people who bring you flowers?" Allison grinned as she presented me with the bouquet of my own blossoms.

"Which you ripped out of my garden without permission." But her grin and happiness were contagious, and I couldn't help but laugh as she tried once again to hug me. This time, I let her.

"This is cute," Melba said as she looked around the living room. "You want to show us the rest, or can we do a self-guided tour?"

I gestured toward the hallway.

"Help yourself. There's not much to see, but it's home, and I love it."

Beth slid an arm around my waist and kissed me on the cheek again.

"I will not apologize for crashing in on you," she said. "We had a feeling you wouldn't come over tonight, so we brought the party to you."

"Happy birthday." I gave her a hug. "It's good to see you again. How are you?"

"I'm good," she said. "Allison said you have a garden. The front looks beautiful. Your green thumb is back. Sandy would love what you've done."

I looked away and tried to swallow the lump in my throat. Beth rubbed my back before joining Allison in the kitchen to put out the spread they brought. Before I could join them, my cellphone rang. I shook my head when I saw the caller ID and stepped into the hallway to answer it.

"Hi, Tam," I said.

"Hi, yourself. I was calling to talk you into going to the social with me. I know we're both nervous, but we can be each other's encouragement."

"I'm sorry, but a load of insanity arrived at my door a little bit ago." Raucous laughter echoed through the house from the kitchen. I couldn't see what was going on and wondered if I wanted to.

"Oh, you have company." The disappointment in Tam's voice was palpable. "I'll let you go."

"Wait a minute," I said. "These guys didn't warn me they were coming over. I was supposed to go to their house for dinner, and they decided I probably wouldn't show up, so they brought it over here, uninvited and unexpected. Would you like to join us? They brought a lot of good food and more than a few bottles of wine. You can come and be the only ray of sanity and help keep me from killing any of them."

Tam laughed, but she sounded nervous.

"Uhm, well, do you want to check with them first? I don't want to crash your party."

"It's my house, and that makes it my party, and I'm inviting you so you won't be crashing it," I reasoned. More crazy laughter came from the other part of the house. "Oh, please come rescue me from these hooligans."

Tam laughed.

"Why does it feel you're throwing me to the lions? But okay. I'll be there in a few minutes."

"Hey," Allison said when she found me still standing in the hall after I disconnected the call. "The hostess isn't supposed to disappear into thin air. Come on. Who was on the phone?"

"A neighbor. She wanted me to go to the community social with her. I invited her to join us instead. I hope you don't mind."

Allison put her hand on her hip and cocked her head.

"I thought you said you hadn't made any friends out here. You're keeping secrets, Janice Halston."

"I barely know her. I met her one day because her granddaughter stopped to admire my flowers when I was working in the yard, and then I went to the little girl's birthday party. Please behave yourself. I think she's straight, but even if she is a lesbian, you know good and well I'm never going to be in another relationship."

She grabbed my hand and pulled me into a hug.

"I'll be good, I promise. But I hope you change your mind about the relationship thing. I hate seeing you alone and lonely."

"I'm not lonely—"

The doorbell rang, cutting off the rest of our old argument. I headed for the door, but before I could get to it, Allison pushed past me and opened it herself. Everyone else had come from the kitchen to see who had arrived. I groaned.

"Hi." Allison opened the storm door for Tam. "I'm Allison, one of Janny's oldest friends. Believe nothing she says about me. It's all lies."

Tam's eyes got big, and a grin spread across her face.

"You mean you're not the smartest, most giving, and caring best friend a person could have?" She winked at me. "Well, hmmm. Okay. I refuse to believe it."

The look on Allison's face was priceless as everyone else burst into laughter. Tam stepped around Allison and gave me a hug.

"Good one," I said into her ear. "You may have neutralized her."

I guided her into the living room.

"You guys, I'd like y'all to meet my neighbor from around the corner, Tam Murphy. Tam, you've already met Allison. This is Beth, Allison's eternally patient partner. And this is Charles and Danny, and Carmen and Melba."

Tam sucked in a breath, and I glanced at her. Tears welled in her eyes as she held her hand out to Danny. He took it and wrapped his arms around her, his face wet with tears.

"Momma Tam," he said into her hair. "I'll be damned. Momma Tam."

CHAPTER FIVE

The rest of us, except for Charles, looked at each other. Everyone's face mirrored the confusion I felt. Charles put his hands on Danny's shoulders and massaged them.

I started trying to herd the others into the kitchen, but they stood as though they were glued to the floor. Tam stepped out of Danny's embrace and turned to me.

"I'm sorry." She swiped at the tears wetting her face. "I'm going now. I'm sorry."

"Don't go." Danny grabbed her hand. "Please stay."

"I can't, Daniel," she said. "It hurts too bad."

Her knees gave out, and Danny and I both caught her and led her to a chair. She sat in it with her face in her hands. I kneeled beside the chair and rubbed her back.

"Tam? What can I do for you?" I said in a low voice.

"Turn back the clock."

Danny sat on the ottoman and pulled it as close to her as he could.

"I wish we could." He put his hands on her wrists.
"Please. We need to talk about this. Please."

"Come on, y'all." Beth held the kitchen door open.
"Let's give them some space."

I was grateful when the four women left the living room.
I was about to follow them when Tam grabbed my hand.

"Please stay," she whispered. "Danny and I need to talk,
but I don't want to be alone."

Panic gripped my heart, but seeing her so devastated, I
knew I couldn't leave her. I took her hand and squeezed it.
Danny sat next to me and took her other hand.

"Momma Tam. I've missed you so much. You look
wonderful."

"You always have been a terrible liar." She tried to smile,
but the sorrow in her face overruled it, and she continued to
cry.

I wasn't sure what I could do to help her, so I sat in
silence, rubbing her hand with both of mine. Danny glanced
at me.

"I didn't know you knew Tam," he said, his voice low.

"We just met a few weeks ago. How do y'all know each
other?"

He glanced at Tam, who had her head bowed. He leaned
over and whispered in her ear. At first, she shook her head
but then nodded.

"You tell her," I heard her whisper.

He kissed her on the forehead before looking at me. He
moved to sit on the arm of Tam's chair, and Charles stood
behind him, his hands on Danny's waist.

"Momma Tam is the mother of my first love, Aaron,"
Danny said, a catch in his voice. "We met in high school and
fell in love with each other almost immediately. We had to

hide it, of course, but everyone knew we were besties. Tam and Darla figured it out almost immediately, and accepted and encouraged us, and held us when things were hard."

Who's Darla? I wondered but said nothing. Danny took a hard breath, and Charles whispered something in his ear before putting his cheek next to Danny's for a moment.

"Aaron's dream was to join the Army as soon as he graduated from high school." Danny's face was so full of pain, I wished I could take it from him. "Even though it was the furthest thing from anything I wanted to do, I joined with him. Oh, we argued about that. I tried to talk him out of joining. He tried to talk me out of joining. But we both lost the argument. Oh, God."

Danny turned and put his head on Charles' chest. I jumped up, retrieved a box of tissue, and a couple of damp washcloths from the bathroom. I handed one to Charles for Danny and the other to Tam.

"Thank you," Tam said. She wiped her face. "Aaron and Mae are the lights of my life. When Aaron brought Danny home, I could see his light shining so much brighter. And we all fell in love with Danny. He was welcome in our home as our second son. When the boys joined the Army, we were so proud of them and scared to death at the same time. I expected them to get assigned to different posts when they came out of boot camp, and I knew it would crush them. But they were stationed at Fort Bragg in the same battalion and ended up going to Iraq, and then Afghanistan, together."

She covered her face for a long time with the washcloth. The house was so quiet I could hear the Regulator clock ticking. Danny once more perched on the armrest of the chair and kissed Tam on the head.

"While we were on our second tour of duty in Afghanistan, we got the news that Darla died. But the Army wouldn't give Aaron bereavement leave since she wasn't his birth mother. I argued with the captain for days, trying to get him to understand that Darla was as much Aaron's mother as Tam was. But it didn't work." He stopped and bent over and put his cheek next to Tam's. "I tried, Tam. Really. I'm so sorry."

She patted his cheek.

"I know, love. Aaron wrote me all about it and how you almost got in trouble. Thank you for trying. I know you loved her, too."

Danny nodded and sat up. He pinched the bridge of his nose.

"I'm sorry to interrupt," I said into the thick silence. Even though I was pretty sure I knew the answer, I asked anyway, "Who was Darla?"

"Darla was Aaron's other momma," Danny said. "She and Tam were partners—"

"She was my wife," Tam said in a strained voice. "We got married in Canada before it was legal to get married here."

She drew in a long breath and swallowed hard. I patted her on the knee, and she gave me a weak smile.

"Darla and I were two sides of the same coin." She squeezed my hand. "We both knew we wanted children. We asked a friend of ours to be our sperm donor, and we were over the moon when we found out I was pregnant. First Aaron and later Mae."

She paused and wiped her face again.

"Darla got real sick right after the boys were sent overseas the second time. The doctors couldn't figure out what was going on until it was too late. She had cancer of the peritoneum, the lining of the abdominal wall. She only lived three months after her diagnosis. Losing her was the hardest thing I had happen to me to that point in my life. And Aaron not being able to come home for her funeral made it even more difficult. We were all the family she had, and she was so quiet, such an introvert, that we didn't have many friends. There were only twelve people at her service, and most of them were employees of the funeral home."

My face was wet with tears. I pulled Tam into a tight hug.

"Oh, Tam," I said, barely above a whisper. "I'm so sorry. So sorry."

She buried her head in my shoulder briefly before sitting back again.

"I was afraid Aaron was going to fall apart," Danny said, "but he was stronger than I thought, and together we moved on and worked hard to stay safe so we could come home. But one day…"

Charles squeezed Danny's shoulders as his voice trailed off, and Tam buried her face in her hands.

"We were on patrol in a small convoy of three Humvees. Aaron and I were in the last one. As we headed back to camp, a little boy threw something under the second Humvee, and it exploded. We tried to save our friends, but insurgents opened fire on us from the village. Me and another soldier were able to pull some of the guys out as everyone else tried to cover us. One of our helicopters flew over and put a stop to the firefight. When I looked around for Aaron, I didn't see him. He was sitting in our Humvee, bleeding. I pulled him out and screamed for a medic. Oh, God. I tried so hard to put pressure on his wound, but I was too late. He died in my arms, and a huge part of me died with him."

I took a sharp breath and watched as Tam doubled over with her face on her knees and sobbed. Danny had turned to Charles again. After a long while, Tam sat up and reached for him. He took her hand but stayed in Charles' arms.

"This man was a hero that day," Tam said in a strangled voice. "He saved four men's lives so they could come home. And the Army allowed him to bring Aaron home. We hung on to each other for several months, but we were both changed people. Things were different between us, and having him around wasn't helping me or Mae to heal. I finally asked him to stay away. That was eight years ago, and today is the first time I've seen him since then."

Tam struggled to her feet and turned to Danny, who moved into her arms.

"I still love you, son," she said. She glanced in my direction. "Would you mind if we have some privacy? Charles, you stay."

I squeezed her hand as I passed her on the way to the kitchen. It surprised me to see Allison and Beth were still there. I collapsed into a chair and put my head on the table. Allison pulled a chair next to mine and put her arm over my shoulders.

"Did you hear everything?" I turned my head to glance at her.

"We eavesdropped," she said, gesturing at the pass-through window. "We probably shouldn't have, but we were worried about you."

"I knew her son died in Afghanistan, but I was unaware of the rest of it." The darkness I'd lived with for so long, but which had started to dissipate, crowded my heart, mind, and soul. I wanted to hide. Sandy's breeze was absent, much to my chagrin. "She's got a lot of pictures hanging on her walls, but I don't remember seeing any with Danny in it. There were a couple of pictures of Aaron and another young man in their football uniforms and another one of Aaron and the same boy grinning at the camera while they played video games. But the kid didn't look anything like Danny."

Allison pulled her cellphone from her pocket and, after a moment, held the phone so I could see it.

"Was this the kid in the pictures?"

A picture of a pale, gangly boy with a big grin stared out of her phone at me. He had a shock of sandy brown hair hanging over his blue eyes. Freckles dotted his nose and cheeks. It was definitely the same boy that was in the pictures on Tam's wall. I nodded.

"That's Danny at sixteen," Allison said. "His sister recently sent me a lot of pictures of him for a bulletin board I did at work for his thirty-fifth birthday. I couldn't believe how much he changed."

The Danny in the living room had dark brown hair, and I often wondered if it came from a bottle. He had a deep tan he worked hard at maintaining, and he was muscular and strong without a hint of a freckle. The only thing that was the same were those blue eyes. There were times those blue eyes had a faraway, almost lost look in them, and I had often wondered why. I studied the picture further and mourned for the boy who appeared to be full of joy. I took a deep breath.

"Did Carmen and Melba leave?"

"Yeah. They slipped out the back and left through the side gate." Beth rubbed my shoulders. "Are you going to be okay if we do the same?"

"I'm sorry about your birthday." I stood up and kissed her on the cheek. "I had no idea this was going to happen."

"Don't worry about it," she said. "But please promise to come see us soon. We miss you."

They each hugged me after I walked them to the gate. When I returned to the house, I flopped on my chaise lounge on the patio and put my arm over my eyes. I heard the slider open but didn't look up even as someone took my free hand.

"Are you okay?" Charles asked.

I peeked out from under my arm at him.

"The question is, are you okay? And Danny? Danny said you knew the story. Did you know all of it?"

Charles leaned back and rubbed his face as he nodded.

"There are times Danny still has nightmares. The next few nights are going to be anything but restful. I hope I can talk him into calling his therapist on Monday."

"Where is he right now? Are he and Tam still talking?"

He nodded.

"I left them sitting on your sofa holding hands with their heads together. I'm not sure if they know I left." He glanced at me. "You didn't answer me. Are you okay? This took a lot out of you."

I didn't say anything as I turned and looked out over the vegetable garden. A cool breeze settled beside me.

"Tam is going to need a good friend." Charles looked over his shoulder. "Here comes Danny. I'm going to take him home."

He stood up and leaned over and planted a gentle kiss on my cheek.

"I'm sorry all this happened today. Thank you for being a safe place for him to tell his story. He's needed to say it out loud to someone other than me and his therapist."

I stayed in my chair while the sound of the men moving around in the kitchen faded away, and silence followed. When Tam came outside and sat in the chair Charles had been in, I sat up and turned so that I faced her. I took both of her hands.

"Rough day, huh?"

She nodded and grinned the ghost of a grin.

"Understatement," she said. Her eyes drooped, and I could see the depths of sadness in them. "Janice, if I'd known Danny was here, I wouldn't have come. I'm sorry I cut y'all's party short."

"It's okay. Are you going to be okay?"

She shrugged, and a part of my heart broke for her.

"I need to tell Mae I saw him, and she's not going to be happy about it. She still blames Danny for Aaron's death. We had a lot of therapy, but she still harbors ill feelings toward him." Tam rubbed her face. "Janice, I can't be alone right now, but I don't feel like talking anymore. Can I just sit here for a little while?"

I turned around and stretched out on the chaise lounge as I moved over and patted the cushion beside me. She joined me, put her head on my shoulder, and we sat in silence.

CHAPTER SIX

I struggled over the next few days. Even though I hadn't expected them Saturday, my friends had come for a fun, positive experience, and the afternoon had been anything but. Guilt plagued me, and I had one more thing to add to my baggage. My soul was dark, and I had a hard time seeing through it. The comfort of the cool breeze was absent, and I was alone.

I didn't visit Tam, or check on her, after she returned home that evening. I would see her and Ocee stroll past the house, sometimes pausing to look at my flowers, but she made no move to come to the door, and I respected her privacy.

It was two weeks later that Allison called me. Her hours at work could be chaotic, so the silence between us wasn't unusual. When she did call, she was uncharacteristically subdued through our greetings.

"How are you doing?"

41

"I'm okay," I lied. "I'm just puttering around the house and garden. Life as usual."

"I don't believe you."

I didn't confirm or deny her suspicions.

"How's Danny doing?" I asked.

Danny and Allison worked together at the LGBT center at the university and she saw him nearly every day.

"It's hard to tell." Allison's voice was so low I could barely hear her. "Charles told me Danny started seeing his therapist again, but Danny has had little to say to me or anyone else. A bunch of us went to lunch the other day, and he didn't say five words. I'm worried about him. What about Tam? How's she doing?"

"I have no clue. I haven't talked to her since that day."

"Why not?" Allison's voice went from one extreme to the other and was now shrill. "She's your friend. Don't you think you should check on her?"

"We're not close, Allison. Before the other day, we'd only seen each other three times and two of those were only in passing. Until she called that Saturday, we hadn't spoken to each other since her granddaughter's party."

"None of those things matter, Janice. She trusted you, and you know she's hurting and probably needs a friend, but you haven't checked on her. You didn't used to be this dense or uncaring. Sandy would be appalled, and so am I."

"I'm hanging up now, Allison." I fought back the tears. "You obviously have forgotten what today is, and I'm not in the mood to be called out. I miss Sandy with my whole being and soul, and I'm on my way to visit her grave in a few minutes. Go to hell."

Without waiting to see if she had anything else to say, I disconnected the call. I grabbed my basket and my clippers and ventured out front to begin choosing flowers to take to Sandy. I had to stop several times because I couldn't see through my tears. Finally, I sat on the sidewalk and gave in to the tears. I jumped when I felt hands on my shoulders.

"Miss Janice, why are you crying?" Ocee's sweet voice whispered in my ear. "Why are you so sad?"

I looked up at Tam's worried face and almost started crying all over again. She offered me a hand and pulled me up. Putting an arm around my waist, she guided me to one of the rocking chairs. Ocee followed us and leaned on my knees once I sat down.

"Did you fall and hurt yourself?" Concern covered her little face. I touched her cheek with my hand.

"No, sweetie. Today is someone's birthday, and I can't spend it with her, and that makes me sad."

"Doesn't she like you anymore?"

"Oh, she still likes me. But she's in heaven now…"

I choked on the tears that threatened again. Ocee climbed on my lap and hugged me. I held her close.

"I'm sorry, Janice." Tam squatted beside my chair. "Is there anything we can do to help?"

I shook my head.

"No. But thank you for asking."

Her face looked haggard, with circles under her eyes, her hair brushed back and held with a headband instead of styled like the last few times I'd seen her.

"I should have been asking you that for the past couple of weeks. I'm sorry I haven't been much of a friend."

She stood up and rubbed her knees before leaning on the porch post with her back to me. Silence engulfed us except for Ocee's quiet humming. Tam finally turned back around and held her hand out to the child.

"We need to head home," she said.

Ocee gave me a sweet kiss on the cheek before climbing off my lap and taking her grandmother's hand.

"Your friend in heaven still loves you," she said. "And so do a whole bunch of people who are still down here."

I stayed in the chair for a while after they left before gathering the basket of flowers and clippers and going inside.

I was having a hard time getting out the door to go to the cemetery. I hadn't missed one of Sandy's birthdays, our anniversary, or the anniversary of her death since we buried her almost seven years earlier. When I finally got in the shower, I ran the water as hot as I could, using just enough cold to keep from getting scalded, and tried to wash away the hairy cloak of grief and uncertainty. By the time I climbed out, my skin was lobster red and tender to the touch. I dressed in a pair of pressed khakis and Sandy's favorite shirt, the one she bought me on our one big splurge of a vacation to Hawaii. Just as I finished tucking my shirt in, the doorbell rang.

I was surprised to see Tam standing on the threshold. She had styled her hair and changed into a pair of sharply creased jeans and a button-down shirt.

"Uhm, hi. I have a feeling you're headed to see Sandy. Would you like a ride to the cemetery? I know how hard it can be to see to drive home after. . .well, after. And I brought a picnic lunch. I thought we could go to the park and talk when you're done, uh, visiting."

Tears came to my eyes when I looked over her shoulder and saw her red minivan parked at the curb. I held the storm door open so she could step inside.

"Thank you. I appreciate your offer, but what about you? Won't it be hard for you, too?"

"I haven't been to the cemetery in a long time. I can check on Darla and Aaron while you visit Sandy. We'll muddle through together." Tam shrugged and answered without truly answering.

"Let me grab my wallet and keys and the flowers."

The drive to the cemetery was quiet. I sat back and enjoyed letting someone else drive for once. It didn't happen often, especially since Sandy died. I surrendered to the temptation to go back in time and remember my tall, dark-haired beauty. She could make me laugh even when I was mad or upset about something. Her positive attitude never waned, even as the end of her life loomed.

"What section?" Tam's voice broke through my memories and brought me back to the present.

"Sixty-two," I said.

I swallowed hard. I gave Tam directions to the road closest to Sandy's grave. She pulled to the side and turned the car off. I looked over at the gravestones and shivered. Every time was almost like the first time, and my grief threatened to take over my thoughts and actions. She touched my arm.

"Would you like me to come with you?"

I took a deep breath and shook my head.

"It's sweet of you to offer, but you want to go check on your family. I'll be done soon."

"They're buried in section sixty-one." She pointed to the opposite side of the road from where I was going. "Let's plan to meet back here at the car. Don't hurry, Janice. Take all the time you need."

She took my hand and squeezed it.

"Wish your lady a happy birthday for me." She climbed out of the van and headed across the street, her hands shoved deep in her pockets.

I watched her for a moment before climbing the slight hill toward Sandy's resting place. My heart clenched as it did every time I came to visit. There were new pebbles and a few more coins on top of the headstone, and fresh flowers lay at its base. I noticed something taped to the front of the gravestone, and I grew angry at the thought of someone defacing Sandy's memory. I ripped the note off and started to wad it up before I saw my name on the outside of the folded piece of paper.

Hey, girl.

I'm sorry I upset you on the phone this morning. I know today is Sandy's birthday, and it's a hard day for you. Please know our arms are wrapped around you even if you can't feel them. Cut yourself some slack and take a bunch of deep breaths. Call us if you need us. We love you, precious lady.

Allison & Beth

Tears stung my eyes as I shoved the note in my pocket. I squatted in front of Sandy's stone a moment before arranging the flowers I brought in the built-in vase beside the marker. Once I had completed that task, I sat cross-legged on the ground and rested my head against the gravestone.

"Gawd, I miss you, Sandy," I whispered.

A cool breeze blew between me and the stone and whispered through the flowers in the vase.

"I know you're with me. I love you so much."

The tears overflowed, and I let them fall and darken the base of the stone. I sat like that a long time, my mind blank, overloaded with grief for what I had lost and what could have been, and with a desire to go back in time. Someone touched my shoulder, and I jumped. Tam and Danny looked down at me, their faces full of sympathy. Danny held his hand out, and I accepted his help to my feet. He gathered me in a tight hug and rocked me.

"I wish I had known her." He kissed the side of my head. "I can see how much you love her. Allison, Beth, and Charles talk about her all the time. They tell me how special she was and how much she loved you."

I stepped from Danny's embrace into Tam's.

"I know," she whispered. "It's hard, harder than it should be."

I nodded, and we headed for the van. Danny opened the door for me and kissed me on the cheek once I settled in the seat.

"Thank you for the other day," he said. "I'm sorry we blindsided you. You could have told us to take it someplace else, but instead you opened your heart and home to us."

I put my hand on his cheek.

"You're welcome. I hope telling your story helps you heal some more."

He nodded as tears slipped from his eyes.

"Charles told me he was proud of me, but it hurts so much. Janice, I miss Aaron. I hate telling Charles how much I miss him."

"Oh, honey." I got back out of the van and hugged him again. "Charles loves you so much. I'm sure he understands or at least tries to. Missing Aaron is natural, and there's nothing wrong with it. I miss Sandy more than I can express. Don't be ashamed of your feelings."

He nodded again. I climbed back into the van, and he closed the door behind me. Tam was already sitting in the driver's seat, and she reached across the console and squeezed my upper arm. Danny appeared beside her, and she turned to hug him.

"Are you sure you don't want to join us for lunch?" she asked him. "I packed extra, so I know there's enough."

"Thank you, Momma Tam." He glanced at his watch. "I'm already late getting back as it is."

"I'll write you a note to give your boss," I offered with a grin.

He laughed and shook his head.

"Like that would work with my boss. You two have a good picnic. I love you both."

We watched as he headed back across the cemetery toward Aaron's grave. Tam glanced at me.

"Who is his boss, and why was that such a joke?"

"Allison is his boss. They've worked together since he was a student at the University. Allison took him under her wing when she found out his family had moved out of the area, and the two of them became pretty close. Anyway, one day I was at the Center giving an art lesson. She couldn't get away to go to lunch with me, but he could. We got carried away discussing music, and he was late getting back, so I wrote him a note asking her to excuse his tardiness, and it's been an ongoing joke ever since."

"Why do I think you and Allison have a bit of a history?" Tam guided the van through the maze of roads to the cemetery exit. "Do you have a preference for which park to go to for lunch?"

"How about the Arboretum?" I suggested. "Yes, Allison and I do have a history dating way back to elementary school. I've known her forever. We were best buds through seventh grade, but we lost touch when her family moved to Charlotte. She came back here for college, and she and

Sandy became friends before I knew she was back. Sandy couldn't wait to introduce me to this crazy new friend she'd met at the Student Union, and the friend turned out to be Allison."

I laughed at the memory of the look on Allison's face when she saw me holding Sandy's hand.

"Neither of us knew the other was a lesbian, and by the time we found out, Sandy and I were already getting close. Allison had hoped for a chance with Sandy, but Sandy chose me. It became an ongoing reason for us to tease and torment each other."

Tam laughed.

"I can see you have a lot of good memories. I'm glad. They make facing each day a little easier."

"And sometimes harder."

"I'm sorry." Tam looked at me out of the corner of her eye. "If you want to talk about it, I have wide shoulders."

"Thank you. Maybe someday, but not right now."

When we arrived at the Arboretum, Tam was lucky enough to snag a parking spot close to the gate. We found a bench under a couple of huge live oak trees and spread our lunch between us.

"Oh, my." I finished the first bite of my roast beef sandwich. "Damn. This is good. What did you do to make it so marvelous?"

Tam covered her mouth and laughed. When she finally swallowed her own bite, she grinned at me.

"Homemade bread, homemade mayo, homemade horseradish sauce, fresh lettuce from Duke's and Mae's garden. Everything else came from the store. I wish I'd had another of those tomatoes you brought to Ocee's party. I've never had one that tasted so good."

"Come in when we get back to the house. I've got an overabundance of all kinds of veggies I'd love to share. Do you like cucumbers? Zucchini? Peppers?"

"Yum. All of the above."

Our conversation flitted from subject to subject like the butterflies among the plethora of flowers in the Arboretum's garden, a cool breeze occasionally tickling the hairs on the back of my neck.

"I hate to cut this short." Tam checked her watch. "It's almost time to pick Ocee up from school, and if we don't get moving, I'm going to be late, and her highness will not let me hear the end of it."

I laughed as I helped her repack the basket.

"I didn't realize she was in school. Summer got away from me."

"Oh, she's in year-round school. She goes in the afternoon three days a week. I've been keeping her this week while Mae and Duke are at some gardening conference."

"Where's the baby?"

"He's with the kids." Tam grinned. "He's still nursing, and Mae will not let him out of her sight yet. Ocee's been moping around because she misses him so much. I asked her if she missed her mom and dad, and the little imp had to stop to think about it."

I laughed. By then, we were at her minivan.

"I can take you home before I go get her if you would like."

"Oh, I don't mind riding along," I said. "You can't be late picking up the princess."

We rode in comfortable silence for a few blocks. I glanced over at her and admired her thick hair, small, turned-up nose, and full lips that made me lick my own. I did a mental head shake.

"Are you always such an overachiever?" I asked to get my mind on other things.

"Huh? What do you mean?" Tam glanced at me with a confused look on her face.

"Homemade bread, homemade mayo, homemade horseradish sauce," I said, repeating what she said about the sandwiches.

The smile on her face seemed private, and I didn't pursue the subject. After a few blocks of silence, she glanced at me again.

"Darla taught me how to cook. My mother was a hands-off, distant person and didn't teach me much about anything. We had hired help, and they didn't teach me anything either. I couldn't wait to get my own place, and I was muddling through with no idea how to survive on my own when I met Darla at a local laundromat. It was the first time I had to do laundry. I was throwing everything helter-skelter in the washer. Darla stopped me and explained why that wasn't a good idea and showed me how to sort the clothes and the proper way to add soap, etcetera, etcetera. While we were dating, she taught me all the things most kids have probably learned how to do by the time they're eleven or twelve. When we got together, she taught me to cook and bake bread and a lot of other stuff. I don't bake as much since I have an empty nest unless my memories are in overdrive like they've been lately."

I stared at her, a bit caught off-guard by her story. It was the most she'd said at one time since we met.

"What?" She pulled the minivan into the pick-up line at Ocee's school. "Why are you looking at me like that?"

"I was trying to reconcile that Tam with this Tam. You don't seem to be an undomesticated being," I said with a grin.

"'An undomesticated being?'" She laughed. "I'm going to have to remember that."

We were quiet for a moment.

"How was it that Danny was at the cemetery?" I asked. She shrugged.

"I didn't know he was there. He was sitting on the bench at Aaron's grave, just sitting there with his elbows on his knees. I touched his shoulder, and he about came out of his skin. He was so far away he didn't hear me walk up."

"How are you doing?" I put my hand on her upper arm.

"I'm okay." The tone in her voice made me think otherwise. "Oh, good. The line is moving. Be prepared for an onslaught of five-year-old energy and a motor mouth."

I watched as a whirlwind carrying a pink bag with a unicorn horn on it threw open the backdoor and clamored into the van.

"Miss Janice! I didn't know you were going to be with Grams. Y'all won't believe what James called me. Miz Baker made him stand in the corner and threatened to call his mother. I already knew everything Miz Baker taught today. I'm still waiting for her to teach me something I don't know."

"Ocee," Tam said sternly, even though she was grinning. "Get in your seat and buckle your seatbelt, please."

"Oh, yeah. Okay. I'm hungry. Can we stop and get some chicken nuggets somewhere? Miss Janice, are you having dinner with us? Grandma put pork chops in the sink this morning. She makes the best gravy—"

"Ocee, breathe." Tam pulled the van out of the school and headed for our neighborhood. Ocee took a deep breath and started talking again. Tam shook her head, and we both grinned all the way home.

Chapter Seven

Since Ocee hadn't unwound from her day at school, Tam didn't come inside for her promised vegetables when she dropped me off. I gathered some cucumbers, tomatoes, and peppers I harvested that morning and packed them in a basket with plans to take them around to her the next day.

But the weather the next day was abysmal, with rain and thunder and lightning and the threat of tornadoes. I watched out the patio door and fought back the tears as the hard downpours and hail pummeled the garden. I loved those plants almost as much as I loved anything else. They had become a part of me. The dark weather took a toll on my mental health, and I curled under a light blanket in the corner of the sofa, not eating, only moving if absolutely necessary. After three days of thinking Noah's flood had returned, I was relieved when the weather began to clear, and soon the sun was so bright it was blinding. I ventured from my cave and looked out the windows as the steam rose from the leaves of the plants and the sidewalks out front.

As I inspected my garden and harvested what had survived the onslaught, I remembered I promised to provide Tam with some fresh veggies. I tried to call her when I returned to the house, but the call was sent to voice mail. She didn't return the call, and my paranoia took over. Maybe she didn't want to be my friend after all. The emptiness returned. I neglected to eat, and the cool breeze was absent.

Over the next week, I tried to call her once more, and one time, I walked around the block, but Mae's car was at Tam's house, so I turned around and walked back home without knocking on her door. I tried to forget about her but found I was driving the long way home so I could pass her house, but I didn't have the courage to stop.

One day, as I was driving by, she was standing beside her car. She waved when she saw me and made a "come here" motion with her arm. I parked at the curb and sat there for a moment, wondering what I should do. Before I could think about it too much, she was standing at the driver's side window.

"Hi," she said a bit breathlessly. "I'm sorry I haven't returned your calls. Life has been a bit more than chaotic lately. The storm last week did a lot of damage at Mae's and Duke's nursery, and I've had the kids while they cleaned up. Leona took them a couple of days, and I went to the nursery to help. I hope you didn't think I'd dropped off the face of the earth."

"Breathe." I grinned at her. "Is the nursery back up and running yet?"

"Yeah. Their insurance is covering most of the damage and the cost of putting things back together." She glanced at me, tilting her head. "Why are we talking out here when it's a lot cooler inside, and I have a pitcher of fresh brewed tea in the refrigerator?"

I climbed out of the SUV, and Tam hugged me. The hug felt so good that I almost melted.

"Did you have any damage from the storm?" she asked.

"My poor garden took a beating, but since I've cleaned it up, everything seems to be fine." I didn't know what else to say, so I just enjoyed us walking in sync with each other.

The house was nice and cool after the humidity outside.

"Come with me to the kitchen," she said. "I have to wash my hands, and then I'll get us something to drink. Are you hungry? It's been too hot to bake, but I stopped at the bakery yesterday and bought some fresh bread."

"That sounds good. What can I do to help?"

She looked over her shoulder from the sink where she was washing her hands.

"Roast beef and ham is in the bottom left drawer in the fridge, and the lettuce is on the right. It's too bad we don't have any fresh tomatoes."

She wagged her eyebrows at me, and I laughed.

"I had a basketful of veggies for you, but the weather kind of interfered with me bringing it over. Are you going to be home tomorrow? I can bring you some then."

"I have Ocee tomorrow." She returned to the table with two plates and the loaf of bread. She opened the fridge and returned with a couple of mason jars. "Roast beef or ham? Mayo or horseradish?"

"Ham and mayo, please." I sat back and watched her efficiently make two sandwiches.

"Diagonal or across?" She held a knife poised above my sandwich.

"It doesn't matter," I said with a laugh.

"Oh, if you have grandkids, it does." She cut the sandwich on the diagonal. "Ocee won't touch a sandwich unless it's cut like this. Doesn't matter what's on it. It doesn't taste right if it's cut wrong."

We laughed and talked as we shared our lunch and companionably cleaned up when we were done.

"Are you in a hurry to get somewhere, or would you like to stay and visit for a little while?" she asked as we went back to the living room.

"I'm not going anywhere. It was too hot to walk to the mailboxes, so I drove."

Tam sat in her chair with a leg tucked under her.

"Wasn't coming down my street a little out of your way from the mailboxes?" She grinned at me. "Or were you checking on me?"

I blushed and looked everywhere but at her. I noticed there were more pictures on the wall. I walked to the wall to get a closer look.

"These weren't here the last time I was." I studied Danny's high school senior picture and one of his formal Army photos. Tam joined me as I looked at some of the other photographs of Danny which had joined the collage of family pictures, including one of him and Charles.

She shook her head as she reached over and lightly tapped one of them to straighten it.

"No. I hadn't hung his pictures when I moved in," she said. "It was too painful. But now it seems right to include him. Danny and Charles are becoming an important part of my life."

"How is Mae doing with that?"

"She's not happy and doesn't even like to sit in here when she visits." Tam shook her head. "I don't know why she blames him. All the information provided by the Army confirmed that there was nothing anyone could have done to save Aaron. But Mae can't get past the fact Danny came home and her brother didn't."

I put my arm around her shoulders and gave her a one-armed hug when I heard her voice crack. She lifted Aaron's picture and traced his face with her finger before replacing it and rearranging his dog tags.

"Well, that conversation got a bit off kilter." She smiled at me through her tears.

"I'm sorry," I said. "One of these days, I'll learn to mind my own business. Maybe I ought to take off."

Tam put her hand on my shoulder.

"You don't have to leave unless you want to. I cry over my son at least once a day, so don't feel bad. Let's sit back down."

We spent the next hour or so chatting about all kinds of stuff until her cellphone rang with a call from Mae. I waved at her as I headed to my car and back home, where a cool breeze met me at the door.

CHAPTER EIGHT

The next morning, I decided to enjoy my morning coffee and mini bagels on the front porch. Heat was already beginning to radiate from the asphalt of the street, but it wasn't too unpleasant yet. I leaned back, closed my eyes, and reminisced about the times Sandy and I sat outside on the deck of our house, telling each other about our plans for the day or, in the evening, how our day had gone. I missed the camaraderie we had almost as much as I missed our intimate times. Her cool breeze caressed my face and swept over my shoulders.

"Hi, Miss Janice!" Ocee yelled.

I opened my eyes to see her waving at me from the sidewalk. When I waved back, she pulled her hand free of Tam's and ran to me.

"You look like you feel better than you did the other day. It made me sad to see you sad."

I smoothed her hair, leaned over, and kissed her on the forehead.

"Thank you, precious," I said. Until Ocee came along, I had never felt close to a child before. I looked up as Tam joined us. "I collected a basket full of veggies for you as soon as I got home yesterday. Would you like to take them now?"

"That would be good," she said. "Mae is getting Aaron from Leona's this afternoon and bringing him over."

"I get my Aaron back today. He spent yesterday with Maw-Maw." Ocee had a huge grin on her face. "I missed him. He makes me laugh and feel all squishy inside."

I laughed.

"That's a good way to feel sometimes, isn't it?" I said as I stood up. "Y'all come on in, and I'll get the basket for you."

I held the door open for them and, once inside, led them to the kitchen.

"Your house looks almost like Grams' house," Ocee said. "Except you don't have any pictures on the wall. Don't you have any family?"

"Ocee, you're being nosey," Tam said, flicking the little girl on the head. "We've talked about asking inappropriate questions, and that's one of them. What do you say to Miss Janice?"

Ocee's face fell, and her bottom lip trembled.

"I'm sorry, Miss Janice," she said, her voice shaking. "I didn't mean to hurt your feelings."

"Thank you, Ocee," I said. "Would y'all like something to drink? I have juice and fresh coffee."

"That's kind of you, Janice," Tam said. "But we have a lot of chores to do that we haven't done properly since the storm, so we need to get back."

"What about school?" I asked.

"I don't go to school on Thursday." Ocee wandered around the kitchen. She looked at the colorful towels hanging from a shelf on the wall opposite the sink. "Those are pretty."

I swallowed hard. Tam tilted her head at me.

"My friend I told you about the other day gave me those for Christmas right before she died," I said. "They're very special to me, and I only use them on her birthday."

"Maw-Maw says you should use the special stuff and not save it for a special occasion. She says why not enjoy them all the time instead of just once in a while?"

I sat down and pulled Ocee to me.

"When I'm not using them, those towels hang there where I can see them every day. Your Maw-Maw is very wise, though, and I agree with her. Most of the time, special things are meant to be used. But if I use the towels all the time, they'll get worn out, and then I won't have them at all. So, I only use them once a year, and I enjoy seeing them hang there the rest of the time."

Ocee nodded.

"That's a good plan." She threw her arms around my neck.

I gave her a tight hug as a sweet happiness I never had before spread through me. Tam gave my shoulder a light squeeze. I patted her hand and stood up.

"The basket is right here." I crossed to the counter.

I opened it so Tam could see what I included. She reached in and pulled a cucumber out.

"Oh, these are beautiful. Do you like pickles? If you have more of these, I can make you some."

"Dill pickles make me pucker too much, and sweet pickles don't appeal to me," I said, puckering my lips.

"Have you ever had homemade dill pickles?" Tam beamed at me. "The only plants I grow are herbs. My favorite is dill, and I have a bumper crop this year. I can't wait to use it to make some pickles."

"You light up when you talk about cooking. Did you know that?" I grinned at her, reached into my vegetable drawer, and pulled out a couple of handfuls of cucumbers. "My cucumbers are overachieving this year. I just slice and eat them, and there is no way I can eat all of these."

"Oh, my." With her hand on her chest, she grinned the biggest grin I'd seen on her face in the short time I had known her. "Are you sure? I mean, that's a lot of cucumbers."

I laid the cukes on the counter and crooked my finger at her. She took Ocee's hand, and they followed me out the back door to the garden. The three cucumber plants were still full of fruit, even after the storm.

"I have plenty," I said with a laugh. "I have a lot of squash and zucchini, too. My tomatoes are about at the end of their growth cycle, but I still have a lot of them and peppers."

"You have quite the green thumb." Tam gave me a one-armed hug, and I found I wished it was a full embrace. I mentally shook myself and remembered that I didn't plan to get into another relationship.

"Momma and Daddy would like your garden." Ocee carefully touched one of the peppers, which was ready to harvest.

"If you can get it off the plant, you can take it to them."

I watched as she gently twisted the pepper until it popped off into her hand. She grinned at me.

"My daddy taught me to do that. He knows all about plants."

"We need to get back to the house and get ready for your momma and baby brother," Tam said. "Let's get the goodies Miss Janice is giving us and get out of her hair."

I pulled a canvas shopping bag out and filled it with the cucumbers and a few more squash and zucchini. I found a smaller bag for Ocee to put her pepper in.

"This bag is heavy," I said as I handed it to Tam. "Are you sure you can carry it?"

She acted as if the bag was so heavy it caused her to stumble, and she laughed when I attempted to catch her. She easily hefted the bag to her shoulder.

"Thank you, Janice. I'll bring you some pickles in a few days."

I walked them out to the sidewalk and watched them head for the corner. Not for the first time, I admired Tam's well-shaped butt. Once again, I shook my head, but this time physically, before heading back inside. Sandy's spirit raced ahead of me and met me at the door.

CHAPTER NINE

Over the next few weeks, Tam and I got in the habit of talking on the phone at least once a day, every day, and visited each other's houses every few days. When we missed a day, it was as though I forgot to do something important that day.

One day, when she was busy with her family, cabin fever raised its ugly head. The house was so clean it squeaked, the garden chores were done, and I was bored. It had been a while since I visited the swimming pool, and I decided this was as good a time as any to start again.

I put my suit on with my shorts and T-shirt over it. The pool was within walking distance, and I set off with my towel flung over my shoulder and carrying my swim shoes.

"Hi, Janice," the pool receptionist said. "We haven't seen you for a while. I hope you're well."

"I am. Thank you." Once I signed in, she flashed me a smile and a wink.

After I made my way through the locker room to the pool, I chose a storage bin from the cabinet in the corner and deposited my ID pouch, flip-flops, shorts, shirt, and towel in it before donning my swim shoes. After I showered off, I watched the other swimmers for a bit before picking a lane where the only other swimmer swam almost as slow as I did. The water was cool, and I held on to the side until I acclimated to it. I swam a few laps until I was tired and realized how out of shape I was.

I climbed out of the pool, showered again, and checked to see if there was a jacuzzi which wasn't overcrowded. One tub was completely unoccupied, and I climbed in. I settled back and let the bubbles and warm water relax my tired muscles. My mind relaxed along with my muscles and for the first time in a while, I felt somewhat at peace. But the peace was soon disturbed.

"Mind if I join you?" a familiar voice asked.

I opened my eyes and recognized the woman who usually worked the front desk as she settled into the opposite side of the tub. Her bathing suit was so skimpy I wondered why she bothered wearing one, and, unfortunately, it was not a flattering look on her.

"I was just leaving," I said, even though it wasn't the truth. "Enjoy yourself."

"Oh, don't run off, Janice. I've wanted the chance to get to know you since you first came to the pool. You're such a handsome woman and always so courteous."

"Thank you, uh, uhm…"

"Monica. My name is Monica. Don't you think Monica and Janice sound good together?" She shifted in the tub, and her top slipped below her breasts. I averted my eyes and took a deep breath. It was obvious the movement was not an accident.

"Nice to meet you, Monica, but I'm not interested in making any new friends right now."

I got out of the tub and hightailed it to my bin, where I changed out of my swim shoes and grabbed my belongings. But when I turned, Monica was right behind me, smiling what I guessed she thought was an attractive and flirty smile, but it only made me cringe.

"Aw, come on, Janice," she said in a low voice as she stepped into my personal space. "I bet you know how to make a woman scream for mercy."

"You are being inappropriate, and you're harassing me," I hissed at her. "I'm not interested. Leave me alone."

"I can make life hell for you," she hissed back. "Once I tell people what happened at that school, you'll be out of this neighborhood."

I didn't give her the satisfaction of answering her as I walked past with my head held high. In the locker room, I calmly put my shirt and shorts on over my suit, but it took everything I had not to run all the way back to my house. Even before changing clothes, I was on the phone to the community office.

"I need to file a formal complaint against Monica, the receptionist at the pool," I told the woman who answered the phone.

"Yes, ma'am," she said. "I'm sorry you had trouble with her. Let me take the basics from you, but I suggest you go to this website and put it all in writing afterward."

I paused for a moment and outlined what had happened at the pool.

"Do you know what she meant about 'what happened at the school'?" asked the woman who identified herself as Ms. Walker.

"I had a court case last year against a school for firing me without cause and slandering me," I explained, my heart pounding.

"Aww, okay," Ms. Walker said, a strange tone in her voice. "Are you a convicted felon?"

I croaked out a laugh.

"No, ma'am. I was never charged with any crime, and I won my court case. I did nothing wrong, and the courts agreed. Since then, I have kept to myself, and people like Monica are why."

"I'm sorry, Ms. Halston," she said. "I can't imagine how you must feel. Go to the website and report her to corporate, and I'll pass this report on to our president here. You'll find most people here are not like Monica, and you're safe in our community."

"Thank you, Ms. Walters, but I doubt I'll test your theory."

After I disconnected the call, I took a quick shower, then accessed the corporate website and filled out the grievance form. By the time I finished, I was shaking. I checked and made sure all my windows and doors were locked and activated the security system, which I seldom used, before collapsing on the sofa. I covered my eyes with my arm and allowed myself the tears and frustration I had fought for the last few hours.

My phone, alerting me to someone in my front yard, startled me. I was surprised to see it was already almost dark outside. When the phone alerted again, I activated the app to see what was going on. I let out a scream as I raced for the door.

"What the hell are you doing?" I yelled as I threw the door open.

The kid shot the bird at me and jumped into a waiting car, which sped away. I wasn't able to see who was driving or the car's license plate. I almost passed out when I saw the damage the kid did to the flower beds. He had pulled out the flowers and strewn them across the sidewalk and yard. What he hadn't uprooted, he had trampled. How was he able to do so much damage in a short time?

I collapsed in one of the rocking chairs and called both the local police department and the community law enforcement. The community security service arrived first. I showed them the video my security system caught of the vandal trashing my yard. When the police arrived, I showed it to them as well. I wasn't surprised when they told me there was nothing they could do since the license plate on the car was not visible. The security guard took pictures of the damage and promised to drive by the house on a more frequent basis.

After everyone left, I looked at my decimated flower beds and burst into tears. I gathered a hoe, a broom, and a bushel bag from the storage closet off the patio. The porch light and security lights lit the yard as I cleaned out the flower beds, collected the detritus into the bag, and swept the sidewalk. By the time I finished, I had cried myself out and felt nauseous. I hauled the bag to the backyard and almost lost my stomach contents as I dumped the remains of my cherished flowers into the compost pile.

The next morning, I awoke with sore muscles, exhausted, alone, and emotionally depleted. I dreaded looking out my front door, but when the doorbell rang, and I looked at the security app, I knew I had no choice. Tam stood on the porch, her back to the door, staring out at the sidewalk, shaking her head. I pulled the door open, unlocked the storm door, and wordlessly gestured for her to come in. I flopped on the sofa with my face buried in one of the pillows. Tam sat on the edge next to me and rubbed my back.

"What happened, Janice?" she asked. "Why did you clean out the flower beds?"

I took the phone from my robe pocket, accessed the video, and handed it to her.

"The little bastard," Tam said as she laid the phone on the table. "Oh, Janice. I'm so sorry. Do you have any idea who he is or why he did this?"

I sat up and told her about the confrontation with Monica at the pool.

"She may have had nothing to do with this, but it sure is a strange coincidence if she didn't."

"Okay." Tam paced the living room. "You can't see the license plate, but the make, model, and color of the car is pretty clear. Let's drive to the pool and see if a car that matches the description is parked there. If there is, take some pictures, and we'll go to the office and show it to security."

I sat and stared at her. This was not the Tam I was getting to know. This Tam was a take charge, grab the bull by the horns, person. She stopped pacing and turned and looked at me.

"I'm sorry. I guess I should ask you what you want to do."

"First, I need a cup of coffee. Second, I need a shower. And third…" I paused, stood up, and put my hands on her shoulders. "Third, I have a deep desire to kiss you."

I drew her closer to me but didn't kiss her. I waited to see what she would do. To my relief, she wrapped her arms around me and leaned her forehead against mine, a smile tickling her lips.

"Well," she said, "kiss me."

CHAPTER TEN

Unfortunately, I didn't have time to. I started to cover her lips with mine, but the doorbell rang. I gently kissed her on the cheek before checking to see who it was. The neighbor from across the street stood there holding his phone in his hand.

"I can't believe what that twerp did to your garden," he said without preamble. "Our security camera caught most of it. I'll be glad to send you a copy of the video, but I don't know your email address. Heck, I hate to admit, I don't even know your name."

My next-door neighbor joined the man on my porch.

"Why did you take your garden out?" she asked. "It was so beautiful."

Throughout the morning, people from the neighborhood stopped over to ask what happened. One lady was driving by, came to a screeching halt, reversed her car, and stared, her mouth hanging open. I was sitting on the porch and watched as she parked and walked up the sidewalk.

"I go out of my way to drive by and see your flowers," she said, tears in her eyes.

For the umpteenth time, I explained what happened.

Thank goodness for Tam. The only reason I had time to shower was because she stayed and fielded the shock of my neighbors. Later, she made a lunch run and brought back Italian subs and soda pops for us. By the time the onslaught was over, I was exhausted, but I had videos from three of my neighbors and a slew of new contacts and email addresses in my phone.

"Thank you for helping," I said when I finally closed my front door again. "I did not know so many people enjoyed my foray into flower gardening."

"Are you going to plant more flowers?" She handed me a fresh glass of tea.

I shrugged.

"I had planned to plant some mums and other fall flowers, but until I figure out what the asshole was doing, I'm not sure I'm going to. It's a lot of money and work just to have it ruined."

Tam rubbed my arm.

"On my way back from getting the sandwiches, I drove by the pool." She pulled out her phone and showed me the pictures she had taken. "Here's what I found. I think I hit the jackpot."

Not only did she have pictures of a car similar to the one in the video, but in one picture, Monica was climbing into the driver's seat.

"I need to email these videos and pictures to security," I said. "I'm going to get my laptop."

It was only a moment before I was back and had the computer positioned in front of me. I powered it on and waited a few moments before the opening screen appeared.

"Oh, my." She reached over, picked up the laptop, and studied the screen. "Is this one of your paintings?"

I nodded, surprised to see tears in her eyes.

"What's wrong?"

"It's so beautiful it takes my breath away." She set the laptop back on the table. "I'd love to see some of your work, the actual paintings. Why don't you hang them, Janice? You are so talented."

I signed into the internet and opened my email without answering her. But I was having a hard time seeing the screen through my own tears. I leaned back and rubbed my face. The cool breeze brushed across my wet cheeks.

"Everything is in my back closet. After what happened with the school, I hit a brick wall, and I can't even stand to look at my work. The only reason this one is on my computer is because it was Sandy's favorite. It was the last painting I did before she died. She was bedridden, and we all knew it wouldn't be long before she was gone. One day, she was perfectly lucid for the first time in months, and she asked me to take her to the Arboretum, which, of course, was impossible. A hospice worker was at the house, so when Sandy fell back to sleep, I took my paints and a canvas, and I went to her favorite spot at the gardens and painted this. I did it so fast I wasn't sure it was even worth looking at, but when I showed it to her the next day, she cried. And then she smiled. And I hadn't seen her smile in such a long time. We displayed the painting at her memorial service. I wanted to cremate it with her, but Allison and Beth wouldn't let me."

Tam had slipped her arms around me while I was talking, and I turned into her embrace and sobbed. She murmured in my ear, rubbed my back, and caressed my head. As I calmed down, I leaned back and looked at her. She wiped the tears from my face and gently placed a hand on each of my cheeks. I thought she was going to say something, but instead, she leaned forward and kissed me. The kiss was gentle and sweet but also seemed full of promise.

"Oh, wow," I said as I sat back. I touched my fingers first to her lips and then mine. "I want to kiss you some more, but I need to send these emails."

She smiled at me but didn't say anything. We sat in silence while I composed the emails to the security company, the front office, and the corporate office. I attached the pictures and the videos and hit send. I turned back to Tam.

"We need to talk before we kiss again," she said.

CHAPTER ELEVEN

"I've wanted to kiss you for a while now." Tam wiped a tear from her face. "But I wonder if I should have. I wonder if we should have. It seems we're both still deep in mourning and my grief for my son is so close to the surface again since Danny came back into my life."

She paused and studied her hands in her lap a moment before looking at me.

"And what does the kiss mean? I kissed you, and I'm not even sure."

The question exploded in my head because I knew I should consider the same thing, but all I wanted was to kiss her again. I jumped up and paced the living room for a few minutes. She watched me in silence. Finally, I sat on the coffee table in front of her and took her hands.

"Will we ever not be in mourning for the people we loved? It's been seven years since I lost Sandy, and what? Eight, nine years since Darla died? And eight since you and

Danny and Mae lost Aaron. Some people would say we should be past it by now, but I don't think I'll ever be. Or you. Or Danny. But can't we support each other when the grief becomes too much for us to handle, like you just did for me? And like I did for you when Danny was here?"

I took a breath.

"Look, does it matter what the kiss means? I swore off ever having another relationship after the mess I found myself in a few years ago. But that was before I met you. I've felt a connection with you since the first time we shook hands. Am I ready for an intimate relationship? I have reservations, but I am certain I want to kiss you again and hold you. But I'll back off if that's what you need."

Tam reached out and put her palm on my cheek.

"I felt the same connection. I was reluctant to let go of your hand that day. It was the first time since Darla died that I experienced anything like that, and it confused me and exhilarated me. You let me and Danny reconnect without judgment, and you held me with so much compassion that afternoon, compassion Darla wasn't always able to show."

It was her turn to take a breath.

"Janice, I'm so confused. On the one hand, I want to kiss you, hold you, and maybe touch you. But on the other hand, I want to bolt out the front door and lock myself in my house to protect myself from the possibility of being hurt again." Tears fell from her eyes as her breath became ragged. "I can't stand the thought of losing anyone else in my life, and face it, neither of us is young. We're not old, but it won't be long before we are."

"Allison would call us both cowards," I said with a strangled chuckle. I moved over to sit next to Tam on the sofa. I embraced her, and she laid her head on my shoulder.

"Let's just do this for right now, and we'll handle the rest of it as it arises."

I kissed her on the forehead and settled back in the corner of the sofa with her in my arms. And it felt good in a way I'd never experienced. We didn't expect our cuddling to morph into sexual intimacy, and I could relax. And Tam relaxed, too.

We sat in silence until my bladder forced me to break the mood. When I returned from the bathroom, I saw Tam was on her phone. I smiled at her and went into the kitchen, where I poured us each a fresh glass of tea and put together a small plate of cut veggies. I was about to head back into the living room when she came through the kitchen door.

"That was Mae," she said, her voice hard. I instinctively stepped away from her, but Tam didn't seem to notice. "She wants me to go with her to Ocee's school next week for a meeting with Mrs. Baker and a couple of other people. Ocee is being bullied to the point she was in tears when Mae got her from school. Oh, damn, this pisses me off so bad. Why do people have to be like that?"

Her anger radiated off of her. At first, I wanted to bolt, but I knew it wasn't me she was angry with. I wasn't sure whether to hug her or to let her rage. Tam paced around the kitchen, her jaw and fists clenched, her arms tight at her sides. After several passes, I stepped in front of her and took her by the shoulders.

"Sweetie, how do you need to be comforted when you're this angry? Should I hug you or give you space?"

I could almost see the wheels grinding away inside her head, but I didn't move or say anything else. After a bit, she visibly started to relax and hugged me. I rocked her a bit and hummed a wordless song in her ear. She stepped back and gave me the oddest look.

"No one has ever done something like that for me before." She dropped into a chair. "Darla never asked what I needed when I was angry about something. She stayed out of my way and taught the kids to do the same thing. I wasn't aware I needed comforting until now. How did you know to do that?"

I pulled a chair around so that we were facing each other, and I put my hands on her knees.

"Sandy taught me," I said. "My mom taught me a lot of stuff, made sure I knew how to tie my shoes, make a bed, drive a car, balance a checkbook. But she never comforted me when I was hurt, distraught, sad, or angry. I was just left out to hang. But Sandy. . .Sandy always seemed to know what I needed, whether it was space or to be held, silence or a song, and she was always available with a hug. She was a big hugger. I learned to hug people because of her."

Tam leaned forward and hugged me. A cool breeze circled us and was gone as quick as it came. I wasn't sure Tam felt it until she sat back and looked around.

"I felt the strangest draft," she said. "I thought it was your AC, but it was different somehow."

I sat back and watched her as she relaxed a bit more.

"Can we go cuddle some more on the sofa?" she asked in a quiet voice.

I rose, offered her my hand, and led her back to the living room. Once we settled on the couch, she sighed, and I placed my hand on her head.

"We have a lot to learn about each other," I said. "Can we talk about what we need and don't need when we need comfort?"

"I've never considered it. Darla was undemonstrative. There were times I didn't know what she was thinking or if she even knew I was in the same room. I know she loved me, but sometimes she was so distant. I figured it was because she was such a strong introvert. She avoided me when I was over the top with my emotions, no matter what those emotions were. And she seldom showed me how she felt, so I seldom needed to comfort her."

She put her hands over her face for a moment.

"I make her sound so cold, but she wasn't. Once I calmed down, we could talk things out, and she had a lot of love, wisdom, and insight into things. And our love life was strong. Until she got sick, we never had a bout of lesbian bed death."

She twisted around to look at me.

"I'm afraid I won't know how to comfort you when you need it." Her eyes were bright with tears.

I kissed her on the forehead and pulled her to me.

"I find your presence comforting," I told her. "Just being with me, being available, is all the comfort I need, at least for now."

We once again settled into silence. Her head was against my chest, and I could feel her heart beating against my belly. It was a strong beat, and I held her tighter. I remembered too clearly holding Sandy and feeling her heart skipping and rattling.

"I never told you what happened to Sandy," I said in a quiet voice.

Tam leaned back and touched my cheek with her hand.

"I'm listening whenever you're ready, Janice. If it hurts too bad, don't worry about it. If it will help you talk about it, I'm right here."

"Can I tell you now?"
She nodded.

CHAPTER TWELVE

"One night, after we made love, I was holding Sandy. She was almost asleep, but her breathing had a strange rattle. I also realized her heart beating against my side didn't feel normal. Instead of the steady, strong beat she usually had, her heart stuttered and missed a beat way too often. It didn't feel right, and I was scared.

"I lay awake the whole night, monitoring her heartbeat against my body and the odd way she was breathing. When our alarm went off the next morning, I was exhausted. Even though she had slept through the night, she was dragging through her preparations for work.

"I tried to get her to call her doctor, but she was so stubborn. Her skin was slightly blue around her lips, and she was pale. I took her hand and led her to the bathroom mirror and showed her, but she blew me off and headed to work.

"Over the course of the next couple of months, I watched as Sandy deteriorated, but she still refused to make a doctor's appointment. But she started growing forgetful. She usually had a memory like a steel strap, almost a photographic memory. One day, I found her standing in front of the open refrigerator, crying.

"When I asked her what was wrong, she told me she couldn't find her keys, and she had a meeting at work she needed to get to. I reminded her the meeting was the day before and it was Saturday. I made the decision on the spot that I would schedule her an appointment Monday morning, regardless of her arguments.

"But Sunday afternoon, I had to call nine-one-one. Sandy collapsed and hit her arm on the side of the table. The EMTs wouldn't tell me anything other than she was having a cardiac episode and her arm was broken. They took her to the heart trauma center at the hospital.

"The police officer who responded wouldn't let me drive since I was almost in hysterics. She helped me get what I would need at the hospital, such as our powers-of-attorney, Sandy's meds, and so on. She also had me call Allison to meet me at the hospital, and then the officer drove me there. I was so scared.

"Sandy had advanced cardiovascular disease, which caused a stroke and brought on severe dementia much faster than any of her physicians had ever witnessed. They recommended I put Sandy into a memory care/assisted living facility, but I knew she would not be happy or comfortable in a place like that. Beth helped me get home health care and hospice care.

"I watched my beautiful, intelligent, head-strong partner weaken to a shell of herself. Her heart had to work harder and harder to pump blood through her body, and her brain began to shut down because of a lack of oxygen. I stayed at her side as much as possible, singing to her, reading to her, reminding her of the wonderful life we had shared for over thirty years.

"One day, when Sandy was sleeping, Beth practically forced me to go get a breath of fresh air. Our bedroom had a private patio, so I headed out there to take a break. I hadn't been there for long when Beth yelled for me to come back inside. The hospice worker was bending over Sandy with a stethoscope to Sandy's chest, shaking her head.

"Later, Beth told me Sandy opened her eyes, looked around, closed her eyes again, and took one last breath.

"Sandy's memorial service was standing room only. There were people she knew from high school and college; there were people from every job she ever had. People she had met in passing but was kind and caring to, saw her obituary and came to pay their respects. Our small circle of friends—Allison and Beth, Melba and Carmen, and Charles—tried to surround me with their love and support, but it wasn't enough.

"Two days after we buried Sandy's ashes, I visited her and told her I would see her soon. On my way home, I stopped at the liquor store and bought four bottles of Sandy's favorite whiskey. I lined them up on the coffee table, changed into her favorite sweats, and turned on a recording of her favorite music that I had composed over our years together. I poured her coffee mug full of whiskey and saluted my favorite picture of her with it.

"Even though I wasn't a fan of whiskey, I downed mug after mug of it. I had emptied the last of the second bottle into my mug when someone started pounding on the door. I don't know how they figured out I needed help, but Allison and Beth came over in what was probably the nick of time.

Fortunately, I didn't have alcohol poisoning, but I was getting close to it.

"They took me home with them, sobered me up, and warned me they would take me to the hospital for a psychiatric evaluation if I ever did something like that again. I haven't had an alcoholic drink since, except for an occasional glass of wine with friends."

I took a deep breath and let it all out in one long whoosh. My face was wet, but I didn't know if it was from sweat or tears or both. My mind and my soul were on the precipice of the darkness I escaped to when things were too hard. Tam went to the bathroom, came back with a damp cloth, and bathed my face.

"Oh, Janice," she said. "I'm so sorry. I won't say I know how you feel, but I know what it's like to lose someone you love so much. How are you doing now? Are there times you still want to join her?"

I nodded.

"Not as much as I used to, but I have a tendency to feel hopeless and lost, especially since the court case. I withdraw when I get overwhelmed, but I won't ever intentionally do something to myself. I have too many friends who care too much for me."

"Including me," she said as she leaned her forehead against mine.

I pulled her to me and kissed her, feeling zings in parts of my body which had been neglected for far too long. It was all I could do to keep my hands in a platonic place on her back.

"Mmm, that felt good," she said when she sat back. She turned and moved away from me a bit. "But if you kiss me like that very often, we'll have to talk about intimacy sooner than later."

"Are we ready for that discussion?" I cocked my head at her.

"Are you?"

"It's been a long time since someone touched me intimately, since the year before Sandy died." I rubbed my face. "My relationship with the woman from the school was one-sided—I did all the touching. She never once touched me."

Tam looked shocked. I stopped talking before I put my foot in my mouth.

"And you're horny as hell," she said, finishing my thought for me. She gave me a weird look as she moved to sit closer to me. She put one hand on my abdomen, dangerously close to my breast. "Do you believe in friends with benefits?"

Her voice was raspy, and her eyes dilated. I had to be careful of my answer.

"It works for some people," I answered, barely above a whisper. "But I think I want more from you, and neither of us are ready yet."

She looked down, but not before I saw the tears in her eyes. I used my forefinger to lift her chin, but she closed her eyes.

"Look at me, Tam." I kept my voice as gentle as possible. When she opened her eyes, I planted a gentle kiss on her lips. "We'll know when the time is right. This has been a weird day with the shit about my flowers, finding out about Ocee being bullied, and me telling you about Sandy. Our emotions are all over the place, and it's too easy to step over lines we shouldn't be stepping over yet. Let me treat you to dinner somewhere."

I rose and offered her my hand. She stared at it for a long moment before taking it. I pulled her up and hugged her.

"Let's take a raincheck for dinner," she whispered. "I need to go home and think a while."

"Okay." I was disappointed, but I would not stop her from doing what she needed to do. "At least let me take you. It's late and dark."

"If I can borrow a flashlight, I'll be alright. I'd rather be alone right now."

I nodded and retrieved a flashlight from the utility closet. I walked her out to the sidewalk, where we hugged again. Once she turned the corner, I trudged back to my empty, lonely house and my empty, lonely soul. I knew in my heart no one would ever want me, and I didn't blame them. After a hot shower, as hot as I could stand, I sank into bed and deep into the darkness that wasn't quite sleep.

CHAPTER THIRTEEN

I didn't hear from or see Tam for the next several days. I tried to call her a few times, but my calls went to voice mail. My heart dropped a little further each time. I knew I had to find something to lift my spirits, or I might sink so far I wouldn't be able to find my way out.

One day, I stared at the opening screen on my computer and the painting I did for Sandy. Every time the screen saver started to come on, I would stop it and stare some more. The cool breeze flitted between me and the screen. Finally, I dug through the closet in the back bedroom and started pulling my paintings out. I spread them on the bed and leaned them against every available surface.

I walked around the room, studying my work. Some of the paintings had hung in places of honor and prestige in galleries and offices around the city, but when the scandal broke, they were all unceremoniously returned to me. I took Sandy's painting to my bedroom and leaned it against the mirror on the dresser.

"Should I hang your painting in here?" I asked out loud.

I turned and looked at each wall, trying to decide where to put it. While I had my back to the dresser, I heard a sound behind me like someone dropped something. I turned, and the painting was lying face down on the dresser. I figured I didn't balance it properly, so I replaced it and returned to studying each wall. But this time the painting didn't merely fall over, it fell completely off the dresser. I retrieved it and made sure it wasn't damaged.

"Okay," I said. "I get the message. I won't hang it in here."

The cool breeze caressed my face and was gone again.

I returned the painting to the rest of the collection. After contemplating some more, I chose two seascapes and several still-life paintings of seashells and sand dollars and carried them to the living room. It took me a while to decide on their placement, but by the time my stomach was growling for dinner, the pictures hung in my living room, making it a bit more homey, and my spirit was lighter.

It had been a few weeks since my last trip to the grocery store. My pantry and refrigerator were near empty. I still had plenty of vegetables, but one can only eat so many before being vegetabled out.

"Pizza for dinner."

I pulled my phone from my pocket, but before I could call the pizzeria, the doorbell app alerted me to someone on my porch. When I checked it, I jumped up, ran to the door, and threw it open.

"Hi," I said breathlessly. Tam looked as beautiful and put together as usual. "Would you like to come in?"

She smiled at me and stepped inside the house. Before I could say more, she had pushed the door closed and had me in her arms, kissing me in a way that told me she had made some decisions.

"Hi," she said as she pulled my T-shirt out of my pants. She slid her hands under it and began caressing my back.

"Tam." My voice cracked as I took her hands and pulled them out of my shirt. "Damn, woman. You've caught me completely off-guard. We need to sit down so I can catch my breath."

I led her into the living room and settled on the sofa, her hands still in mine.

"Talk to me," I said. I was surprised when her eyes filled with tears.

"Janice." She looked at her hands and then back at me. "Janice, I've realized over the past few days that I want more than a friendship with you. I want a relationship. I'm not ready to say those three little words, and I don't think you are either, but I hope we get there someday."

She placed her hands on my cheeks and kissed me lightly on the lips.

"I'll understand if you tell me to hit the road, but I hope you don't."

"Uhm, wow. I need to pace a few minutes. I'm sorry. Let me try to clear my mind. Okay?"

I paced around my living room wanting to pull on my hair, but I refrained from doing so because I was afraid it would give Tam the wrong message. After a few circuits of the room, I sat down beside her. I took her face in my hands and kissed her, long and deep. But my growling stomach ruined the mood.

"Haven't you eaten today?" She leaned back and looked at my middle. "In fact, have you eaten since the last time I saw you? It looks like you've lost weight."

Her complexion changed from ruddy and flushed to pale in a split second, and she backed away from me.

"Why are you losing weight?" she whispered. "Are you okay? Are you sick?"

"Tam, honey." I reached for her. She leaned out of my reach and jumped to her feet. I moved between her and the door. "Tam, I've hardly eaten anything except for the vegetables out of the garden for almost two weeks. I had my yearly physical a few weeks ago, and Dr. Patel said I'm as healthy as can be expected for a nearly sixty-one-year-old woman. I'm okay. I promise."

"Why are you only eating vegetables?" Tam asked, still pale and obviously frightened.

"Because I've been too scared to go grocery shopping. I haven't wanted to leave the house since the yard was vandalized, so I've subsisted on what I had available. I was about to call out for pizza when you came to the door. What do you like on yours?"

I pulled my phone out again and waited for her to answer. Instead, she sat on the sofa and put her face in her hands.

"I'm sorry, Janice," she said, her voice muffled. "Maybe this isn't such a good idea after all if I'm going to panic every time something seems a bit off."

I sat beside her and wrapped my arms around her.

"Look, babe. It's okay. It shows me you care. And I'll probably be the same way if you ever cough or clear your throat. I believe it's natural under our circumstances. Right now, I'm starving. We either need to go get something to eat, or I need to call out for food."

"No. You need to come home with me. I have leftovers in the fridge from when Mae and Duke and the kids were over a couple of days ago."

She looked at my bare feet.

"Go put your shoes on, grab your keys, and come on."

Twenty minutes later, I sat at Tam's kitchen table with a plate of roast beef, potatoes, carrots, and homemade rolls in front of me. Tam sat with her elbows on the table and her chin in her hands, watching me as I dug in. The food was so good, and I was so hungry I was wordless until I sopped the last of the gravy off my plate.

"Oh, damn," I finally said. "That was marvelous. Thank you."

I crooked a finger at her as I scooted my chair back. She came to me, and I pulled her on my lap and kissed her the way she had kissed me when she first arrived at my house. She moaned, and the zings hit me again in all the right places. It was my turn to push her shirt up and caress the bare skin of her back until I reached her bra. I looked at her, and she nodded. It had been ages since I had unhooked another woman's bra. I was delighted when I did it without fumbling.

Tam stood up and took my hand. I followed her to her bedroom and watched as she stripped out of her clothes. I caught my breath as her full breasts invited me to touch them and kiss them and suck on them. But before I could, she pulled my shirt over my head and pushed my pants to my ankles. I stepped out of them as she deftly unhooked my bra. She caught me off-guard when she bent and grabbed the center of my bra with her teeth and pulled it off. I laughed, amused at how playful she was.

"Mmm," she said as she placed a hand on both of my breasts. "You are as beautiful as I imagined you would be."

With her hands on my waist, she pulled me to the bed, where she sat with me standing between her legs. Her hands cupped my butt cheeks while she sucked one of my breasts into her mouth. I threw my head back and arched into the sensations I was feeling. She released me and fell back on the bed, pulling me with her. I started to explore her body, but she stopped me.

"No, Janice, not yet. I want to make love to you first." She leaned over and took my lips in hers and kissed me while her hands found all the spots that made me whimper in pleasure, spots that had been neglected far too long. Her fingers were gentle but insistent.

"That's it, precious lady," she whispered. My body bucked and arched as an orgasm grew until I exploded with hot currents racing from my core to every nerve ending in my body. "Come for me, love. That's it. Oh, yes, hon."

Finally, I stilled her hand, breathing hard and covered in sweat. My body continued to react, even though she was no longer touching me. She lay beside me and nuzzled my neck as she laid her hand on my chest, just below my breasts.

"Are you okay?" she whispered.

I nodded, still unable to talk because of the sensations racing from my groin outward and then back again. I involuntarily bucked a bit, and she giggled.

"Was I really that good?" she asked as she rose on her elbow and looked down at me. "Or has it been so long—"

I stopped her words by flipping her on her back and lying on top of her, kissing her. I straddled her on my knees and admired what I saw. Her breasts beckoned me, and I bent to them and caressed them and kissed them and licked them until her back was arching. I scooted back until our clits met.

"Wait, Janice," she said, a bit breathless.

She turned and reached into the side table drawer for a tube of lube. After she laid back again, she put a small dollop on her clit. I once again introduced our clits to one another, and she groaned. I started grinding against her, but she grabbed my hips and took charge. It didn't take long before we were close to having simultaneous climaxes.

"Oh, dear God," she screamed as she pushed up and I ground into her. My climax followed, and I collapsed on top of her. I rolled to one side and watched while she reached for her clit and started masturbating. Her legs spread wide, and I moved to lie between them.

I traced a finger around the outer edges of her vagina, and she leaned into it. I looked at her and smiled when I saw her looking back at me.

"May I?" I let my finger dip a bit inside her.

She nodded as she used her free hand to move the lube within my reach. I lubed a couple of fingers and gently slid them into her. Her hips started moving faster, and she let out a screech as my fingers kept pace with her.

"Oh, my God, Janice," she yelled.

The decibels of her moans continued to rise as she came closer to climax. I'd never been with anyone so vocal, and I wanted to do everything I could to keep those moans coming. Finally, she pushed me away and closed her legs tight, even though her hand was still between them. She turned on her side and bucked against it a couple of times before pulling it out.

"Oh, God," she said. "Damn. Come here and lie beside me."

I slid up the bed, put my head on the pillow next to her, and caressed her head.

"Thank you," I whispered, suddenly feeling like I was going to cry. I turned over so she wouldn't see me, but she caught me and held me as the tears came.

"Oh, Janny," she said. "Oh, honey. It's okay. I'm right here. Hold on to me. You're okay."

Her crooning soothed me through my tears. A cool breeze blew across my body as I fell asleep.

CHAPTER FOURTEEN

Tam and I spent a lot of time together through the following days, either in her bed or mine. But reality returned, and Tam had to pay attention to and spend time with her family, and Allison and Beth were clamoring for my attention. They kidnapped me one evening and took me to dinner.

"Why are you hiding away?" Allison asked as we enjoyed our meal. "You're not going to disappear on us again, are you?"

I shook my head but managed not to grin like a wild woman. Tam and I weren't ready to share our relationship with anyone yet.

"No. I've been busy in my garden and learning how to preserve my vegetables, and I've been going through my artwork and re-cataloging it."

"You're kidding." Allison's eyebrows rose to her hairline. "Are you thinking of showing again?"

"Uh, no," I said, shuddering at the thought. "It's something to keep me busy. I hung a few on the wall, though. You'll have to come in and see them."

It was good to spend time with my friends, but it was even better to go home and wait for Tam to join me for the night.

The following week, she invited me to join her and her family for their weekly dinner. I loved it when Ocee was excited to see me and wanted to sit on my lap while we waited for Tam to tell us dinner was served.

"Are you going to plant some more flowers, Miss Janice? I cried when Grams told me a bad person ruined your flower beds."

I pressed my lips against the side of her head and hugged her tighter.

"I don't know, kiddo. They still haven't caught the bad guy, and I don't know if he will come back and do it again."

"You need a watchdog."

Mae and Duke guffawed, and I looked askance at them.

"She's after us to get her a dog, and since we said no, she's been working on everyone else to get one so she can play with it." Mae scowled at Ocee. Even though I couldn't see the child's face, I could tell she was grinning.

"Well, that someone won't be me. Dog fur makes me sneeze and itch."

"A poodle's wouldn't." Ocee turned and looked up at me. "They have hair instead of fur, and it wouldn't bother you."

It was my turn to guffaw.

"I'm not going to get a dog, baby girl."

Tam saved me from any more argument by calling us to the table.

Once again, she amazed me with her cooking. She had roasted two chickens, made mashed potatoes, steamed broccoli to perfection, and baked two loaves of fresh bread. And then she surprised me with a birthday cake, complete with candles in the shape of a six and a one.

"It's not my birthday," I said in protest as everyone clapped when Tam lit the candles.

"Not today," Tam said with a gentle smile. "But I peeked at your driver's license, and it seems you neglected to tell me it was three days ago. It surprised me that your friends didn't do anything for you."

I groaned. I had purposely spent the day at Tam's house and put my phone on silent as well as made a new voicemail message telling everyone I was unavailable. By the time I got home, I had fifteen missed phone calls and almost as many voicemails, plus a dozen text messages. There were also five birthday cards taped to the front door and several gifts stacked on the porch chairs. I had a feeling that I would hear about it when I saw them the coming weekend at Allison's birthday party, which I'd neglected to tell Tam about even though the invitation was extended to her as well. I knew it was necessary to say something soon.

"Thank you," I said after I blew out the candles. The red velvet cake and its cream cheese icing melted in my mouth, and I wished I could take Tam in my arms and thank her for it in a much more personal way.

Later, after her family left, I did just that. As we lay in bed after our lovemaking, I decided now was as good of a time as any to tell her about my birthday.

"Thank you for making me a cake today," I sat up and leaned against the headboard, drawing my knees to my chest. "I'm sorry I didn't tell you when my birthday was."

Tam sat up too and ran a finger from my shoulder to my elbow.

"What's wrong, Janice? It's obvious something is bothering you."

"I don't like celebrating my birthday." I took a deep breath.

"Why not?" Tam stopped her tracing and put her hand on my arm. "It can't be because you don't appreciate your age."

"No." I shook my head. "Nothing like that."

I rested my forehead on my knees and tried to stay calm. Tam stroked my head but didn't say anything.

"My parents threw me out on my eighteenth birthday. In my infinite immature wisdom, I thought my birthday party with all of my friends, family, and extended family in attendance was a good time to come out of the closet. I figured with all those people present, my parents wouldn't lose their cool and all would be well."

Tam stayed quiet and massaged my neck.

"I was phenomenally wrong." The memories threatened to overwhelm me, and I had to take several deep breaths. The feelings of abandonment and emptiness were close to the surface and threatened to drown me.

"Shhh, hon." Tam took me in her arms. "I'm so sorry that happened to you. No one should have to go through that. But you're safe now."

I nodded.

"My fiends, I mean friends, have practically forced me to celebrate ever since. Sandy always threw me a birthday party and invited anyone who could hear to come. It was always a big deal to everyone but me. I wanted to hide, but I had to pretend to be happy and enjoying myself. It was one of the few things Sandy did that truly pissed me off.

101

"Anyway, Allison and Beth have tried to keep it going, but instead of a birthday party, they usually try to blindside me by coming to the house with a cake and gifts and a string of friends in tow."

"Why didn't they do that this year?" Tam asked.

I giggled.

"Because I outsmarted them and spent the whole day with you. I put my phone on silent and ignored it, and I had my voice mail tell them I was out of touch for the day and to leave me the hell alone. My voice mail box was almost full of indignant messages, and I had a ton of text messages, too. Plus, when I got home, there were gifts on the porch and birthday cards taped to my front door."

Tam leaned back and looked at me, her mouth wide open. After a moment, she started laughing.

"Oh, my. What will they do to me if they find out where you were?"

"There's more," I said. "Tomorrow is Allison's birthday, and they're having a get-together at their house on Saturday. I've been told if I don't make an appearance with you in tow, they're going to hunt me down and hog-tie me and haul me back to their house. And I wouldn't put it past them. We can run away—go to the beach or something where they can't find us."

I looked at her in hopes she would agree it was a good idea, but she was shaking her head.

"You've been a recluse for too long, Janice Kirsten Halston," she said. "We're going to the party, and I bet you have fun in spite of yourself."

It was my turn to be surprised.

"How do you know my middle name?"

"It was also on your driver's license." She let out a screech when I goosed her and pulled her back to the bed.

Saturday, when Tam and I arrived at Allison's and Beth's house, I groaned when I saw the number of cars parked in their yard and along the street.

"I don't know if I can do this, Tam." I trembled, and my heart was about to pound out of my chest. "There are too many people. What if some of them. . .?"

Tam got out of the car and came around to the driver's side. She opened the door and squatted beside me.

"Give them a chance, sweetheart. It's been a long time since all that shit happened, and there's been a lot of other stories in the news since then. But I'll tell you what—if someone harasses you, first, they'll have to contend with me, and second, I'll take you home."

I couldn't help but smile at her when she offered to take care of anyone who messed with me. It shouldn't have surprised me that she was quite the momma bear. I leaned over and kissed her.

"Thank you." I let her take my hand and pull me out of the car. I hugged her, glanced around, and kissed her again.

"Why are you being so furtive? Don't you want anyone to know about us?"

I raised my eyebrows.

"Do you want them to know? I didn't think you were ready for that."

"Let's play it by ear. We'll be natural with each other and see who catches on first."

I laughed as I pulled Allison's birthday gift out of the back, and we headed for the house. We were at the base of the steps when Danny and Charles caught up with us. After trading hugs all around, Danny and Tam linked arms and headed inside. Charles put his hand on my arm, and, grinning, stopped me.

"I saw y'all hugging and kissing," he said in a low voice. "Does that mean what I think it means?"

"Just keep your mouth shut about what you think you saw." I took his arm. "How are y'all doing?"

"He's back to his old self. In fact, I believe he's better than he was. He and Tam have become close, and I'm finding out more about their relationship. She stepped into the mother role with him when his mom passed away, and his dad kind of left the kids to their own devices. He told me she and Darla fed him and his sisters more than once because there wasn't food in their house."

"I believe it." I allowed myself to fall for her a little more.

"Well, I'll be damned." Allison met us at the door and hugged me a little harder than necessary. "You not only came, but you brought Tam. Or did Danny and Charles bring her?"

"She rode with me." I jumped when Charles goosed me with a huge grin on his face before wandering off.

"What was that about?" Allison asked, watching him walk away.

"Who knows?" I rubbed the spot on my side where he got me and glared at him when he looked back at us.

"Is this for me?" Allison took the gift from my hand and raised an eyebrow. "This looks like a canvas. Are you painting again?"

I waggled my eyebrows at her and headed inside to find something to drink and see where Tam got off to. I didn't get far before Beth and Melba accosted me and hugged me.

After some small talk with them, I took a few more steps before having to give someone else hugs.

"Are you going to sing for us today?" Cheryl, an old friend from church, asked me. "We so miss your voice at church. I wish you'd come back."

"I doubt I'm going to sing," I said, cringing at the idea of being the center of attention. "Thanks for the invite to church, but only look for me if you see the whites of my eyes."

After several more encounters, I was on overload and feeling like I was being torn apart by a pack of wolves. I made a U-turn and headed back toward the front door, but I hadn't taken three steps before Tam was standing in front of me with a red plastic cup of tea in each hand.

"Hey," she said in a voice low enough only I could hear it. "Are you okay?"

I took one of the glasses and took a long drink. My hands were shaking so hard that I sloshed some of the tea on my arm. Tam took my elbow and cleared a path for me to the French doors and out onto the patio. She shooed someone out of a chair and urged me to sit down. She squatted beside me and rubbed my back.

"Do I need to take you home?"

I shrugged. I didn't trust myself to open my mouth. It was too tempting to start screaming and not stop. I covered my face and continued to tremble.

"Is she okay?" someone asked.

I couldn't hear what she said, but it was only a few minutes before someone put an ice cold cloth on the back of my neck. I knew it had to be Allison. She was one of only a few people who knew I needed either an extreme of hot or cold to calm myself. I pulled the cloth around and buried my face in it.

"You better not be having a nervous breakdown at my birthday party." Allison's voice in my ear made me jump, but I still didn't look up. "Tell me who put you in this condition, and I'll throw them out."

I glanced at her and tried to grin.

"Bye."

"Huh?" The look on Allison's face was priceless.

"Just being here makes me nervous, Allie." I shuddered again. My heart had finally slowed to a reasonable pace. "At least five people asked me if I'm going to sing today. Please tell me you didn't tell them I would. You know I can't sing in public anymore."

"All I said was it would be the best birthday gift anyone could give me if you could sing, but I didn't say you were. I'm sorry, hon. I didn't know a simple comment would cause you so much pain."

I sat back and studied her face for a moment and realized she was serious. I pulled her into a hug.

"Don't worry about it. I'll be okay in a few minutes."

I looked around again.

"Where did Tam go?"

"I'm right here." She rested her hands on my shoulders, and I looked up into her worried face. I pulled her around and onto my lap and buried my face in her shoulder.

"Uhm, y'all?" The tone in Allison's voice made me giggle.

I peeked at Tam, and she was grinning at me. She leaned over and kissed me, leaned back, and then kissed me again.

"Well, I'll be damned," Allison said. I looked at her, and she was grinning like a madwoman. She put her arms around both me and Tam and hugged us. "Both of y'all deserve to be happy, and I'm so happy for you. Oh, damn. I'm going to cry."

Tam got to her feet and let me up so I could give my oldest friend a genuine hug. I dried the tears from Allison's cheek with the pads of my thumb before pulling her into my arms.

"Sandy would be so happy for you," she whispered in my ear. "I'm proud of you. You'll have to tell me how and when this happened when we go to lunch this week."

I laughed as I stepped back.

"Do we have a date for lunch?"

Allison nodded, grinning. "We do now."

"What's going on out here?" Beth asked from the door. "Did y'all move the party out here and forget to tell the rest of us? Hon?"

Beth came out on the patio and hugged Allison.

"Why are you crying, babe?" She leaned her forehead on Allison's.

"They're happy tears."

Allison pointed at me and then at Tam. Beth looked at us, a frown on her face. Tam stepped over, took my hand, and leaned her head on my shoulder. Beth's face lit up, and she held a hand out for me. I took it, and she pulled me and Tam into a hug.

"It's about damn time." She, too, started crying. "Oh, shit. Oh, God. I have to go have a good cry. Please excuse me."

She took off at a trot toward her shed. I watched as she disappeared inside, and I shoved my hands in my pockets. Tam placed a hand on my elbow.

"What's going on? Why is Beth so upset?"

107

"She and Sandy were best friends before I met Sandy. I mean, joined at the hip best friends. Sandy's death hit her as hard as it did me."

"Does she think we shouldn't be together?"

I looked at Tam's worried face and turned and hugged her.

"It's not that, hon. After Sandy died, and they had to take care of me, Beth had a bit of a breakdown. Our relationship took a few years to get back to some semblance of normal."

Tam hugged me without saying anything.

The cool breeze I was used to feeling and looked forward to feeling wrapped itself around me and Tam. Tam shivered a bit, and I rubbed her arms. I leaned forward so I could whisper in her ear.

"Sandy approves of you. I'm going to check on Beth. I'll meet you back inside."

We shared a quick kiss before I headed for the shed. I tapped on the door and pushed it open. Beth sat in her recliner, one arm thrown across her eyes.

"Hey, sister." I sat on the arm of the chair. "Are you okay? Should we have waited to tell you?"

Beth sat up and looked at me.

"Is this serious? Or is it just because you both have needs?"

"It's serious, Bethany." I stood up and put my hands on my hips. "I can't believe you would think I'd make the same mistake again, especially with someone like Tam."

"Do you love her?"

I hesitated. I knew what I wanted to say, but Tam wasn't ready for me to yet.

"Janice. Do you love her?" Beth stood toe to toe with me. "You promised me you wouldn't get into another relationship with someone you didn't love. You promised Sandy before you promised me, and then you broke your promise. Are you doing it again?"

"Please stop reminding me." The pain of the memory was almost too strong for me to handle. I would never forget lying in bed next to Sandy on one of her lucid days and promising her I'd find someone to love. "I've paid for that sin over and over, and I'm still punishing myself for it. I'm not making that mistake this time. But Tam isn't ready for me to say it out loud."

I felt a hand on my back and turned to see Tam standing behind me.

"What am I not ready for you to say out loud? Did I hear you tell her I'm a mistake?"

I reached for her, but she stepped away.

"You didn't hear the whole thing, Tam," Beth said. "She was talking about what happened when that bimbo almost ruined her life. That was the mistake she was talking about."

She stepped between me and Tam and put her hands on each of Tam's arms.

"I asked her if she loves you, and she wouldn't answer me out of respect for you." Beth looked at me over her shoulder and then back at Tam. "Tam, this woman has the biggest heart in the world, and she had a partner whose heart was even bigger. I don't want her hurt ever again. And that's why I asked her. Her answer is between the two of you."

Beth looked at me again and left. Tam and I stared at each other.

"What am I not ready to hear you say out loud?" Tam asked in a low voice that caught in her throat as she spoke. She took a step toward me and held out her hand. I took it and pulled her into my arms.

"I love you," I whispered into her ear. "I almost said it last night and again this morning, but you told me you weren't ready to say those words yet, and I was afraid if I did, you would feel pressured. But I can't hold back anymore. I love you, Tam Murphy."

She tightened her hold on me, but she said nothing, and my heart broke.

"Let's go back to the house." I stepped out of her embrace. "I have a surprise for Allison, and then I need to get out of here."

I left the shed without looking to see if she was behind me. When I got to the house, I found Melba and whispered in her ear. She disappeared into the first bedroom and reemerged with her guitar and a stool. Without a word, she sat on the stool and began to play. I hummed along with her for a moment to make sure we were in the same key. As the chords of the guitar floated through the air, the drone of voices dropped. When it was mostly quiet, I held my hand out to Allison, who already had tears rolling down her face.

After three long years, I sang in public. I serenaded Allison with a medley of her favorite songs, with Melba following along on her guitar the way she always had when we performed together. At the end, I led the group in a rousing rendition of *Happy Birthday*, which ended in cheers, applause, and hugs for both me and Allison. I made my way through the crowd to the front door. Once there, I turned and looked around at the group and knew I'd made a tremendous step forward in part of my life but had possibly made a gigantic step backward in another part.

I didn't see Tam anywhere, so I made my way to the car and leaned on it, a minute before unlocking it and sitting in the driver's seat. I reclined the seat all the way, covered my face with my hands, and released the emotions which had built while I was singing. After a few minutes, someone climbed in the car with me, laid on top of me, and began kissing my hands. I peeked through my fingers into Tam's eyes.

"I love you, too, Janice," she whispered. "Let's go home. I'm tired, and I bet you're exhausted. I'll drive."

She rolled off of me and helped me to sit up and then stand up. I stared at her for a long moment before pulling her to me and kissing her and holding on to her for dear life.

CHAPTER FIFTEEN

Tam took me home, tucked me into bed, and then returned to her house even though I begged her to stay.

"We both have some more thinking to do." She kissed my forehead. "Get some sleep, and I'll talk to you soon."

But "soon" wasn't the next day or the next few days. She sent me one text message asking me to give her some space. My heart was in turmoil, and the door to the dark place was opening again. What *thinking* was I supposed to be doing? I knew I loved her and wanted her in my life. I had no questions about those facts. But I respected her need for space and didn't call or go to her house even as I sank into my doldrums and ate next to nothing.

"Melba, I only sang at Allison's party as part of my gift to her," I told her when she called a week and some days after the party.

"You should still get your keyboard out again. Let me come over with my guitar, and we can practice together. We sounded pretty good the other day, but we both got lost a time or two, and that's only because it's been so long since we practiced together." Melba sighed. "I need someone to sing with me while I play. I need the practice. Please, Janice?"

"Oh, alright. But don't get the wrong idea. I have no interest in performing anywhere for any reason. And besides, if I did, and the billing had my name on it, no one would come."

"You are so damn paranoid. Or vain." I could almost see Melba shaking her head.

"What do you mean?" The ire in me built, and I was ready to change my mind about practicing with her. It took everything in me not to lash out at her.

"I'm not going to explain," she said. "Think about it. I'm off tomorrow, so I'll see you in the morning. I'll be there at nine. Have a pot of coffee ready, okay?"

Before I could say more, she disconnected the call. My keyboard was hidden in the guest bedroom closet. I uncovered it, pulled it to the living room, dusted it off, and plugged it in. I got a dining chair, sat at the instrument, and stared at it. There was a time when I could put my fingers on the keyboard, and instinct would have them dancing their way through a song. But now my fingers had two left feet, and I wasn't eager to hear how bad I sounded after several years of neglecting my love of making music.

After taking a deep breath, I shook out my fingers and touched the keyboard. I ran through the scales and groaned when I missed a couple of notes. I also pulled some sheet music from the file cabinet. I chose a piece at random, put it on the keyboard's music stand, and studied it for a moment. After a couple of false starts, the music came back to me, and

I closed my eyes and swayed with the song, which was etched in my memory and now flowed from my fingers to the keyboard. When I finished, I realized my eyes were wet with tears. A cool breeze blew by and lingered on my face before wafting across my fingers, still resting on the keyboard.

"Thank you, Sandy," I whispered. "I love you, too."

I spent most of the day practicing and reacquainting my spirit with the art of music. When I finally went to bed in the wee hours of the morning, my soul was smiling and was truly at peace in what seemed like forever, and I fell into a restful sleep. The alarm clock didn't even piss me off by having the gall to wake me earlier than I had become accustomed to. I vocally ran through my scales as I showered and discovered my bathroom had horrible acoustics. But it didn't stop me from singing to my reflection in the mirror as I got dressed and combed my hair.

Melba, as was her habit, arrived at nine o'clock sharp. She laughed when I threw the front door open and pulled her inside and into a hug.

"Why do I think you've decided you're excited about this after all?"

"Oh, Melba. Thank you," I smiled at her. "I spent all day yesterday playing my keyboard, and it seems like I've turned a corner I didn't realize I needed to turn. Let me get you a cup of coffee, and let's talk about where you want to start. I pulled out some folk music and some jazz, as well as Tret Fure."

"Sounds good. Let me drink a cup of coffee, and we'll get started."

I was in my element for the next several hours. Melba and I played duets, and then I sang while she played her guitar. We finally collapsed on the sofa with glasses of iced tea and grinned at each other.

"You still got it, girl," she said, clinking glasses with me. "Are you sure you don't want to perform? There's an open mic at Carson's next Thursday. Why don't you think about it? I'm going regardless."

Before I had time to panic, my doorbell rang. When I peeked through the peephole, my heart raced, and I had to remind myself to be decorous as I opened the door. Tam stood there, a hesitant smile on her face.

"Hi," I said. I stepped aside for her to come in.

"Oh, no," she said. "You have company. Ocee insisted I bring some things she thought you needed. I'll leave my wagon, and you can bring it back around later."

"My company is Melba. I'm sure she'd love to say hello to you. And what did Ocee decide I need?"

I peeked around her at the canvas wagon sitting on the sidewalk and had to laugh even as tears stung my eyes. The wagon was full of mums and fall-blooming daisies. I stepped outside to look at them and saw a piece of paper shoved between two of them.

"Plant your flowers, Miss Janice," Ocee had written. "I love you." Flowers drawn in the primitive way of a kindergartener surrounded the words.

"Oh, goodness. She is so precious."

"She's angry because you weren't at dinner last week." Tam rubbed my arm, and it was everything I could do not to pull her into an embrace. Instead, I ran my hand over the top of the multi-colored mums waiting to be planted.

I laughed as the strains of *Tiptoe Through the Tulips* came from a rocking chair on the porch. I joined Melba and tried to reach the high notes, but my alto voice failed miserably, and the three of us dissolved in laughter.

"Hi, Tam." Melba pulled Tam into an embrace. "We've been practicing, and it's getting to be time for me to head out."

"Oh, not yet," I said. I turned to Tam and smiled. "Can you come in, or are you in a hurry?"

"I have time. I'm having company tomorrow, but I already have everything ready."

My heart dropped a bit when I realized *company* didn't include me, and I worried where her thinking had taken her. Inside, I freshened Melba's and my tea and got a glass for Tam.

Melba was sitting on the coffee table, strumming her guitar. I sat down at my keyboard, listened a moment, and joined her. After a few bars, I started singing Tret Fure's *Grace of God*, the song I sang at Sandy's funeral. Tears poured from both Melba's and my eyes, but we didn't miss a note. When we finished, I covered my face with my hands. Arms encircled me from both sides.

"I guess I should have played a different song," Melba said in my ear. "I'm sorry."

"No. I'm glad you played it." I shook my head. "I haven't sung it in a long time, and it helped to sing it now. Thank you."

Melba kissed me on the cheek and started packing her guitar in its case. I turned to Tam, who kneeled beside me.

"I miss you," I whispered. She caressed the back of my head before rising and hugging Melba.

"Y'all sound amazing together."

"I'm trying to talk her into coming to open mic at Carson's on Thursday," Melba said. Once again, I shook my head.

"I'm not ready." Panic built in my chest.

"Yes, you are," Melba said. "We sounded amazing singing *As If by the Wind* a while ago and *Grace of God* just now. Come on, Janice. It's time you put the shit behind you and step back into the limelight where you belong."

"I'll come with you." Tam rubbed my arm. "I want to hear you sing some more. You have a gift you should be sharing. Please?"

I put my arm around her as I took a deep breath. I was relieved when she didn't pull away.

"For you, I'll do it. But if I have a nervous breakdown, it's on y'all's backs."

Melba hugged me before heading out the door. As soon as she was gone, I turned to Tam and studied her face.

"I want to kiss you," I said, my voice husky. "But what do you want? Why have you been avoiding me? I miss you so much."

She took my hand and led me to the sofa. Once we sat down, she leaned over and gave me a light kiss on the lips.

"I missed you, too. But I had to figure out what I missed most—you or the sex."

"What did you decide?" I held my breath as I waited for her answer.

"Breathe, silly." She grinned as she poked me in the side. But her face turned serious again. "Janice, I missed both you and the sex, but I missed you the most. I missed your hugs, your understanding, your ability to listen with your whole body, your wise words when I need to hear them, and your silence when I need to be quiet."

"But? I hear a 'but' coming."

Tam began to pace the living room, wringing her hands in front of her. I didn't move except to watch her as she traversed the room several times. My patience was waning, and my heart was breaking before she finally sat in front of me on the coffee table and took my hands.

"But I'm scared. I'm so insecure, and every time you make a sound I'm not familiar with, you sneeze, or even belch, I get scared. I've fallen in love with you, and the thought of losing you…Oh, it hurts. It hurts so bad."

I pulled her over to sit on the sofa beside me and let her sob herself out, holding my shirt in her fists. Finally, she sat back. I reached past her and snagged the box of tissue from the side table. I used several to dry her face.

"The reason I cried when I sang *Grace of God* is because it's the song I sang at Sandy's funeral." I grabbed a few tissues for myself. "I'm not sure why Melba chose to play that particular song, but after I finished singing, Sandy's spirit sat on my shoulders and then blew away, taking what felt like a load of bricks with her."

Tam started to speak when I paused, but I put two fingers on her mouth.

"I'm scared, too, Tam. Whenever I'm holding you and can feel your heart beating against me, I count the beats and try to figure out if their rhythm is right. Even though I know it's just your nature, and you don't have dementia or a heart problem, my heart skips twenty or thirty beats every time you have to stop and search for a word or idea you can't remember. So, baby, I understand. When I lose a little bit of weight or have a tummy ache because I either ate too much, not enough, or something that didn't like me, I watch as you struggle with the pain and uncertainty. I don't know what to tell either of us except to love each other with all we have and keep an eagle eye on each other."

"That's what I meant when I said you always have wise words when I need to hear them." She fell into my arms.

I shifted until I was resting on the sofa with her on top of me, and I smoothed her hair off her wet face. I used the tips of my fingers to dry any tears I could before drawing her closer for a kiss. The kiss we shared was gentle and spoke tons more than any words could say.

She rose to her feet and extended her hand to me. I took it and followed her to the bedroom, where we consummated the message which accompanied the kiss.

CHAPTER SIXTEEN

"I have to get home," she said later that evening as we finished eating dinner. "My company is coming for lunch, and if I stay here tonight, I might not get back in time to look presentable."

"Is the family coming over?" I pushed the last of my salad around my plate.

"No." The tone in her voice made me look up. Frustration oozed from her as she shook her head. "No. Danny and Mae are coming over. Mae is still not happy he's back in my life, so I decided to put an end to her idiocy by trying to play mediator. If you hear a nuclear explosion come from my house, please come rescue me."

"Oh, goodness." I watched as her ire built behind her eyes and her jaw clenched. "Sweetie, you might get mad at me for asking, but is it your place to do this? Isn't it Mae's decision how she handles her grief, even if she's still at the anger stage?"

Tam's eyes flashed for a moment, and I readied myself
for an onslaught of angry words. Then her shoulders
slumped, and she put her hands over her face.

"Damn you and your wise words." She peeked at me
through her fingers. "What should I do now? They're already
planning on being there, and it's too late for me to call either
of them. I guess I could send them a text message."

"Let them come over. But let them decide how to handle
being in the other's presence. And if they can't, and one, or
both of them, leaves, let them go, but call me, and I'll come
sit with you as you try to process things."

She paced the kitchen. I gathered our dishes and dodged
her as she continued on her path. She embraced me, her arms
encircling my waist, as I scraped the leftovers in the compost
bowl. I turned so I could gather her in a proper hug.

"I'll be glad to walk you home."

She shook her head.

"No, because I'd want you either to stay or let me walk
you back home."

"I can take you. Even for fall, the skeeters are pretty
bad."

"Well, if they carry me off, I won't have to face the
disaster I planned for tomorrow."

I kissed the side of her head.

"But I wouldn't have you either."

She turned her head so that she could take my lips in her
own. Her kiss made me weak in the knees, and for an instant,
I considered begging her to stay. Instead, I walked her to the
front door and to the end of my sidewalk. We exchanged
another hug. I watched as she walked to the corner, where
she turned and waved at me before disappearing toward her
house.

It was late, but restlessness overwhelmed me. I stared at the wagon of flowers. Even though it was dark, I got my hoe and trowel and a bottle of root stimulant. Back in the front yard, by the light of the security lights and the light on the porch, I arranged the pots of mums and Marguerite daisies along the sidewalk, rearranging several times until I was happy with the combination of colors and set to work. It was good to get my hands in the soil. It always brought me peace.

When I finished, I stood on my little porch and smiled in satisfaction. Once inside, I turned the porch light off and made sure the security lights were no longer illuminating the yard before I took a long shower and thought about Tam. I hoped her lunch with Mae and Danny wouldn't be too stressful for her.

It was past the wee hours of the morning when I finally fell into bed and into a sleep full of odd dreams, where Sandy and Tam were sitting at a bar together while I sang from a stage I couldn't escape. I fought my way out of the dream and sat up in a cold sweat.

"What were y'all talking about, Sandy?" I could almost hear her melodious laugh as the cool breeze blew across my breasts, making my nipples stand at attention. "Not fair when I can't touch you, too."

I lay back and remembered Sandy making love to me. My fingers found my clit, but while I fantasized about Sandy making love to me, her spirit morphed into Tam, and it wasn't long before I worked myself into a frenzy. When I climaxed, I cried out, but more from wishing Tam was with me than from the climax itself.

The sun was high when I dragged myself from bed later that morning. Once I was dressed, I dragged my feet to the kitchen, where I started the coffeemaker. I leaned on the counter until it finished brewing. Even though it was tempting to drink it straight from the pot, I managed to pour myself a mug without spilling any. Fixing anything to eat was out of the question. I rummaged through my bread drawer and was happy to find I still had some mini bagels.

With my cup of coffee at my elbow, the bag of bagels beside me, and my tablet in my hands, I lay on the sofa and browsed the news channels and Facebook, but soon, the tablet seemed to weigh a ton. I put it on my chest and closed my eyes, fully intending to reopen them and try to get some housework accomplished. But when I did open them, the light in the room was different, and I wondered what awakened me. But then the doorbell rang, and I knew it had been my phone alerting me to someone on the porch.

I rubbed my face. It took me a few more minutes to be awake enough to answer the door. In the meantime, the bell rang two more times.

"I'm coming," I yelled, aggravation rising into my craw. But when I looked through the peephole, I regretted the sound of my voice. I opened the door with a grin on my face.

"Hi," I said as Ocee started to open the storm door. Mae slapped her little hand.

"We wait until we're invited," Mae said.

Ocee rubbed the smacked hand. She looked at me with the saddest eyes and a trembling bottom lip. I pushed the door open and squatted. She flew into my arms and put hers around my neck.

"Thank you for the flowers," I said as I hugged her. "Did you pick them out all by yourself?"

She stepped back, and I was relieved to see a huge smile on her face.

"Mostly. Daddy helped me. I wanted to get all mums, but he said it would look better if there was something else with them. So we got the daisies, too. They look good in your flower beds."

"When did you plant those?" Tam asked. "They weren't there when I left last night."

I almost fell over laughing at the look Mae gave her mother. She was obviously unaware of our relationship.

"After you left." I stood up, and muscles I hadn't used for a while screamed at me, but I tried to ignore them. "Y'all come on in, and I'll get us something to drink."

"You have a piano." A grin spread across Ocee's little face. "I didn't know you had a piano. Do you know how to play?"

"Oh, she does." Tam gave me a sweet smile. Another strange look crossed Mae's face. "Maybe if you ask her nicely, she'll play something for us."

Ocee folded her hands under her chin and grinned at me. "Please, Miss Janice?"

"Let me get us some tea, and then I will."

"I'll get the drinks. You play us a song," Tam said.

I watched as she headed for the kitchen, and it didn't surprise me when Mae followed on her heels.

"Can you show me how to play?" Ocee was oblivious to the fact both her grandmother and mother had disappeared.

I pulled the chair out from the keyboard and sat as far back on it as I could so that she could perch between my legs. I switched on the keyboard, put my fingers on the keys, and ran through the scales. Ocee turned and grinned at me.

"I want to learn to do that."

"Let's begin with something simple." I took her finger and pressed a key. "This is the main note on a piano. It's called middle C."

Keeping her finger in my hand, I guided her through *Twinkle Little Star.*

"Oh, cool. I want to do it myself."

"Okay. I'll point at the right keys, and you play them."

By the time we had played the song a few times, Ocee was bouncing on the chair.

"I think I can do it myself. May I?"

"Go right ahead." I couldn't help but smile. It had been quite a while since I gave a music lesson, and I'd almost forgotten the satisfaction I had when a student "got it."

Ocee flawlessly picked out each note in the little song using only her forefinger. We were both surprised when we heard applause behind us. She jumped off the chair, turned to face her family, and bowed at the waist two or three times. I laughed, pulled her onto my lap, and gave her a tickle.

"Miss Janice!" she yelled. "Not fair. Let me go."

I set her on her feet and patted her butt as she scooted over and hugged her mother.

"I really need piano lessons." She took her mother's face in her hands. "Please tell Daddy I'm talented, and I really need them."

Mae took Ocee's hands and pulled her into another hug while she scowled at me. And it wasn't a teasing scowl. I leaned back to get away from the anger coming from her.

"Uhm, I'll be back in a minute."

I tried not to rush as I passed the sofa and headed to my bedroom and bathroom. Sitting on the end of the bed, I rubbed my face. Confrontations scared me, and I wondered if it was safe to go back to the living room. I flinched when I felt a hand on my shoulder and flinched again when I saw Mae looking at me.

"I'm sorry, Janice. Is it my fault you're upset? I shouldn't have looked at you like that."

"I shouldn't have taught Ocee anything without your permission."

Mae shook her head as she sat beside me.

"It's okay. That's not the problem."

She looked at her hands before taking a deep breath and glancing over at me.

"How long did you and Mom think you could keep it a secret?"

"I didn't know it was a secret. I left it up to Tam to tell you. We never discussed it."

"Mom is still grieving for both Darla and Aaron." Mae's eyes were bright with tears. "I'm putting you on notice, Janice Halston. You better be good to her, and you better not hurt her."

I put my arm over her shoulders and pulled her into a hug and softly kissed her on the side of her head.

"Miss Mae, I'm falling head over heels in love with your mother. I know she's still grieving. I'm still grieving for Sandy, too. Tam and I are learning how to support each other through the grief and not let it rule everything else. Honey, I can't imagine ever doing anything to intentionally hurt her. I promise."

Mae nodded and took another deep breath.

"She's going to think I'm back here strangling you if we don't get back out there."

We hugged each other again. I laughed when I heard the strains of *Twinkle Little Star* being played again.

"She picked it up a lot faster than most kids. What would you say if I give her an occasional lesson in exchange for a few hugs?"

Mae laughed.

"I'll talk to Duke and see what he thinks." A frown marred her face for a moment. "The only problem is we can't afford to get her a keyboard to practice on."

"Leave it to me, sugar."

By then, we were back in the living room. Tam turned on the sofa and smiled when she saw us standing arm in arm and watching Ocee experiment with pushing other keys on the piano.

"My turn," I said. I reclaimed my chair at the piano. Ocee leaned on my knee. "I can't play with you right there, sweets. Go sit with your grandma."

She gave me a quick kiss on the cheek before scurrying to the sofa. I stretched my hands out and put them on the keyboard. I hoped I remembered how to play one of my favorite songs. Almost as if on their own, my fingers flew over the piano in *Flight of the Bumblebee*. I was breathless when I finished. I turned in my chair and blushed when Tam, Mae, and Ocee jumped to their feet, clapping their hands.

Not much later, Mae settled Ocee in the wagon and headed back to Tam's house. Tam and I watched until they turned the corner and then went back inside. Once the front door closed, I took her in my arms and kissed her, but not a lusty, passionate kiss, although I did plan to do that later.

"Mmm," she said. She started swaying, and I moved my feet with hers and, to only the music of our hearts, we slow danced to the sofa where we sat and snuggled.

"Tell me what happened this morning," I said into her hair. She shuddered, and I held her tighter.

"It was pretty intense. Danny came ready to reconcile, but Mae was still on the warpath. I had fixed a simple lunch of sandwiches and potato salad because I wasn't sure if they would actually eat. When Mae refused to say hello to Danny, he hugged me, went to the table, helped himself, and sat down to eat. I stood back to see what happened next.

"Mae sat down at the table too, but she leaned toward him and asked him how he could eat when he knew what he did. He put his sandwich down and took her hands. She tried to pull away, but he wouldn't let her.

"'What I did,' he said, 'was love your brother with all my heart and try to save his life from a wound no one could save him from. What I did was hold him while he slipped away, telling him I loved him the whole time. What I did was ride in the belly of a loud military airplane with fifteen coffins, bringing Aaron home to y'all. What I did was watch the two of you break into too many pieces for me to put back together. What I did was step away from you when I realized how much my presence hurt you. What I did, and what your mother did, was lay our hearts open so that we could reconcile. What I do every week, without fail, is go see Aaron and talk to him. Lately, Charles has been going with me, which makes me love him more than I already do. What I do now is make sure your mother knows I never stopped loving her, and I do the things Aaron would if he was here, and I always will. What I do is grieve that you and I can't get to that point, too. But it has to be up to you. And what I'm going to do right now is finish my sandwich, hug your mother, and leave. But I'll always be here, Mae. Whenever you're ready, I'll always be here.' And he finished his sandwich, hugged me, and drove away."

I handed her the box of tissues and grabbed some for myself.

"What did Mae do?"

"She sat there and watched him eat. I kept praying she would say something, anything, or would hug him before he left, but she didn't. She cleaned off the table, put the leftovers away, and called Duke and asked him to bring Ocee over so we could come visit you, and that's what we did. I have no idea how she feels about what Danny said. She didn't tell me, and I didn't ask."

"How are you?"

"Worn out. I didn't sleep very well for worrying about today and wishing I'd stayed here. But it looks like you would have put me to work if I had."

"Oh, those flowers wouldn't have been planted if you had stayed."

I turned so that she could lie on the sofa beside me, and I gave her the lusty, passionate kiss I wanted to earlier. To my surprise, she shook me off and snuggled up to me.

"I'm so tired, Janice. Will you just hold me? Please?"

"Do you want to go to bed?" But before I finished speaking, she was asleep. I pressed my lips to her forehead, closed my eyes too, and reveled in the feeling of holding this woman I loved. A cool breeze settled on us for a moment and then was gone.

CHAPTER SEVENTEEN

The following Thursday, I stood to the side of the small stage at Carson's, trembling, heart pounding. Melba laid her hand on my arm and squeezed it. I tried to smile at her, but my nerves were getting the best of me.

"Next to perform are Melba and Janice," the emcee said. "Melba graces us with her presence regularly, but those of you who have been around just short of forever will remember Melba and Janice performing together way back when. If you're not familiar with them, be prepared to be mesmerized by these two beauties." The emcee turned to us. "The stage is yours, ladies."

Melba gave me a bit of a push, and I moved to sit behind the keyboard while she plugged the amplifier into her guitar and perched on the stool the emcee put beside the microphone stand.

"Hey, y'all."

"Hey, Melba," the crowd responded, applauding and cheering.

"Y'all all know me and are probably tired of seeing me every week—"

"No, we're not," Allison yelled, causing everyone to laugh.

"Like I was saying before I was so rudely interrupted by someone in the peanut gallery, tonight, I brought an old friend who has been hiding for far too long. Y'all say hello to Janice."

I blushed when our friends, including Tam, Mae, and Duke, jumped to their feet, hooting and hollering. I bowed my head toward the keyboard and didn't look up again until Melba strummed a few chords on her guitar. She gave me a bit of a nod when I glanced at her, and I joined in on the keyboard. I sank into the music and forgot everything else. I always hated when we got to the end of a song, and this time was no different.

The response of the audience stunned me. They were still cheering when Melba started again, this time playing a song we had decided I would sing. It took a couple of tries, but once I opened my mouth and let the words out, I was in my element. We got three standing ovations and played two more sets before I held up both hands and walked off the stage, heading for the restrooms, tears pouring from my eyes. An arm snaked around my waist, and Tam helped me find a private place where I could hang onto her and cry so hard I had the hiccups.

"What happened?" she asked once I could get hold of myself.

"I'm not sure. I got so overwhelmed."

131

"Janice, you were amazing." She lightly brushed her lips against mine. "I'm so proud of you. Everyone loved you. You and Melba put on a wonderful show. Come on now. Come back to the table, and I'll treat you to a drink."

"Just a soda," I said. "Thank you."

She took my elbow and led me out of the hallway and back into the dark cavern of the bar. When we arrived at the table, everyone shifted around so I could sit next to Tam. We spent the rest of the evening in happy camaraderie.

I was so exhausted I could barely hold my head up, and I was glad I'd ridden to the bar with Tam rather than drive myself. Sleep overtook me as soon as I buckled in. At her house, Tam got me inside and to her bedroom, where she helped strip out of my clothes and slip between the covers. I remembered nothing else until I woke early the next morning with her back pressed against mine. I turned over, spooned her, and fell back to sleep. When I woke up next, I was alone in bed.

I checked the bathroom, but it was empty. I put my clothes on and headed down the hallway. The aroma of French toast and fresh coffee pulled me to the kitchen.

"Hi," Tam said when I pushed through the door. She came over and gave me a light kiss. "Sit down and I'll get you some coffee."

"Can I do anything to help?" I wasn't used to being waited on.

"You can sit down and drink your coffee." She set a mug on the table. "Breakfast is almost ready, so just relax. Did you sleep okay?"

The coffee was so rich and delicious I decided Tam must have stirred it with her finger.

"I don't know what time I woke up the first time, but it was nice to wake up next to you," I said as I nodded.

"When you turned over and hugged me, I felt so loved and secure." She smiled at me as she pulled a pan from the oven. "I hope you like oven-baked French toast."

I held out my arms, and she came to me after setting the pan on top of the stove. She sat on my lap, and I kissed her as I slid my hand up her shirt and found a full breast to caress. The moan she filled my mouth with caused zing after zing from my groin throughout my body. She pushed away from me and got off my lap.

"Food first," she said with a crack in her voice. She cleared her throat as she served the food. When she sat down, I found her leg with one of my bare feet and ran my toes from her calf to the back of her knee and down again. "Stop, Janice. Oh, God. Damn it all."

She took my hand and dragged me back to the bedroom.

CHAPTER EIGHTEEN

Over the next few weeks, life settled into a sort of routine. Tam and I bounced between each other's houses, only occasionally spending the night apart, usually when Ocee was staying with her. Whenever Ocee was at Tam's, she hounded her to come over for a piano lesson. She always paid me with multiple hugs, and I enjoyed it almost as much as she did.

Ocee proved to be an easy student. She picked up reading music and the correct placement of her hands within a couple of lessons. I dug my spare keyboard out of the storage locker and had it serviced. When I gave it to them, Mae and Duke insisted they had to pay me. To keep them from being embarrassed about receiving what they perceived as an expensive gift, I suggested we come to an agreement for them to provide me with plants for my spring garden, which they were glad to do.

The flower garden was filling in again, and the neighbors would smile and wave when they saw me out working in it. A couple of weeks earlier, Mrs. Walters at the community office had called me and let me know Monica was let go because of numerous complaints against her. The company also banned her from any neighborhood owned by them. But they couldn't do anything to her about the vandalism to my yard since they couldn't prove she had anything to do with it, especially since there were many cars similar to hers in the area. They were kind enough to compensate me for the plants I lost, and I had to be satisfied with their response.

Melba and I continued to practice together and perform at open mic nights around the area. Soon, both clubs and individuals were approaching us to perform at parties, weddings, and other events. I balked. It was one thing to perform in the small clubs where most of the audience was friends and family, but quite another to perform where we most likely wouldn't know anyone.

"Janice."

I looked up from studying the new sheet music we chose to work on. The look on Melba's face surprised me. She seldom frowned or looked worried, but both now marred her complexion.

"What's wrong, Mel?" I crossed the room and put my hand on her shoulder. "Are you coming down with the bug that's going around?"

Melba shook her head and gestured at the sofa. We curled on opposite ends, and I waited for her to tell me what was going on.

"Janice, Carmen and I are broke," she finally said. "A lot of things came due all at once, and we've been robbing Peter to pay Paul, but we're at our limit."

"I can help, you know." I pulled out my phone. "I'll put some money in your account. How much do you need?"

"No. No. No." She shook her head so hard her glasses ended up crooked on her nose. "We don't want a loan or a gift. Not when there's a solution, and you're part of the solution if you'll agree to it."

I had a feeling I knew what was coming, and my heart was already pounding.

"If we take a few of these gigs, we can make enough money between now and the new year to get us out of the hole. Shoot, the gig we've been offered on New Year's Eve would be ample to pull us out on its own, but we can't wait that long. Janice, one gig a week would help so much, and it would allow me to earn the money instead of having someone bailing us out. Please."

By the time she finished speaking, I was pacing the living room, trying not to hyperventilate. Melba jumped off the sofa and stood in my path. When I stopped, she laid a hand on each of my upper arms.

"What are you so afraid of? Is it still because of the shit from a few years ago? No one knows who you are anymore, and besides, no one ever uses our last names. I doubt we'd even know anyone at any of these things."

"That's part of the problem," I whispered. "I hate the idea of being among total strangers. The thought makes me sick to my stomach."

Melba led me back to the sofa.

"I didn't know your social anxiety was so severe. And I've been pushing you to do things that probably make you uncomfortable. I'm sorry."

"Just when I believe I'm going to be okay, something scares me again. As long as Tam is there, I can get through it because she can see when I'm getting overwhelmed, and she gets me out of the crowd until I calm down. But at these paid gigs, she won't be there. What if I panic and make a fool of us? I can't take the chance of ruining any opportunities you may have."

Tears stung my eyes. I looked away from my old friend. She put a box of tissues on my lap and gave me a one-armed hug.

"Maybe there's a solution. Hmmm, I believe there is. What if we ask Tam and Carmen to be our assistants? Carmen can take care of all the admin stuff, like making sure we get paid and keeping track of where we're supposed to be when. Tam can help us set up the equipment and pack it when we're done. That way, she'll be there for you, and we won't have to explain her presence. And with Carmen taking all the paperwork hassle out of our hands, we can concentrate on our music. Do you think Tam would go for it?"

"The only way to find out is to ask." I was relieved Melba had found an idea that made sense. "I'll call and see if she can come over so we can ask her. She's got a little while before she has to get the princess from school. Which reminds me, I promised Ocee a lesson this afternoon. You would not believe how fast she's learning the piano. We're already on the third book in level one, and she's getting bored with the simplicity of the pieces."

"Do you realize how much you glow when you talk about that kid?" Melba grinned at me. "You'd think she was your grandchild."

I blushed as I nodded.

"She's pretty special. And she's so different from any other kid I was ever around."

"Well, call your lady and see if she's free to come over."

Within fifteen minutes, Tam and I sat side by side on the sofa while Melba explained her idea. Tam looked at me and seemed to gauge my reaction.

"What are your thoughts on it, babe? Do you think you can handle doing this if I'm there?"

I shrugged.

"Just the idea of performing in front of strangers makes me choke. Which doesn't make sense since I used to do solo gigs all the time. I could do a reading from my books and enjoy every minute of the interaction with my readers. Gallery showings didn't turn me into a puddle of anxiety. I looked forward to discovering people's opinions of my work. And I loved singing for anyone who would listen. And now the thought of doing any of those scares the shit out of me."

Tam turned on the sofa so she was facing me.

"Did you talk to your doctor about this when you saw her last week? I know you were there to have your allergy medicine tweaked, but you promised you'd talk to her about your anxiety."

I studied my hands as I turned red.

"You didn't, did you?" Tam took a sharp breath through her nose, and I knew I was going to hear about it. "I have to go get Ocee, but we need to have a talk. Melba, you can probably count on me. I'll let you know. See y'all later."

And she was gone without hugging me, kissing me, or saying those three little words.

"Uh oh," Melba said into the silence Tam left in her wake. "I think you better call and make a doctor's appointment before she gets back. And I think it's a good idea, too."

"They'll give me some pills to take, and I already take more than I want to."

"Janice, you are as dense as a doorknob. Both Carmen and I take antidepressants, and I know Danny does, too, and I believe Beth does. It makes all the difference in the world. At least talk to your doctor about it before you decide."

She packed her guitar while she spoke. After giving me a quick hug, she was gone, and I was left to contemplate her words. I pulled my phone out and accessed my contacts.

An hour later, Tam was back at the house but without Ocee, which didn't surprise me since I knew Tam rightfully planned to ream me. I met her at the door with my hands in the air.

"Don't shoot until you hear me out."

She came in and took her jacket off without a word. After she sat on the sofa, her arms crossed over her chest, I tried to explain.

"I'm sorry I didn't talk to Dr. Patel about my anxiety. It sounds weird, but I was afraid she would want to send me to a psychiatrist, and I'm not willing to do that. The first therapist I saw after Sandy died. . ."

I swallowed the lump in my throat and turned away from Tam.

"She was a royal bitch and basically told me grief for a same-sex partner wasn't worth getting so upset about, but if Sandy had been my husband, well, it would have been a different story."

I heard Tam gasp, but I didn't turn back to her.

"I'm afraid a psychiatrist will tell me I should be over my fear of people knowing who I am and reacting to it, like all my friends keep telling me. While my brain knows they're right, the rest of me doesn't, and I cringe whenever someone looks at me wrong. Plus, I'll be looking out at a crowd of people I don't know and performing."

139

I took another deep breath.

"Shit. I take pills for my allergies, pills for the arthritis in my knees, and pills for my blood pressure, which isn't even that high. I'd rather not add any to the list. But when I told Melba, she basically called me a coward and told me she and Carmen, as well as a few other people in our circle, take antidepressants."

"Ump hmmm." Tam cleared her throat, and I finally looked at her. She had her hand in the air. "Me, too, Janice. I've taken them since Darla got sick. You wouldn't want to be around me if I didn't take them. And Mae recently started taking them. She didn't tell me until a few days ago that she's seeing a grief counselor again, and the counselor recommended them. Janice, I wish you would make an appointment to talk to your doctor. She might have a different solution, but you won't know if you don't ask."

"My appointment is Monday at ten. I was hoping you would go with me."

Tam put her hands on my shoulders.

"Thank you, sweetheart. I'll be glad to go with you. I love you, and I hate seeing you like you get after you perform. I already called Melba and told her I'd go with y'all to any gigs you book."

I laid my head on her shoulder, fighting back the emotions which threatened to swamp me. She led me back to the sofa, where she sat down and urged me to rest with my head in her lap. She bent and kissed my forehead before sitting back and stroking my head. Before long, I relaxed and dozed off. When I awoke, my head was on a pillow, and I could hear Tam puttering around in the kitchen. I sat up and stretched before I joined her.

"Hey, sleepyhead," she said as I hugged her. "Feel better?"

I nodded and tried to kiss her, but she laughed and turned her head.

"Every time you kiss me in the kitchen, we end up not eating for a couple of hours. That's not going to happen tonight. Have you stopped eating again? You look skinny."

"I don't eat as much when we aren't together," I said. I pulled her back into a hug. "It's easier to grab a snack than fix something."

"Janice, you have to start eating." Her voice cracked, and I stepped back and looked at her. "You worry me when you don't. I'm always afraid you're getting sick. That's something else you should talk about with your doctor. Your appetite fluctuating like it does isn't normal."

I sat her down in one of the chairs and squatted in front of her, both of her hands in mine.

"I love you for worrying about me. But I wish you could talk to my mother or Sandy. They would tell you this is how I've always been. Sometimes, I can't get enough to eat, no matter what. Other times, food doesn't appeal to me. I've had my thyroid tested, and I don't even know what else. Hon, it's just the way I am."

She leaned forward and put her forehead against mine. I dried the tears from her cheek with the pads of my thumb.

"I worry about you just as much. And when you get this upset thinking I'm sick, I worry if it's because something is wrong with you. Are you okay?"

"I'm fine. I have my well woman appointment right before Thanksgiving. My doctor will take a gallon of blood, but if things go as usual, I'll be told I have borderline everything but nothing to worry about because it's common for someone in their mid-sixties.

"You're not sixty-five yet."

"No, but I will be in January." She planted a soft kiss on my lips. "My pan has probably boiled dry before I even put the noodles in it. Let's go to the diner and get dinner. Then we can come home and play. Mae doesn't need me to watch Ocee tomorrow."

"Now that sounds like a plan." I pulled her to her feet and into my arms. "We both have to figure out a way not to worry about each other so much. It takes too much of our energy."

"After you see the doctor Monday, I'll start working on it," Tam said with a grin.

CHAPTER NINETEEN

Two weeks later, Melba and I had our first paid performance in over three years. Even with an antidepressant and an antianxiety medication on board, I was nervous. I kept running my hands through my hair until Tam threatened to tie them behind my back until it was time to perform.

"Sit down and let me comb your hair again," she said as she pulled the comb from her back pocket. After she fixed my hair, she gave me a quick kiss. "Now sit on your hands until it's time to go on stage. Once you get into your music, you'll be okay."

And she was right. Regardless of what genre we were playing on any given night, the music calmed my spirit. But when we stopped, my nerves kicked back into overdrive, and, more than once, Tam had to rescue me from myself. I kept hoping it would get easier, but while the anxiety wasn't as intense as it once was, it was still there.

"One more performance, Janice," Melba said when we were backstage on New Year's Eve, preparing for the largest gig we'd done to date. "Then we'll take three months off to recoup and learn some new music. Carmen already put it on our website that we're taking the time off, but we're still getting requests. We could book something every night of the year if we wanted to."

My eyes felt like they were going to pop out of my head.

"Unh-uh." Panic rose in the back of my throat. "I can't handle more than once a week. I have to have time to visit Sandy and go to the beach and just fucking breathe."

"Do the last one now," Tam said as she joined us. "Carmen and Melba already have the days on their calendars for when you need the time off. Your time with Sandy is sacred, and I won't let anything get in the way of that. And what's this about going to the beach?"

I face-palmed myself. "You weren't supposed to hear that part."

"Ladies and gentlemen, welcome."

For once, I was relieved to be introduced by the emcee so that I didn't have to explain myself to Tam. Melba and I stepped onto the stage to polite applause. We glanced at each other, and I was suddenly even more nervous. We were used to a much more raucous crowd.

"Thank you," Melba said. "We're glad to be here to help y'all welcome in the new year. If you have any requests, let us know, and, if we can, we'll be glad to honor them. First, Janice and I would like to perform some original music which we wrote. I hope y'all enjoy it."

Melba began strumming her guitar, and I joined her on the keyboard. I watched as the crowd paired off and began to dance. Melba nodded at me, and after a few more bars of instrumental music, I sang. Some people stopped dancing and turned to listen. Soon, no one was dancing. All eyes were on me. I had to look away or my nerves would have taken over, and I wouldn't have been able to finish. When I sang the last note, there was a long, uncomfortable moment of total silence. Out of the corner of my eyes, I saw Tam sidle toward the stage. In that moment, applause and cheers of "Bravo" filled the room. Melba and I exchanged looks, our mouths wide open. It took a few minutes before we could collect ourselves and play the dance music we were hired to play. Tam smiled at me and mouthed *I love you* before moving back to her spot backstage, where she was out of the way but could keep an eye on me.

We played slow dance music, dance music which elicited some interesting movements from some of the younger attendees, and even country line-dance music. By the time our long break came at ten-thirty, I was bordering on exhaustion.

"How are you doing?" Tam offered me a bottle of water, which I gladly accepted.

"I'm tired, but I'm okay. I have one more solo to do, and it's a song I sing a lot, so I'm not worried about it. And after *Auld Lang Syne* at midnight, we'll be on the downward slide to a shower and some sleep."

"Only sleep?" she whispered in my ear. I grinned and pulled her to me. There were too many people around, or I would have kissed her.

As I headed toward the snacks the party organizers provided for the entertainers and workers, someone tapped me on the shoulder. I turned, expecting to see Melba or Carmen. I almost threw up when I found I was face-to-face with the one person I never wanted to see again.

145

"You look good, Janice." AnnaMarie put her hand out to touch me. I moved out of her reach so fast I stepped on Tam's foot, but I caught her before she fell.

"Get me out of here," I hissed. "Please."

"Wait," AnnaMarie called as I tried to hurry away. "I'm single now. Can't we talk?"

I wanted to get away from her, and my stomach was roiling around, threatening to spew its contents of fear, anger, and regret. Tam led me to the bathroom, where I darted into the first empty stall and wretched.

"Oh, hon." Tam wet a paper towel and handed it to me. "Who was that?"

"Is she okay?" the occupant of another stall asked. "Do I need to see if there are any medical personnel available?"

I reached behind me and pushed the door closed as I wiped my face with the towel. I didn't move in case I had more to lose. It wasn't long before I heard the door to the restroom open and close and then the lock thrown.

"It's only me now," Tam said. "Can I come back in?"

I got to my feet and opened the door. She took me by the arm and led me to the sinks, where she wet another paper towel for me. I washed out my mouth and washed my face. When I looked in the mirror, the woman staring back at me was not the same woman who left my house that evening. My color was off. My eyes were wild. My hair stood on end.

"Sweetie, can you tell me who the woman was and why you got sick?"

I almost cried when I looked at Tam and saw the worry etched on her face.

"AnnaMarie Curry. The bitch who ruined my life. I can't go back out there. Will you go tell Melba?"

"Janice, if you don't finish, y'all don't get paid, and Carmen and Melba need the money. You'll be letting that woman win. Please try to pull yourself together and do the best you can."

I shook my head even though I knew she had valid points. Someone knocked on the door, and Tam unlocked it.

"What's going on?" one of the organizers asked. "Someone informed me one of our performers is ill."

"I'm fine." I joined Tam at the door. "I choked on a bite of food, and it made me sick to my stomach, but I'm fine now."

"Are you sure?" The woman gave me a hard look.

"I need to comb my hair and have something to drink, and I'll be ready. Thank you for checking."

Tam took my elbow and led me to where Melba and Carmen stood together near the stage. Melba gave me a hug.

"I saw that bitch talking to you. Are you able to keep going?"

I nodded, even though I knew it was an abject lie.

"I'm fine. Let's get this over and done with."

But before we could take the stage, someone else stepped to the microphone, and I almost got sick again. Tam rubbed my back.

"Hi, y'all," AnnaMarie said. "I want to let you know Janice is Janice Halston of Gregson's School of Art and Music fame. Let's welcome her and her partner, Melba, back to the stage."

She turned and looked at us, clapping her hands. It took everything I had not to bolt, but I followed Melba onto the platform to the applause of the partygoers, although I could see the strange looks on many of their faces. I sat at the piano and ran through the scales on the muted keyboard before turning it on.

"Are you sure you can sing?" Melba whispered in my ear.

I smiled the best I could and nodded. She patted me on the shoulder and returned to the microphone.

"We're back, folks," she said with a forced grin. "Janice will perform another song for y'all, and afterwards, we'll dance until it's time for the countdown to midnight. Janice, are you ready?"

The worried look in her eye steeled me to do my best. I hated to disappoint her. I nodded and played the opening notes to the song. Melba joined me, and we played several bars of introduction before I began to sing. Applause rose from the crowd when they recognized the song, and most of them started dancing again. I got through the song, and my smile when I finished was genuine as almost everyone turned to look at me and applaud. I took a small bow before Melba and I once again played the standard dance music.

Tam appeared at my side with a bottle of water and a smile.

You did good, she mouthed. *I love you.*

Her encouragement and belief in me helped put the confrontation with AnnaMarie behind me, although I had a feeling it would not be the last of her. And I was right. When we finished at one o'clock, she was waiting at the side of the stage. Melba approached her.

"Please get lost. You're not welcome here."

"I beg your pardon," the bitch huffed. "I can be sure you never perform around here again."

Carmen grabbed Melba's arm and pulled her away as Melba stepped into AnnaMarie's personal space. Tam had joined me on the stage and stood between me and the confrontation happening just feet away. She made eye contact with me and kept it, helping me stay calm and grounded. But when AnnaMarie stepped onto the stage, grabbed Tam by the arm, and tried to move her out of the way, I was unprepared for what happened next.

Tam made a quick move and freed her arm from AnnaMarie's grasp, and, before I could blink, AnnaMarie was flat on her back on the floor. The look on her face almost made me break into hysterical laughter.

"You keep your filthy hands off of me," Tam hissed in a tone of voice I'd never heard before. "And you leave Janice alone. She wants nothing to do with you, and it would behoove you to just move on."

"Someone call nine-one-one," AnnaMarie screamed. "This bitch assaulted me."

Two of the organizers helped her to her feet. One of them rushed her away while the other turned to us. I was struggling to keep my stomach under control. Tam wrapped an arm around my waist and pulled me close. Melba had materialized on the other side of me and also slipped an arm around me.

"We are so sorry this happened," the organizer said. "Mrs. Curry had no right to accost y'all in that manner or to make the unapproved announcement before your last set. Mrs. Towson and I saw what happened, and there will be no legal ramifications from us. What Mrs. Curry does, though, may be another story. If she takes legal steps, let us know, and we'll make sure the authorities are aware of what we saw."

She stopped and grinned at Tam. "I wish I could move like you do," she said. "Every woman should be able to defend herself, and I, for one, don't want to make you mad."

Tam stepped forward, her hand outstretched. The organizer shook it and then patted me on the shoulder.

"Janice, I followed the whole ridiculous case when it was happening. I admired you at the time, and I still admire you for the class you showed through it all. My apologies for what happened this evening. Don't stop singing."

My brain was reeling too fast for me to have the ability to grab any words.

"She really is able to talk." Tam grinned at me. "I think she's overwhelmed right now, and we all need to go home. Thank you for coming to our rescue."

The organizer left the platform, and we breathed a sigh of relief in unison. Without a word, we broke down our equipment, put it on the hotel luggage carrier, and took it to our cars. Once it was loaded, we stood and stared at each other.

"Well, that was an interesting start to the new year," Carmen said, shaking her head. "I checked our account, and the money for tonight is already there. Janice, I'll transfer your half when we get home. You were wonderful tonight. In fact, you were better than I've ever heard you."

I blushed as the other two agreed with her. After hugs all around, we were finally on our way home. Tam drove since I was both exhausted and wound up. I couldn't sit still if my life had depended on it.

"Want to go to the All-Nighter and see if they have an empty booth and get some dinner?" Tam covered my hand with one of her own as I fiddled with the heater settings and then the radio tuner of my SUV. "You won't be able to sleep until you calm down."

"I would rather not be around any more people," I said. "Let's go home. A hot shower usually helps calm me. I don't know why I'm so jittery."

Tam let out a sharp laugh.

"Hmmm, could it be you just encountered some unnecessary drama, and I scared you half to death?"

"Uh huh." I turned in my seat to look at her. Her face was lit by the dim lights of the dashboard dials and, at the same time, was silhouetted by the lights of the buildings we passed.

"How did you do that? I mean, damn, girl. What did you do? It happened so fast, I really don't know."

"It was a self-defense move I learned way back when Darla was still alive. She got mugged and roughed up pretty bad at a concert, and she insisted we take classes. Until tonight, I've never had to use anything I learned, and I have to admit I surprised myself when I remembered the move."

"I'm glad you can defend yourself," I said as I patted her on the arm. "Did that bitch hurt you when she grabbed your arm?"

"I have a couple of bruises from where her fingers dug in. We need to take pictures of them when we get home, so we have some documentation in case she takes legal action."

I caught my breath. AnnaMarie had changed drastically since I'd last seen her at the courthouse. That was after the decision about my settlement against her and the school was announced. She had been mousy and timid as her husband, now ex-husband, shouted epithets at me and had to be held back. If this had taken place then, I doubted the bitch would have taken action, but with this new AnnaMarie? I wasn't sure what to expect.

"Don't worry about it, Janice." Tam pulled into my driveway. "Let's get your keyboard and stuff inside, and then you can take your shower, and I'll fix us something to eat."

I nodded, and together, we made quick work of emptying the SUV and setting the security system on the house. She rested her hands on my shoulders and guided me to the bathroom. I turned and took her in my arms.

"Shower with me and wash my back." I spread kisses down her neck as I was unbuttoning her shirt. My hand slid inside her shirt and found her breast. She took a sharp breath as she arched into my touch.

"When you put it like that, how can I say no?" she said. She put both hands on the sides of my face and kissed me. "You are so sexy when you're like this."

I pushed her out of the bathroom until the backs of her legs hit the bed. It didn't take long before we had both shed our clothes and were celebrating the new year as any couple in love should.

CHAPTER TWENTY

In mid-January, we celebrated Tam's sixty-fifth birthday with her family and friends. It did my heart good to see how much everyone loved her. Ocee had learned to play *Happy Birthday* on the keyboard and did so with some flourishes which caught me off-guard. She received a standing ovation and soaked it in as she bowed several times. I definitely needed to raise the difficulty of her lessons.

After everyone left, and it was only the two of us, I gave Tam the birthday gift I prepared for her. I wrote the music for a song, and Melba helped me write lyrics for it. I played the song on the keyboard and sang it to her.

When I raised my eyes from the keyboard, I looked into the tear-filled eyes of the woman who made me a bit more whole every day. She pulled me out of my chair, and we kissed our way to the bedroom.

Later that night, as we lay in each other's arms, Tam trailed her fingers along my arm, and I could tell her mind was on something.

"Do I need to offer you a penny for your thoughts? Are you thinking about how much work I need to do to your song? It's not finished or polished, but I wanted more than anything to sing it to you tonight."

"The song is perfect just the way it is." She gave me a sweet kiss on the cheek as she turned on her side and put one arm over my torso. "No, I was thinking about something else. We're not doing it on purpose, but we're hiding our relationship from Ocee, and I think she realizes something is different between us. Mae said she's been asking a lot of questions."

"Such as?"

Tam chuckled.

"She asked if we're having sleepovers. You left a shirt here a couple of weeks ago, and she saw it in my laundry. She didn't say anything to me about it, but she gave Mae an earful. And she saw us touch hands when we were both in the kitchen doing something."

"Is she upset about it?" I slid down so that we were face-to-face. "I hate the idea of doing anything to hurt or upset her. She means too much to me."

Tam traced my jawbone with her forefinger.

"I think you love her more than you knew it was possible to love a kid," she said with a gentle smile. "And the love is mutual. If she comes over and we don't go see you, or you don't come over here, she mopes around like she lost her best friend."

She was quiet for a long moment.

"We need to figure out a way to tell her we love each other, but that it doesn't take away our love for her. And I'm not sure how to tell her that, while it's okay for two women to love each other, she can't announce it from the rooftops. And you know she's going to want to."

I leaned my forehead against hers and hoped our combined brainwaves would bring one of us a solution. We lay in silence for a while before Tam snuggled close to me.

"It's getting colder outside. Hold me, and let's get some sleep. We can talk about it again tomorrow."

I pulled the quilt to just below her chin before tightening my hold on her. She shivered once and relaxed into sleep. I could feel her heart beating against my body and counted the beats. Once I knew her heart was beating as it should, I, too, slipped away into sleep.

We woke the next morning to the unusual silence of a world blanketed in snow. Together, we stood at her front window, wrapped in her quilt, and watched as the snow continued to fall.

"I'm glad we don't have anything we have to do today," Tam said, leaning on my shoulder. "And it also means Ocee probably doesn't have school today, and the kids won't open the nursery. Which means you and I have the whole day to ourselves, uninterrupted, hopefully undisturbed."

She turned and wrapped her arms around me and kissed me like we'd been apart for weeks, and I realized I still hadn't talked to her about the beach. But I returned her kiss, and we made our way back to the bedroom, putting off the inevitable until later.

We each had to answer our phones once. She answered a call from Mae, telling her what she already knew about Ocee and school. I had to tell Allison, no, I wasn't interested in going sledding with them. I reminded her we were sixty-one years old, that she had osteopenia, and that put her in danger of breaking bones. She poo-pooed me, called me a spoil-sport, and hung up on me.

"She'll never grow up." I fell back on the bed after putting my phone back on the side table. "I guess in a way it's a good thing, but sometimes I wonder when I'll get the call from Beth telling me Allison pushed a step too far."

"Don't think about that." Tam slid her body on top of mine. "Don't think about anything but this."

I moaned as she trailed her lips from my neck south.

We finally dragged ourselves out of bed when growling stomachs forced us to go find something to eat. It had stopped snowing, but I could tell there was ice on top of the snow, and there was no way I could attempt to go home.

"It's a good thing I did my grocery shopping the other day," Tam said as she pulled eggs and bacon from the refrigerator and a loaf of homemade bread from her bread drawer. She handed me a cutting board. "Do you mind chopping some veggies? I'll make us omelets."

We were discovering we were a pretty good team in the kitchen with me as the prep chef and Tam wearing the chief chef's hat, literally since Melba and Carmen had given her one with a matching apron for her birthday. Working together, we soon had breakfast for dinner sitting on the table in front of us. She surprised me when she reached over and took my hand before we ate.

"I am so grateful you are in my life," she said with a bit of a catch in her voice. "The song you wrote keeps resonating with me. I know you said it's not finished or polished, but I love it, and I love you. Thank you, my darling. Thank you."

I dried the tears from my face and leaned over and kissed her lightly before putting my cheek next to hers.

"I love you, too, Tam. You really do complete me. You've taught me so much and you've supported me so often. What would I do without you?"

After we ate and cleaned the kitchen, we cuddled on the sofa, watched the local news and weather reports, and were once again glad we hadn't had to go anywhere that day. The next day was supposed to be substantially warmer.

"My yard is going to be a muddy mess," I muttered.

"Were you planning on working on it? Isn't it kind of early to do that?"

"I need to prepare for my early spring crops. But I can't do that when the yard is soupy. I do want to get some of my plants started, though. I bought shelves and grow lights, but I've been kind of busy doing extracurricular activities and haven't put them together yet."

She reached inside my robe and tweaked one of my nipples, causing it to harden.

"You mean these kinds of extracurricular activities?"

I pushed her back onto the sofa and opened her robe. Even at the age of sixty-five, she had a wonderful body that I had a hard time keeping my hands and lips off. I shed my robe and covered her body with mine.

"Mmm, you feel good on me," she said, as her eyes dilated with desire. She arched her body so more of her body was against mine. "Make love to me, Janice."

She didn't have to ask twice.

CHAPTER TWENTY-ONE

The next day, I waded home through the slush and muck and discovered my backyard was a mess. I knew I had to wait until it had dried out some before tackling it and beginning to get it ready for the year's garden. But I constructed my shelves and connected the grow lights to them. Once I was done, I pulled out my collection of seeds and started sorting them to decide which ones to start soon. I was so engrossed in what I was doing that I almost screamed when my phone rang with Tam's ringtone.

"Hi, beautiful," I said. "Miss me?"

"The bitch did it," she said without any preamble. "I was served with papers from AnnaMarie Curry's lawyer. She's suing me for, and I quote, 'endangering her health and well-being by physically assaulting her with no provocation' and 'for causing her undue mental stress and anguish.' I've already called my lawyer, and I have an appointment to go see him the day after tomorrow at one. I emailed him the pictures of the bruises on my arms and the names and phone numbers of everyone who was present, but I really need you to come with me. Please?"

I was on my feet, putting on my jacket, and heading out the door before she finished talking. The sidewalks were still wet and slick, and I had to keep from running so I wouldn't fall.

"I'm on my way over, sweetie. Try to take a deep breath. I love you."

By then, I was on her sidewalk, and she threw her front door open and flew into my arms, crying almost hysterically. I guided her back inside and to her sofa. I held her while she cussed and spewed and hung on to me. When she finally settled down, I got her a damp cloth and a glass of water. She almost grinned when she glanced my way.

"Aren't you going to take your coat off?"

"It's not like I had much of a chance to." I shrugged out of it before I sat beside her and rubbed her arms. "I'm sorry she's doing this. It's all my fault."

I covered my face with my hands and put my elbows on my knees.

"It was a given this would come back and bite me on the ass. I hate she's going through you to hurt me. I'm so sorry."

"Come back here." Tam pulled me back in her arms. "Number one, stop trying to make this all about you. This time, it's all about her and me. Number two, you didn't cause it. She did, and she's going to pay for it. And number three, don't use this as an excuse to go back into your shell. You're a lot happier since you emerged into the sunlight."

I had to stop myself from lashing out when she told me not to make the situation all about me. Her words stopped my thinking in its tracks.

"Is that what I do? Do I really make things all about me?"

Tam rubbed my back.

"Sometimes, my love, you do. Especially when you're feeling insecure or scared, and especially if you feel insecure or scared because of what happened in your past." She stopped for a moment. "You've never told me everything that happened. I know the school fired you for having a relationship with her and because of some paintings you did. But that's all I know."

I stiffened as she spoke. The thought of rehashing the whole story made me shudder, but the rational side of my brain told me that if I wanted a relationship of trust and openness with Tam, it was only fair for me to fill in the blanks.

"You don't want to hear about it right now, do you? You're already on overload because of her suing you."

"And that's exactly why I need to know. Otherwise, I'm going to see my lawyer without a good grasp on why this happened."

I jumped to my feet and started pacing the living room. I stopped beside the keyboard Tam had bought so Ocee could practice when she was staying there. I switched it on and played a few notes before turning it off again.

"Gregson's School of Art and Music. It was the premier place to work. Only the best of the best students attended it, partly because it was expensive and partly because it had the reputation of putting out the best musicians and artists in the area. I hit the jackpot when they hired me. Sandy's death still had me reeling. I had just sold our house and bought a tiny little cottage east of town, and I had, for the most part, withdrawn from all our friends. Getting the job was a step in the right direction.

"For the first couple of years, it was great. I began to heal, and I let Allison and Beth back in my life, and they slowly dragged everyone else back, too. And I started making new friends among the staff at the school. I also started painting again. A good friend of mine who shall remain nameless, and no, it wasn't Allison, asked me to paint some boudoir pictures of her which bordered on X-rated to give to her partner. The way I paint portraits, or much of anything for that matter, is I take pictures and paint from them. That way, subjects don't have to pose for hours on end, and I had no desire to look at her private parts up close and personal for an extended amount of time. So, we took an afternoon, and I took some pretty explicit pictures of her. She chose which ones she wanted me to use, and I got started."

I stopped for a moment and took a deep breath. Tam sat on the sofa with her elbows on her knees and her fists under her chin, watching me but not saying anything.

"Even though I use my good camera to take the pictures, the files are available on my phone, too. Stupid me didn't delete the pictures off my phone like I should have. One day, I was having lunch with AnnaMarie and a couple of other instructors, and I got on my photo app to look for a picture of something else. I don't even remember what, and I scrolled past those pictures. AnnaMarie was the only one who saw them, and I remember her eyebrows rose so far on her head they disappeared under her hair. I immediately closed the app and excused myself. Tam, I was so embarrassed that I thought I was going to be sick to my stomach. I went to the faculty restroom, and when I came out, AnnaMarie was waiting for me.

"She asked me if we could get together and talk after work. I never expected the talk would lead where it led. She asked me why I had pornography on my phone, and I explained it wasn't porn and what it was for. Her face lit up, and she asked if I could do the same for her so she could give them to her husband. At first, I balked, but over a couple of months, she worked on me, and I finally said yes. The biggest mistake of my life up to that point that led to the biggest mistake of my life ever."

"Shhh. Stop a minute." Tam stepped into my path. "Sit down, hon. I'm going to get you something to drink, and I want you to take some deep breaths while I'm gone."

She led me to the sofa and kissed me on the forehead. I buried my face in my hands when she walked away, and I stayed like that until I felt the cool glass of water against my arm. I leaned back and drank half of it in one long swig. Memories of those horrible days swirled around inside my head and gut, and I wondered if I could finish telling Tam what happened. But after a few moments, I continued.

"AnnaMarie came out to the house one Saturday when her husband, Jason, was out of town on a fishing trip or some such thing. She saw pictures of me and Sandy and asked who she was, and I was honest with her. I wasn't in the closet at work, but I had no reason to advertise the fact I was a lesbian, either. Anyway, we talked about what kind of pictures she wanted, and her ideas were even more X-rated than my friend's had been. I tried to steer her toward more tasteful ideas, but she had her mind made up, so I followed along with her. Even though I took about fifty or more pictures, she insisted she come back out to the house the following weekend to take more.

"God, she was so manipulative, and I was such a pushover. On the third trip, she started touching herself even more provocatively than what we'd discussed, and I wanted to touch her, too. I told her it was time for her to leave, and I had plenty of pictures. But she came to me, still nude, and kissed me. An all-or-nothing kiss. You know what I mean. And then she led me to the bed and asked me to take off my clothes, and for some stupid reason, I did. She wanted me to touch her, to show her what it was like for a woman to make love to her. And for some other stupid reason, I did. Weekend after weekend and a few times after work when Jason was on a business trip. In all that time, she never touched me, but I didn't hold back with her. It was sexy and exciting, and so, so wrong.

"Meanwhile, I was painting the pictures my friend had asked for and then the pictures of AnnaMarie. One thing I always did was take pictures of my completed paintings, especially the commissioned ones, since I knew it was unlikely I'd ever see them again. And I did it with these paintings, too. Mistake number one-thousand nine-hundred and ninety-nine. I delivered my friend's pictures, but AnnaMarie didn't want to take delivery of hers. She wanted me to keep them as her gift. She paid me but left the paintings, so I sent her the photographs of the paintings. And we kept getting together.

"One day after school, I drove to her apartment, and she met me outside because Jason had come home early. She had me pull my car around to the back in a shady spot behind the dumpsters and away from the building. She straddled me and unbuttoned her blouse. Stupid, stupid me was working away on her boobs when I heard voices near the car. By the time I could push her off, it was too late. Three boys had seen us and ran away before I could confront them. One of them was a student at the school.

"AnnaMarie tried to blow it off, but I knew if the boy said anything, we would probably both get fired. I was a nervous wreck. And he said something—to the headmaster. AnnaMarie was called in first, and a couple of days later, I was called to the office. There were two police officers waiting for me. The police officers arrested me on charges of forcing AnnaMarie to pose for obscene pictures and for forcing myself on her. She showed them the photographs I took and sent her, as well as the photos of the pictures I painted. I spent the night in jail."

I had to bolt for the bathroom. Tam followed me and rubbed my back while I bent over the toilet. She wet a cloth and handed it to me as I rinsed out my mouth.

"I'm sorry. I hate that I do that when I'm overwhelmed."

"I hate that you had to go through all that. You don't have to tell me anymore."

I shook my head.

"I want to tell you, but I need to rest a few minutes first."

She led me to her bedroom and urged me to sit on the bed. She took off my shoes and had me scoot back so I could lie down. I threw an arm over my eyes and tried to put the trauma of my one and only night in jail behind me, but I knew it would haunt me for the rest of my life. Tam put a pillow under my head and lay beside me, her hand on my chest.

"Allison and Beth bailed me out of jail the next day and helped me hire a lawyer. The school fired me, but not her. AnnaMarie told them and Jason that I painted the picture without her permission. That's where she screwed up. I never do a commission without a signed contract and, if it's a portrait, a consent form. Since I could provide copies of those to my lawyer, Ms. Leonard, as well as some voicemails AnnaMarie left me in which she detailed what she let me do to her that day, or what she wanted me to do to her the next time we were together, all the charges were dropped, and my record was wiped clean. By that point, the headmaster and AnnaMarie had slandered me to every other school from here to the coast and back to the mountains. I couldn't get another job anywhere, not even sweeping floors. And someone leaked it to the media.

"That's when Ms. Leonard referred me to a civil lawyer—she specialized in criminal cases—who suggested I sue the school and AnnaMarie, which I did, even though I didn't have a cent to my name. I lost my house and my car. The bitch made sure I lost everything, especially my dignity."

I sat up and banged my fists against my thighs. Tam sat up, too and took my hands in hers.

"I wondered if I would have to file bankruptcy, but the civil lawyer, Ms. Cranston, told me to wait until after the court case was settled. She also recommended we insist on a jury trial, which made me nervous as shit. My future was in the hands of twelve people I didn't know, who didn't know me, and would hear about what I thought was an extremely private matter. To say the trial was contentious would be an understatement. But that's when I found out who my friends truly were. Either Allison or Beth or both were in court with me every day, and Melba was there as much as she could with her schedule at work. And, Tam, Danny tried to be there, too. It was then that I realized how extraordinary he is. He and Charles had only been together a few years, and he barely knew me, but he supported me and let me cry on his shoulder more than once.

"When the case was handed to the jury," I continued the sordid tale, "Ms. Cranston told me not to be surprised or worried if they took a while to decide the verdict. But after three days, I was on the verge of a nervous breakdown. Allison and Beth wouldn't let me out of their sight. They made me stay with them, and they practically force fed me because I was so distraught I couldn't even think about eating. By the time the jury came back on the fourth day, I had lost a lot of weight between not eating and not being able to sleep or be still. Allison and Beth sat on either side of me, and Danny sat behind me, all of them trying to hold me steady while we waited to hear the findings. When the jury ruled in my favor, I passed out cold. I'd never passed out before. When court was back in session, the judge made it clear he was a little perturbed he had to call a recess while the EMTs revived me. He told one of them to stay with me while he asked the jury what the settlement was. It was a good thing he did because I passed out again."

"Oh my, babe," Tam said. "Do I dare ask you what it was, or will you pass out?"

I smiled at her.

"The figures still astound me, but they haven't made me pass out for a while now."

"Well, what was the settlement?"

I couldn't help but grin.

"Gregson's had to pay me back pay from the time they fired me to the date the trial ended, including vacation and sick pay. They were also ordered to pay me five million dollars for other damages, including losing my house and car, and for mental and emotional trauma."

166

"Oh, my God." Tam's mouth fell open. "Did they actually pay it? I've read about those settlements being contested and either dropped or diminished."

"Not them. They were losing students right and left because of the bad publicity and controversy, and they wanted it over. I had my settlement, less taxes, in my bank account within six months."

"What about AnnaMarie? What did the jury award you from her?"

"According to them, she owed me two million dollars. The judge reduced it to one and a quarter million."

"And have you gotten a penny from her?"

"Some. Since this is a community property state, both Jason and AnnaMarie have their paychecks docked every month, and he has a pretty substantial salary. They also had to divest a certain amount of their assets, with a little over fifty percent of the proceeds coming to me. I knew when Jason and AnnaMarie divorced because the direct deposit from him stopped. The court raised the amount AnnaMarie has to pay every month."

I lay back down, drawing my knees to my chest so that I was in a fetal position, and began to rock. Tam lay behind me, spooned me, and tried to soothe me the way she did Ocee and Aaron when they were having a meltdown. It took a while before I could relax. I turned over so that we faced each other.

"I'm sorry, Tam. I'll understand if you toss me out on my ass for being so stupid and drawing you into all of this. It's so unfair to you."

Tam sat up and looked at me, an unreadable look on her face. After a few moments, she stomped out of the room, slamming the door behind her. I sat up in confusion and looked at the closed door. I jumped when it flew open, and she filled the doorway with her anger.

"How dare you say something like that?" she growled. "I love you. It feels like I've loved you all my life and will into my next life. And I know you love me. How dare you think I'm so shallow I'd toss you out on your ass for mistakes you made years ago, which you didn't realize were mistakes at the time? How dare you?"

And she was gone again, slamming the door once more. I was about to reach for it when the door flew open again and she flew into my arms, almost knocking me down. I held her while she sobbed. She started beating me on the shoulders with her fists, but I grabbed them and held her off.

"I love you, damn it," she said. "Someone else's stupidity and selfishness are not going to take you from me."

I pulled her back to the bed and down beside me.

"Shhh," I said. "I'm sorry I said that. You're not shallow. I guess I'm scared AnnaMarie is going to make a mess of your life, and you'll come to resent me for it. And I wouldn't blame you if you did."

"Can't we wait until something like that happens before we worry about it?" Tam asked, looking at me through her tears. "Can't we wait to see what my lawyer says before we go there? Please?"

I held her until we were both able to breathe again.

"I'm hungry," I said into her hair. "If the roads aren't too bad, you wanna go to the All-Nighter for some dinner?"

CHAPTER TWENTY-TWO

Two days later, I drove Tam to her lawyer's office. She and I were both nervous wrecks and had little to say to each other. Tam surprised me by asking me to accompany her when it was time to talk to the lawyer.

"It's nice to meet you, Ms. Halston," Mr. Dowdry said. "Ms. Murphy emailed me some of your history with Mrs. Curry and why she thinks it could be tied to this suit."

I had given Tam permission to tell him, but having him say it out loud still hit me in the chest like a hammer. She reached over and took my hand when I exhaled hard.

"Ms. Murphy, I reviewed your evidence and called each of the people you listed as witnesses to the episode. They have agreed to write out what they saw and heard, have it notarized, and sent to me. Ms. Halston, may I assume you will do the same?" I nodded, and he continued. "Hopefully, we won't have to depose you or any of them."

He took a breath and looked from Tam to me and back again.

"I believe we have enough to ask the court to throw the case out. I also think we have enough for you to counter sue or to sue for damages due to your injuries and the mental anguish this is causing."

Tam took a deep breath, and I squeezed her hand.

"Let's see if you can get the case thrown out to begin with," she said. "If it is, I want that to be the end of it except to have a restraining order against her for both me and Janice. If it isn't, I'll consider the countersuit."

"Okay, then." Mr. Dowdry slapped his hands on his desk and made me jump. "It's been a short meeting but a productive one. As soon as I have the written and signed statements from each of your witnesses, I'll put the request together and present it to the court. In the meantime, if you have any questions or if Mrs. Curry contacts either of you, please contact me right away."

He pushed himself out of his chair and gestured toward the door. Tam and I looked at each other before we left his office. We waited for the elevator in silence. I was glad when we had it to ourselves.

"Are you okay?" I asked as I hugged her.

She shrugged.

"It seems too easy. I won't relax until I have the paperwork in my hands, saying the case is over and done with."

I rubbed her back. The elevator came to a stop, and we stepped away from each other.

On our way back to the house, my SUV started making an unusual clacking sound. Other than the odd noise, it seemed to run okay until we got to my driveway. It conked out as I pulled in. Fortunately, I had enough momentum to roll close to the house. When the car stopped, Tam and I sat and looked at each other.

"Why, Janice, have you not replaced this clunker? It's not like you can't afford to."

"I didn't see any need," I said. "Until just now, she ran without a hiccup since I bought her. I guess I'm afraid no dealer will want to work with me since I have a repossession on my records."

Tam raised her eyebrows.

"I'm going to ask you a personal question. And I hope you choose to answer it."

"I might." I inwardly cringed since I didn't know what the question could be.

"Please tell me you haven't already spent your entire settlement. I know this house took a chunk of change, but you should still have enough left to buy a new car outright, without having to worry about getting it financed."

I frowned at her. I had plenty of money in my accounts and a good bit of it smartly invested so that I could use the interest without touching the primary funds. And it was being watched over by a financial advisor and accountant whom I trusted to make sure the money stayed safe. But even with those factors in place, it had never occurred to me to pay full price for a car right off the bat.

"Uhm, I guess I could," I stammered. "Sandy was always the one who negotiated prices and stuff. The cottage I lost and this house are the only things I bought on my own, and if my realtor hadn't been a friend, I probably would have been ripped off both times. I'm inept at things like that."

"Oh, good grief, Janice." Tam was laughing at me. "You are so talented on so many levels to be so naïve and incapable on so many others. Since it looks like it's going to be necessary to depend on me or someone else for transportation until you either get this thing fixed or replaced, I'll go car shopping with you and protect you from the big, bad salespeople."

I grinned at her, and a cool breeze swirled through the SUV.

"You're mean, you know that?" I leaned over and gave her a kiss. "But I'll happily accept your offer."

CHAPTER TWENTY-THREE

"You mean you and Grams love each other like Momma and Daddy love each other?" Ocee asked a few days later as she sat between me and Tam. I had just told her I loved her grandmother, which meant she might see us holding hands or even kissing once in a while.

"That's right, precious." I caressed the back of her head. "How does that make you feel?"

She gave me a huge grin.

"So, you're my third grandma?"

I looked over at Tam, who was looking back at me, a smile tickling the corners of her mouth.

"I guess I am."

Ocee jumped off the sofa and onto my lap, throwing her arms around my neck. I wrapped her in a tight hug as I fought back the happy tears. Tam scooted over to sit next to me. She rescued me from being strangled and sat Ocee on her lap.

173

"Now, baby girl," she said, "I need you to listen to me and truly hear what I'm saying. Can you do that?"

Ocee's face got serious as she nodded.

"Not everyone understands when two women or two men love each other. And some people can be mean. Sometimes they call us bad names or even threaten to hurt people like us. It would be best if you didn't tell everyone you meet that Janice and I love each other. It's something we want to keep just between us and in our family. Does that make sense?"

Ocee frowned.

"Paul at school has two daddies, and Gerald has two mommies. Our teacher told us we're not to say anything bad about it because it's okay. Some of the other mommies and daddies got mad about that, and Miz Baker didn't come to school for a long time. None of us liked the new teacher, Mr. Horrible, I mean Mr. Howard, but Miz Baker is back now."

"I'm sorry, sugar," Tam said. "But that's why it's not a good idea to tell everyone. Okay?"

Ocee nodded.

"That's stupid, but okay."

"Ocee!" Mae rose from where she and Duke were playing with Aaron on the floor and flicked her daughter lightly on the head with her finger. "Do you not remember our discussion the other day about using that word?"

Ocee rubbed her head as she looked at her mother with defiance.

"Of course, I remember it. You told me not to call other people stupid. I didn't call anyone stupid. I said it was stupid that other people get mad because two people they don't even know love each other. Good grief."

She crossed her arms over her chest and leaned against Tam. Duke had also stood up, and now he grabbed Mae's elbow as she started to flick Ocee again.

"She's right," he said, low enough for only her to hear even though I caught it, too. "It is stupid. Let it go for now. Okay?"

Mae frowned but nodded as she allowed him to turn her around and hug him. The room was quiet except for Aaron banging a toy on the floor and laughing. I watched as he suddenly seemed to realize he was alone on the floor. He looked around and then got on his hands and knees and crawled across the floor to the sofa. I grinned at him, and he grinned back as he grabbed the knees of my jeans and pulled himself to his feet.

"Uh, y'all," I said. "Look here."

Mae and Duke looked down, and their mouths fell open. Ocee slid off Tam's lap and kissed her brother on top of his head.

"You're standing up," she shouted, clapping her hands, which made him let go and land on his butt. The look on his face was pure surprise, but then he clapped his hands, too, and laughed. Duke picked him up and swung him to his shoulder, which made the child laugh harder.

"Well, I believe it's time we make some sandwiches and eat dinner." Tam headed for the kitchen. "I made fresh bread and mayo yesterday. We have roast beef, pastrami, and ham. Y'all come help yourselves."

Before I stood up, Ocee climbed back on my lap.

"What do I call you now? If you're my new grandma, I shouldn't have to call you 'Miss Janice' anymore."

"Now that's a good question. What do you want to call me?"

175

Ocee shrugged.

"I don't know yet. Can I think about it and get back to you?"

I laughed and hugged her.

"I can't wait to hear what you decide on," I said as I set her on her feet. "Let's go eat."

CHAPTER TWENTY-FOUR

Later the same evening, when Tam and I were once again alone, I told her about Ocee's question.

"I hadn't even thought about it," I said.

"Whatever she decides on will probably be something off the wall and weird," Tam said with a laugh. She glanced at me. "When do you want to go car shopping? Why do you keep putting it off? I bet you don't have any food in the house since you haven't asked me to take you grocery shopping. Unless you asked someone else, in which case I'm going to be jealous."

"I haven't asked anyone else. But I've been over here so much I haven't needed to go grocery shopping." I hesitated a moment before putting my arms around her. "And I think that's something we need to discuss."

"Grocery shopping?" Tam raised her eyebrows.

"Well, the fact that I haven't needed to go grocery shopping," I said. I knew I was being as clear as mud when she sat back and stared at me, her head slightly cocked. "I'm here more than I'm there. The only reason I go home is to check on my plants and try to decide what to do about the garden."

"Try to decide what to do about your garden?"

"Hon, why are you repeating everything I say? Am I truly confusing you?"

"Since I'm not catching on to what you're saying, I guess you are." The tone in Tam's voice changed, a warning sign she was getting aggravated. I started pacing. I could see her watching me and knew I had to have an explanation, so I sat beside her.

"We ought to consider moving in together, either here or at my place. I want to be with you all the time, and I hate when I go home and you're not there. But you shouldn't have to give up your place, and I don't want to give up mine. I can't figure out how we can meet in the middle."

Tam stared at me, her mouth hanging open. I used a forefinger to close it, and then I waited for her to say something, anything. She pressed her palms against my cheeks, leaned in, and kissed me.

"I love you. I was thinking about the same thing the other day. You were at your house working in the garden, and I wanted to come over and sit on the patio and watch you. But I thought it was something you wanted to do alone."

"I wish you had." I smiled at her. "Except I probably would have put you to work."

"Which would have been better than sitting here missing you." I heard the tears in her voice before I saw them in her eyes. "What are we going to do? I love my house. It's the first one I ever bought on my own. Your Sandy and my Darla were a lot alike in some ways. Darla was usually such an introvert, but she was almost always our negotiator. I knew I could do it just as well as she did, but I always let her handle it. It made her happy and helped her feel like she accomplished something important and special."

"I don't want you to move out of your house," I said.

I sat back and closed my eyes for a moment. My house was finally turning into a home as I hung my artwork on the walls. The new bookcase had all my books and awards on it, and my keyboard was in the living room, where I could use it any time I wanted. And the baby plants were flourishing under the grow lights, and the garden in the back waited to be planted. Could I sacrifice all that?

"I can see your wheels turning," Tam said. "Tell me what you're thinking."

Tears stung my eyes. She pulled me into a hug.

"We don't have to find a solution right now. We'll just keep going back and forth until something changes. Why don't we go back to your place for a few days? We've spent most of our time here lately, and I suspect your walls are lonely."

"I have something else I need to talk to you about first," I said. "Something which may change your mind about coming home with me tonight."

"That sounds ominous." She leaned back and crossed her arms. "I'm not going to like this, am I?"

"You probably won't." I rubbed my face. I started pacing again. "Sandy died in early April."

"I know that," Tam interjected. "Why would that upset me?"

"Please, Tam. Let me finish." I covered my face with my hands and took a deep breath before I turned to face her. "When she died, I was inconsolable, like I'm sure you were when Darla died. I told you how drunk I got and how Allison and Beth rescued me. Once they got me sober and decided I wouldn't fall off the wagon again, they took me to Sandy's and my favorite motel out at the beach and left me in the care of its proprietress, Miss Tanner. For a week, she sat with me, dried my tears, fixed Sandy's favorite seafood dishes, made me go for walks on the beach and look for seashells. I've gone out there for the week of the anniversary of Sandy's death every year since then. Miss Tanner died last year a few days before I was due. Her partner, Hannah, and I grieved together, and I promised Hannah I would come back this year. I have to go, Tam. I can't go back on my word, and I need the time to myself."

"Ooo-kay," she said.

"And I have a tendency to not be nice when I get home," I added, almost as an afterthought. "Allison calls it my earthquake week because we all know it's coming, but it happens when I least expect it. I try to stay home and away from everyone until I can find my center again."

Tears rolled down my face, but I did nothing to stop them. But neither did Tam. I stumbled to the coat rack, grabbed my jacket, and headed out the door without putting it on. The cold air froze the tears on my face, but I didn't care. When I got to the corner, I stopped, leaned on the fire hydrant, and put my jacket on. My eyes closed, and I tried to feel Sandy around me, but all the air was cold. I jumped when someone honked their horn.

"Get in the car, Janice." Tam leaned across the front seat and pushed the passenger door open. "You can't just stand there when it's twenty-two degrees outside. Come on."

I stumbled off the curb and climbed into the warm interior of her car.

"You're so silly." She drove the few feet to my house and into the driveway behind my old clunker. "Would you like me to come in, or do you need some space?"

"I always need you," I whispered. "That's why I didn't think you would understand about me going to the beach."

"You are silly," she repeated as she climbed out of the car and came around and opened the passenger door. "It's too cold to talk about this out here. Come on."

She offered me her hand, and I let her pull me out of the car. She stood behind me and pushed me to the front door. I laughed when she reached into the front pocket of my jeans for my keys and tried to grope me while she was at it. Once we were inside, she pushed me to the sofa. Before I sat down, she took my jacket from me and hung it up.

"Now, Janice," she said in her schoolmarm voice, "why are you so insecure I won't understand things? You need to give me a bit more credit."

She lifted my chin and turned my head so we were face-to-face.

"I hate that you'll have to grieve without me there for you, but I'm glad you have a little bit of a support system. And I'm sorry the person you counted on for so many years isn't there anymore. But it sounds like you and Hannah help each other face the hard shit, and I'm glad you're there for each other. My only grievance in the whole thing is your 'earthquake' week. I hope I'm not the reason for your earthquake this year, or the victim, but I can't let you be alone during such a vulnerable and fragile time. We've pledged we'll be there for each other as we grieve, regardless of what form the grief takes. Even anger."

I lay flat on my stomach on the couch, my feet in her lap. She pulled my shoes and socks off and started massaging my feet.

"They're all stinky," I said into the pillow I buried my face in.

"There are parts of every relationship that are stinky," she said. "We have to learn to live with it and tolerate it and forgive it and help each other through it."

She stood up and put my feet back on the sofa. I heard her go to the bathroom, but I didn't think anything about it until she returned, lifted my feet, and sat back down. She had brought back a warm cloth and started bathing my feet, which reduced me to tears. Her hands were so gentle, and her love and care emanated through them and up my legs, through my body, and settled in my heart. A cool breeze caressed the back of my head. Sandy hadn't been around for a while, and knowing she was there with me now, when I was so confused and so low, made the tears flow faster. Tam gently urged me to move over. She laid down next to me and placed her hand on the same spot on my head where Sandy still rested.

After a while, Tam rose to her feet.

"Come on, babe. Let's go to bed. I'm tired, and I know you are, too."

I hugged her before we retired to my bedroom and climbed into bed. Tam spooned me, and I was soon asleep.

When I woke up, I checked the clock. Six-thirty-two in the A.M., and I was wide awake. Tam lightly snored and was sound asleep. I slipped out of bed and shivered. I pulled a set of sweats from the dresser and got dressed. After starting a pot of coffee, I retrieved my laptop from the living room. I settled at the kitchen table and powered it on with my mug of coffee at my elbow.

My writing muse took over my mind and body, and I started typing. I paid little attention to the words as they poured through my fingers and onto the screen. The characters told me their story. All I did was transcribe it. I had written several thousand words by the time Tam pushed through the kitchen door.

"Good morning." She kissed the side of my head.

I waved at her, but I was on a roll and couldn't stop.

"Love you," I mumbled and kept on typing. I was vaguely aware of her refreshing my cup of coffee before she left the room. By the time I ran out of steam, my coffee was ice cold. I stretched and went to find Tam.

She was lying on the sofa, the TV remote on her chest, and some true crime show on mute on the TV. I watched her sleep for a few moments before pulling her robe closed over her exposed chest and putting the sofa blanket over her. I smoothed the hair off her face and kissed her forehead. My brain was in overdrive, and I was fidgety and manic. I didn't quite know what to do with myself. I checked the outside temperature, thinking I would go putter around my dirt patch, which would soon transform into my garden. But the thermometer registered barely twenty-one degrees at a bit after one o'clock in the afternoon.

I checked on Tam when I headed back through the living room. She had turned on her side, and the quilt had slipped off her legs. I adjusted it and proceeded to my spare bedroom to check on my plants. They hadn't changed much since I checked on them the day before. My restlessness was making me nervous and threatening to take me to the edge of my darkness. I couldn't practice my music because it would wake Tam. My writing muse was taking a break. As I looked around the room, my eyes fell on my neglected easel. I pulled it out and dusted it off before setting it near the window. The light wasn't good, even with the plant lights shining from their assigned places. But I didn't care.

I dug through my blank canvases until I found one ready to be used. Once it was on the easel, I went to the dresser drawer that held my oil paints, brushes, and other painting paraphernalia that I hadn't touched since I unpacked the boxes this time last year. The canvas and I stared at each other for a long time before I pulled my phone out of my pocket and opened my photo app. I started sketching with one of my light sketching pencils. Once I got the basic picture drawn, I picked out the colors I needed for the first few layers of paint.

Like with my music and my writing, I entered a place in my psyche and soul where painting was the only thing I was aware of. I let the photo and the paints guide my hands. My eye and my spirit always knew what I needed next. After a while, I sat back and smiled at the little girl who grinned back at me from the canvas. I sensed someone behind me and turned to see Tam leaning against the doorjamb, her hand over her mouth. I went to her and slipped an arm around her waist.

"You did that while I was sleeping? You were in the kitchen tunnel-visioned on the laptop when I came in, and now you've created this beautiful picture of our granddaughter."

My mouth fell open at her words.

"*Our* granddaughter," I whispered.

She nodded, not seeming to be aware of how those words affected me. Overwhelming joy and love flooded my being, almost causing my knees to give way. When I staggered, Tam turned her attention to me.

"What's wrong, Janice?" She put her arms around me to support me.

I smiled at her.

"Our granddaughter," I repeated.

Tam nodded and hugged me.

"Yes, my love. Our granddaughter. I'm curious what she's decided to call you."

"I need to sit down," I said. "I'm suddenly exhausted."

Tam kept her arm around my waist as she guided me to my bed. I sat on the edge of the bed, and she sat beside me.

"What were you doing on the computer this morning? I wasn't even sure you knew I'd come in."

"I waved," I said with a grin.

"Yes, you did." She grinned back at me. "Is it none of my business what you were doing?"

"I woke up needing to write. When the characters tell me their story, I have to write it as soon as I can, or they harass me until I do. If I don't, I'm useless. All I can think of is the story and what happens next."

"Wait a minute," Tam said. "You started a new novel this morning and painted the portrait of Ocee this afternoon? What are you going to do for an encore? Write a new song?"

A tune had been tooling around in the back of my mind as I was writing and painting. It started coming to me faster, and I hurried to find something to write on. Fortunately, there was a notebook and ink pen on the dresser. I penned in the notes and between the lines for two pages before grinning at Tam.

"I have to go see how this sounds on the keyboard," I said.

She shook her head and followed me to the living room. I switched on the piano and ran through the scales the length of the keyboard, practicing crossovers as I did. Once my fingers were limber, I glanced at the notebook before closing my eyes and visualizing it as I let my hands pull the music from my instrument. I stopped a couple of times and listened to the music in my head before playing again. When the melody resonated with me, I opened my eyes and scribbled in the notebook as fast as I could, trying to capture what I heard in my head on paper. A sound behind me caught my attention, and I turned to see Tam giggling.

"What? What are you laughing at?"

"I sat here and called you every name in the book. Your phone rang, and I pulled it out of your pocket and talked to Allison for five minutes. You didn't even seem to know I was in the same room. I wonder if you would hear the fire alarm go off when you're like that. It was the same when you were writing and when you were painting. I've never seen you like this."

It used to bug Sandy to distraction that I was unaware of my surroundings when I got so deep in my art, regardless of which medium it was—writing, painting, or making music.

"I'm sorry." I moved to sit beside Tam. "I didn't mean to ignore you."

"You weren't ignoring me, hon. You were doing what your heart needed you to do. In all the months we've known each other, I've never seen you so happy."

"Months? Have we only known each other for months?" I had to think back to when we first met and when we became friends and finally fell in love.

"Yes, hon, months. Almost a year." Tam looked at me, her eyebrows near her hairline. I caressed her cheek and kissed her.

"In some ways, it feels like I've known you for eternity, and in other ways, like we just met," I said. "I love you, and I never want you out of my life."

I caught my breath when I realized the way it sounded. Tam's eyes got big and her eyes bright. She took both of my hands.

"I love you, too. I've watched you change, and it's all been for good. You're not as afraid of your own shadow anymore, and now look at you. In one day, you've started writing again, painting again, and continued making your music. You need to play your song for Melba. It has to become part of your repertoire."

"My tendency to retreat into myself when I'm in the process of creating doesn't bother you?" I asked.

She shook her head, an incredulous look on her face. She retrieved a video on her phone. There I was, at the piano, swaying and playing, effortlessly doing crossover work, pausing a moment with my face in the air, my eyes closed, and proceeding to play some more. I watched as my eyes popped open, and I feverishly wrote in my notebook before looking up and smiling at the camera. It was the first time I'd seen how I looked when I was in one of my creative trances. I hadn't even known she was taking a video of me as I worked.

"How can I be angry at that?" she asked. "I wish I had taped you while you were writing and painting, too. It's mesmerizing to watch you. I can't be angry when you're in your element. Come to think about it, you get the same way

187

when you're working in the garden. I love you, Janice. I'll never be mad at you for being happy."

"It used to drive Sandy nuts. She would try to talk to me, and I wouldn't acknowledge her, and it would piss her off. I got to where I tried to work after she headed to bed or when she was at work. I even called in sick a few times so I'd have time to work. But I can't decide when it's going to come to me. My muses don't work on a set schedule. I rarely have a lot of warning before I have to create something. But I never remember doing all three on the same day."

"You've healed a lot lately," Tam said. "But let me ask you this. Have you eaten anything today? You didn't drink any of your coffee this morning. When I went to the kitchen a while ago, it was still sitting where I put it this morning."

"Eaten?" I had to think about it. I honestly couldn't remember, and I shrugged. "I'm not hungry, but if I ate, I don't know what I ate."

"You have to eat, Janice." Tam stood up. "If I fix you some eggs, which is all you have to eat in your kitchen, do you promise to eat them?"

I nodded as I looked over the musical notes I'd made in my notebook. I jumped when Tam put her hand between it and my eyes.

"Eat first," she said. "Please."

She gently took the notebook and set it on the keyboard before offering me her hand and leading me to the kitchen.

CHAPTER TWENTY-FIVE

"Your name is Gah-Gah," Ocee said as she settled at the keyboard in my living room and put her lesson book against the book stand.

"Gah-Gah?" I glanced at Mae.

She was trying to get Aaron to sit on the sofa with some of his toys, but he was bound and determined to get on the floor and explore.

"We went online and tried to find what 'grandmother' is in the Ocala language only to find out it's not the Ocala tribe that Ocee is from but the Timucua tribe. Ocali was the name of their village. Anyway, we started looking at what grandmother was in other native people's dialect, and Gah-Gah, which is Lakota, is the one Ocee settled on."

"I like it," I said with a grin. "I think Tam will, too."

"Listen, Gah-Gah." Ocee ran through the scales on the keyboard. My mouth fell open when she started at the high end and worked the entire length of the instrument, crossing

189

her hands as she did. "I watched a girl on YouTube do that, and I watched and watched until I could do it, too."

I hugged her.

"That's amazing, Ocee. A lot of people are never able to learn that their whole lives. I'm proud of you."

"Gah-Gah, this book is too easy." Ocee pointed at the green book sitting on the keyboard. "I can already play all the songs in it. Can we do something else?"

I grinned at her. "I have an idea," I said. "What if I give you a page of music you've never seen and see if you can play it?"

Ocee grinned and bounced on the chair.

"That would be fun."

I had transposed the music I wrote to a computer program that generated sheet music. When I retrieved it from the spare room, I studied it for a moment and wondered if it might be a bit too hard for a novice musician like Ocee. But the more I considered it, the more I liked the idea of letting her try.

"Okay. I'm not going to tell you what this song is or where it came from or who wrote it," I said as I set it on the keyboard in front of Ocee. "It's a lot more complicated than anything I've given you before, so don't worry if you make mistakes. I'm not going to help you the first time through so I can see where you need the most help."

I watched as Ocee studied the sheet music for a bit before returning it to the keyboard. She pointed to some of the more complicated bars.

"How do you do this?" she asked. "I can't start if I don't know what this means."

I bent over from behind her and played the notes she pointed at and explained what I had done.

She ran through the scales a couple more times before taking a deep breath. At first, she was a bit tentative as she picked out the notes on the page. She started over twice, but on the third try, it seemed as if she got a feel for the music. The complicated crossovers stumped her even though I'd shown them to her, but she tried, and when she couldn't get it, she moved on to the next part. I was proud of her for not getting frustrated. Just as she played the last note, Tam pushed through the front door.

"Oh, my goodness. When I heard the music, I thought Janice was playing her song."

"Your song, Gah-Gah?" Ocee said, her eyebrows high on her head and her head tilted.

"Gah-Gah?" Tam smiled. "I like that. Let me go put these groceries away and then I want you to play it again for me, okay?"

"Let me help, Mom." Mae said and took a couple of bags from Tam. "I have something I want to tell you, anyway."

Aaron fussed when Mae left the room, but I picked him up and motioned for Ocee to move. I let Aaron push the keys as long as he was gentle, but when he wanted to pound, I pulled him back and reminded him to be careful.

"Say 'Okay, Gah-Gah.'" Ocee took his hand and kissed it.

I almost dropped him when he said "Gah-Gah" as clear as Ocee did. She started laughing, and Aaron kept saying "Gah-Gah" over and over to keep her laughing. Tam and Mae came from the kitchen, grinning.

"I'm jealous," Mae said. She took Aaron from me. "He hasn't even said 'Momma' yet. He tries to say 'Ocee,' but it comes out 'Okee,' and now here he is saying 'Gah-Gah.' I see where I stand with you, little fellow."

She gave him tummy raspberries, and he threw his head back and laughed the marvelous laugh of a happy baby.

"Eww, you stink." Mae turned her head away from him, grabbed the diaper bag, and headed for my bedroom. "Say 'bye-bye.'"

"Bye, bye, bye, bye, bye," Aaron said over and over as he and Mae disappeared into the back of the house.

"Ocee, I'd like to hear you play Gah-Gah's song for me," Tam said.

"She didn't tell me it was her song." Ocee pulled the chair closer to the piano. "Now that I know, I'll try harder."

I moved to sit next to Tam as Ocee warmed up yet again before wading into the music. When she came to the crossovers, she still stumbled, but after trying twice, she moved on and played through to the end.

"My goodness, sweetie." Tam held her arms open to Ocee. "That was beautiful. Thank you for playing it for me."

"Why are you crying, Grams?" Ocee climbed onto Tam's lap and used her fingers to wipe the tears from her grandmother's face.

"Because my beautiful granddaughter was playing my beautiful lady's beautiful song, and it made my heart sing and brought me happy tears." Tam hugged Ocee until Ocee squealed.

Once she freed herself, Ocee returned to the keyboard and brought the sheet music to me.

"This part still confuses me," she said as she pointed to the crossovers. "Will you show me how to do it again?"

By the time Mae and the kids left about forty-five minutes later, Ocee and I had practiced crossovers until I was tired. She still hadn't quite mastered them, but I could see she was outgrowing what I could teach her. While Tam was getting me a glass of tea, I wondered how to make sure Ocee could continue lessons which I knew her parents couldn't afford. I planned to discuss it with Tam, but when I walked into the kitchen, I found her listening to someone on her cellphone.

"Thank you for letting me know, Mr. Dowdry," she said as she nodded. "Yes, sir. I'll let you know when I receive the paperwork."

She sat staring at her phone for what felt like an interminable amount of time before looking up at me, her face unreadable.

"Oh, no. The court wouldn't drop the case." I reached for her.

"That's not it." She struggled to get the words out. "Mr. Dowdry said the judge was livid when he looked over the case. Turns out AnnaMarie and her lawyer were at the hearing, and the judge lit into them. He not only threw the case out, but he also fined the lawyer for bringing it to court in the first place, ordered AnnaMarie to pay all the court costs *and* my fees to Mr. Dowdry. It seems AnnaMarie's hobby is suing people, and ninety-nine percent of the time there is no case to hear. He threatened to throw her in jail if she did it again."

I sat back in my chair with my mouth hanging open as she spoke.

"And that's not all," she said, shaking her head. "This has been a day of good news."

"What else?"

"Mae told me the school called her this morning. That kid who was bullying Ocee had already been moved to a different class, but as of today, the district has moved him to another school. They warned his parents that if something like this happens again, he'll be sent to an alternative school, and then expelled if it happened after that." She grinned at me. "Our baby is safe."

And then we started laughing and were hanging onto each other, trying to stop. I took a breath and realized Tam's mouth was a fraction of an inch from mine, and I kissed her with a passion that had been missing for a couple of weeks as we struggled to find a compromise between my house and hers. I pulled her from her chair onto my lap and slid my hand into her shirt. She moaned as I caressed her breasts through her bra.

"Let's take this somewhere more comfortable," she said as she got to her feet. We practically ran to the bedroom, where it didn't take long to strip out of our clothes and collapse together on the bed.

"Oh, damn." I arched my back into her touch. I put my hand on hers to stop her, and she giggled.

"Had enough, my dear?" she said.

"For now." Rolling onto my side, I snuggled close to her. "I missed you. I'm sorry I've been so distant. Let's try not to do that again."

"I missed you, too." She leaned her forehead against mine. "I know this is about our housing situation, and I don't see a solution in sight. Will we be okay if we stay with the status quo for now?"

I nodded, even though the status quo was not ideal.

"At least until I get back from the beach. Are you sure you'll be okay while I'm gone?"

"Janice, love, I'll be fine. Danny has already claimed one day while you're gone to help me with minor stuff around the house, and Mae's going to take advantage of the time and *let*—quote, unquote—me keep the kids a couple of days. My hair may be even grayer than it is now when you get back."

"What minor things around the house? I can help you with stuff like that."

"Hush," Tam said with a laugh. "Your jealousy is unbecoming. I don't know what minor stuff yet. Those were his words, not mine. I'll let him put a nail in here or there to hang some more pictures, and I was thinking about changing out the knobs in the kitchen. He can handle that."

I silenced her laughter with a full tongue kiss as I also slid my hand down her body and found her tender spot.

CHAPTER TWENTY-SIX

For reasons I couldn't fathom, I found myself sliding toward the dark tunnel I seemed to have escaped from over the past few months. I didn't tell anyone, and I fought against it, but there were times and days I realized it was a losing battle. Isolation once again became my defense, even though Tam stayed with me as much as she could.

"Honey, what's wrong? Why are you so far away?"

I shrugged one shoulder without looking at her or saying anything. I absentmindedly played the scales over and over again on the keyboard. My music was gone. I couldn't even teach Ocee so I asked Mae and Tam to keep her away for a little while.

"I bet Ocee could make you feel better." Tam gently rested her hands on my shoulders and tried to massage the tension out of them. "Why don't I call Mae to bring her over?"

I wiggled out of her grasp.

"It's not a good idea right now." I flopped on the sofa on my stomach. "I hate when I'm like this, and I don't know why I am now. Go home, Tam. I love you, but please leave me alone. I'm sorry."

She squatted beside the sofa and put her face next to mine, but she didn't touch me.

"I can't do that. You need me even if you don't realize it. And besides, you won't eat a bite if I'm not here. Or shower. Or probably even get out of bed. I'm going to sit in my chair and read some of the library books I have on my tablet and leave you alone. But I'm not going anywhere. I love you too much."

I turned my head over so she couldn't see my tears. She didn't understand, and I didn't know how to explain.

A couple of days later, Allison called.

"Enough is enough," she said. "Tell Tam you need to borrow her car and meet me at the diner in one hour. If you don't come, I'm getting everyone together, and we're coming over to do an intervention."

"I don't feel like going anywhere. I don't want to spend time with anyone. Please, Allison."

"Too fucking bad." I could hear the tears in her voice, but I was so empty they didn't move me. "I'm going to hang up now and call everyone to meet me at your place."

"No, Allison." I squeezed my eyes shut. Although I loved my friends, thinking about having to deal with them was overwhelming. "I'll come to the diner, but I don't think it's going to fix anything. You know I have to wade through this on my own."

"But you're not wading. You're drowning. We'll talk about it when we see each other in a little while. Give Tam your phone. I know she's sitting right there."

I handed Tam the phone.

"She wants me to meet her at the diner, and she wants to talk to you. I'm going to go change clothes."

I don't know what the two most important people in my life talked about, but within twenty minutes, I was behind the wheel of Tam's car on the way to the diner. Allison met me in the parking lot and gave me a long hug that I had trouble reciprocating. She took my arm and escorted me inside.

"Allie, can I borrow y'all's extra car next week when I go to the beach?" I asked after we ordered our food.

She studied me for a long moment before answering.

"I'll let you borrow my car on the condition you let Tam take you car shopping when you get back. I can't believe you've dragged your feet for so long. What is your problem?"

I shrugged and said nothing. I had her answer to my request, and I had nothing else to say.

"There was a time you would have had a new car picked out and in your driveway within seventy-two hours and here it is, almost three months since your car died, and you've done nothing. It's still sitting in your driveway, probably getting tire rot, and you're having to beg rides from Tam or me or whoever else might be available."

I shrugged again.

"So what, Allie?" I decided to make her happy and talk to her. "I've never had to buy a car before. Sandy always handled this side of our lives. The last time I had to buy a car, Charles stepped in and handled things for me. I didn't know how dependent I was on people until recently. Even after Sandy died, I didn't have to make a lot of decisions. You and Beth and Charles did it for me. And sometimes Melba and Carmen. Buying my house was the only thing I made a big decision about, and when I hired Brenda to be my realtor, she took all of it off my shoulders. I'm absolutely lost."

Allison reached across the table and took my trembling hands.

"You're full of shit. You're making excuses. I haven't seen you like this since Sandy died. I know everything's okay with you and Tam, so what is going on?"

We had to lean back when the waitress brought our food, but food and I weren't friends, and I just stared at it.

"You better eat something, or Tam's going to take both of our heads off," Allison said. "She made me promise I'd make sure you ate. You're getting skinny again. You do this every year, and it worries all of us. But it's worse this year. Your shirt is hanging off of you. Eat."

She pointed at my plate, and I picked up a French fry, but all I did with it was smear the ketchup around my plate. I jumped when Allison hit the table with the flat of her hand.

"Goddamn it, Janny," she said, her voice low, almost a growl. "Eat that fucking French fry and then pick up another and do the same and repeat. Then pick up the burger and take a bite out of it. I'm not effing joking."

I stared at her with my mouth open. She grabbed the fry, leaned over, and put it in my mouth.

"Now chew," she said.

I had no choice but to do as she said. It was clear she planned to force feed me if she felt it was necessary. I wanted to be angry with both her and Tam, but I was empty, drained of all emotion.

Once I'd eaten enough to satisfy her, I escaped from her as quickly as I could. I was grateful Tam let me use her car, but I felt guilty that I had left her stranded because of my procrastination.

"I've got a couple of things to do before I come home," I told her over the phone. "Do you need me to bring you anything?"

After we disconnected, I opened the maps app on my phone and let the disembodied female voice direct me to where I wanted to go. I spent two hours talking to people and doing what needed to be done to make some decisions before I returned to Tam's house, mentally, physically, and emotionally exhausted. When I pulled into Tam's driveway, I shut the car off and sat with my forehead against the steering wheel. I didn't even jump when the car door opened.

"Hon? Are you sick?" Tam rubbed the nape of my neck.

"I'm just tired."

"Allison called to tell me you barely ate. Please let us take care of you. Come inside, okay?"

I nodded and reached into the passenger seat for my bag. The thumb drive they gave me, with all my pertinent paperwork on it, fell on the floor. Tam went around the car and got it for me.

"What is this?" she asked as she joined me at the front door.

"If you'll let me borrow your laptop, I'll show you once I've gone to the bathroom and got something to drink."

With her hand on the small of my back, she guided me into the house. While I changed from my jeans to some sweats, she got me a glass of tea and a couple of freshly baked blueberry muffins. I cocked an eyebrow at her because she knew I wasn't hungry. But to make her happy, I picked at them. They were delicious, but I still didn't want to eat.

I turned on Tam's laptop and plugged the thumb drive in. A picture of a maroon Jeep Rubicon appeared on the screen.

"Oh, that's pretty," Tam said. "Would you like me to take you to test drive it tomorrow?"

I shook my head and clicked on to the next screen. Tam picked up the laptop and studied it before giving me an odd look.

"This is the title to the Jeep, isn't it?" She returned the computer to the coffee table.

I nodded and waited for her explosion. But she surprised me by throwing her arms around me and kissing me on the cheek.

"Is this where you were all afternoon?"

I nodded again. Tam took my chin in her hand and turned my head so that I faced her.

"What's going on in that head of yours, sweets?" She leaned her forehead against mine. "I'd think you would be happy, but you look like you lost your best friend. Did you and Allison get into it?"

I shook my head as I leaned back on the sofa and threw my arm over my eyes.

"I don't know what's wrong. Emotionally and mentally, I'm at my tether's end. I have so much I want and need to do, and I can't seem to get it done. Allison read me the riot act about all my excuses for not getting a car yet, so I put on my big girl panties and did it. They'll deliver my Jeep to my house tomorrow at ten."

"I'm proud of you, Janice." Tam leaned back beside me. "I know it had to be hard for you. The key question is, do you love the Jeep, or did you buy the first thing you looked at?"

"Both. I'd already decided I wanted another Jeep but kept putting off asking you to take me to look at them. Mr. Lesley, the salesman at the dealership, was so nice and so patient. I stammered and stuttered, trying to tell him what I wanted, but he never even blinked. I drove this Rubicon first and then two other Jeeps—a Wrangler and another Rubicon—but this one seemed to be the right fit."

"Good. Okay, now what else do you need to do? If you tell me, maybe I can help you." She traced a line from my shoulder to my wrist and back again.

"That tickles." I pulled my arm away from her. I heard her catch her breath but acted like I didn't. I sat up and stretched.

"I have to get back to where I can be around Ocee again." I started pacing Tam's living room. "Master's School of Music is having their spring auditions. If I can get a tape of her playing three different pieces, I can send it in. If she figures out I'm taping her, she'll either get nervous and shut down or show off."

"We talked about this a few weeks ago," Tam said. "Did you talk to Mae about it?

"No. It's like I tried to explain." I turned to look at her. "I don't want them to know until I hear something back. Ocee is good—too good for me to continue to teach. If I can get her this scholarship, all Mae and Duke have to worry about is paying for the music, which I can take care of if necessary, and getting her to the lessons. I don't see what's so wrong about that."

Tam stood up and got into my personal space.

"What's wrong is Ocala is not our child. She's our grandchild. Her parents should make decisions like this. It's okay to do this if they give their blessings. Otherwise, you're stepping over a line you might not be able to step back from."

I knew she was right, but I didn't want to admit it. I also knew our relationship was suffering, in part because of my stubbornness about this, and in greater part because of my depression. We stood toe-to-toe for a long moment before I grabbed my jacket and my bag and quietly left for my house. Once I was inside, I looked around the space and realized it no longer felt like home. I locked the doors and set the security system, before stripping, going to the bathroom, and taking a scalding hot shower. I was numb and hoped the hot water would make me feel something.

When I got out and dried off, I still felt numb even though my skin was bright red and hurt in places, but my emotions and mental capacity were diminished, and I couldn't acknowledge the pain. I laid on top of the bedspread, curled into a ball, and rocked myself to sleep. I jumped when I felt a hand touching me, and I tried to scoot away.

"Janice, it's me." Tam's voice cracked with worry. "What have you done? There are blisters all over your back. Be still while I go get the salve."

"I set the alarm," I said. "How did you get in?"

"Baby, don't you remember giving me a key and the security code? Lay on your stomach, and let me put this ointment on your back. Janice, some of these blisters look like they need more medical care than I can give them. I'm going to call Beth to come look at them."

"No, Tam. Please don't." I knew Beth would tell me to go to the hospital, and I wasn't going to do that. "Just put some ointment and a gauze pad on them. They'll be okay in a few days."

"In a few days, you're going to the beach, and who will dress them for you out there?" I could hear the tears in Tam's voice. "Honey, these are severe burns, not just little blisters. Can't you feel them?"

Burying my face on the pillow, I shook my head.

"I'm numb, Tam. I can't feel anything. My soul, everything, is depleted. I have nothing left."

She lay beside me and rested her hand on the back of my head.

"Is that why you're not making music anymore? And why you're not eating? Do you think it's because it's so close to the day you lost Sandy?"

I shrugged.

"I don't know. Maybe. I don't remember feeling like this except when I first lost her."

"Beth and Allison told me how sick you were, and you've talked about it, too." Tam stroked my head. "Allie was so scared you were going to commit suicide."

"I wasn't. I just wanted to forget everything. But this is something different."

"Look, baby. I know this isn't what you want, but either you let me call Beth or I'm calling nine-one-one. You need to have your back looked at, and you need more help than I'm able to give you. I honestly don't think you should go to the beach yet. Maybe later, after you feel better."

I tried to scoot off the bed and realized my legs were stuck to the blanket. When I tried to peel them off, pain like I'd never dealt with before shot through me, and I collapsed back on the bed in agony. My body was no longer numb, and I wished it was.

"Good God, Janice."

I must have lost consciousness, because the next thing I knew, a man I'd never seen before was leaning over me.

"Ms. Halston, it's going to hurt when we put you on the gurney. I'm sorry. Hang in there, okay?"

Going to hurt was an understatement, and I passed out again. The sound of a siren broke through to me, as did the pain with every jolt and movement of the ambulance.

CHAPTER TWENTY-SEVEN

"Ms. Halston." A soft voice made its way through the void to me. "We're going to change the dressings now."

A cool liquid soaked my legs and back. But when the bandages came off, the pain returned, and I let out a screech.

"I'm sorry, hon," the gentle voice said. "I've got to do this so you can heal. Your wounds are already looking better. I've put some pain meds in your IV. Count backwards from ten...nine..."

†

"Hey, baby."

I could hear Tam's voice and wanted to reach out for her, but I wasn't sure where she was.

"It's okay, love, I'm right here, and they're going to let me stay with you now. I love you so much."

"Tam." I didn't know if I'd spoken out loud until I felt the back of her hand on my cheek.

"I'm right here. Can you open your eyes?"

I blinked and blinked again before my eyelids would cooperate and let me open them a slit. My beautiful lady's face was directly in front of mine. I reached for her but winced when something pinched my arm.

"Shh," she said. "Your IV is in that arm. Try to lie still. Do you remember why you're in the hospital?"

I tried to remember. All I could remember was her telling me I had blisters on my back. But I couldn't remember where the blisters came from.

"You've got severe burns on your back, your legs, and one arm." Tam took a deep breath. "Baby, did you take a hot shower with no cold water? It's the only way we can figure you did this to yourself."

I frowned.

"Don't worry about it right now. The important thing is you're going to be okay, physically."

She kissed me on the cheek.

"Everyone misses you, Janice." A tear dropped off her face onto mine. "Go back to sleep. I promise either me, Allie, or Beth will be here when you wake up."

Time passed in a sort of vacuum, but every time I was the least bit aware of my surroundings, either Tam or one of my two best friends was at my side, drying my tears or rubbing a soothing ointment on my arms. Even when I was not fully aware of what was going on, I could hear their voices talking to me. But Sandy was nowhere around, and I needed to see her, to hear her. I called out to her, but there was no answer.

"She's gone, hon," Allison said in my ear as she dried the tears from my face. "She loved you so much, Janny, but she's not here. Tam is in the hall. I'll go get her for you."

I nodded.

"Okay, sugar. She'll be here in a minute." Allison patted my cheek.

The light in the room was bright, but I blinked my eyes open. I wanted and needed to see Tam. I tried to smile when she came through the door.

"Hi, Janice." She leaned over and kissed my cheek. "I love you."

"I love you, too," I whispered. "I'm sorry."

She pulled a chair close to the bed and lowered the bed rail. She took my hands in hers and kissed each of them.

"There's nothing to be sorry for," she said after a moment. "It's good to hear your voice. I've missed you."

"What happened?"

Tam frowned a bit.

"What do you remember?"

"I bought a car, but I was still upset."

Tam nodded but stayed quiet. I swallowed and realized I was thirsty.

"Can I have a drink of water?"

She held a straw to my mouth, and I sucked the cool water into my mouth and swished it around before I swallowed.

"Thank you." I tried to look at her, but she had moved out of my line of sight. "Where did you go?"

Panic built in my chest until she was back at my side.

"Shhh, baby. I'm right here." She took my hands again. "Do you know why you were still upset after you bought your Jeep?"

I closed my eyes and tried to remember.

"Sandy died. I wanted to save her, but I couldn't."

"Honey, that was eight years ago," Tam said with a catch in her voice.

"You were mad at me." I couldn't remember why. "I took a shower to fix things."

She took a sharp breath.

"I was angry with you, but it didn't mean I don't still love you. Baby, why did you think a shower would fix things?"

"I don't know. I'm tired." I closed my eyes and allowed sleep to take over. But even in my sleep, I knew she was holding my hand.

†

"Goddamn!" I screamed as the nurse took the bandage off the only blister that still needed one. I'd been told the worst of the burns were across my upper back, probably because it was where the hot water hit first and for the longest. "Please stop. Please fucking stop."

"I'm sorry, Janice," the nurse said. "But the doctor has to see it so he can tell if more skin needs to be debrided."

"No." I buried my face in my pillow. "I'm tired of hurting. Please don't do anything else to me. Let me go home. Please."

"Let the doctor do his job, sweetie." The nurse patted my arm as Dr. Dennison came into the room.

"Hello, Janice. Let's take a look at things, shall we?"

"Please tell me I can go home." I was whining, but I couldn't help it.

"We're almost there. These edges still need some tissue removed, but once that's done, you'll be on the path to going home as long as your psychiatrist agrees."

I kept my face buried so no one could see the tears. Too many doctors were poking and prodding me, both physically and mentally. It was time for me to go. My plan was to pack my Jeep and leave Dodge as soon as I got out of the damn hospital. Even my love for Tam wasn't changing my mind. I was tired of hurting and of hurting others. Tam deserved better. But I didn't tell anyone what I was thinking because I knew it would keep me in the hospital longer.

†

A couple of weeks later, I leaned against a pillow on Tam's sofa, free from the probing fingers and probing questions of the hospital personnel. Tam set a glass of tea on the side table in easy reach. She stood and stared at me until I squirmed.

Her stare turned into a glare, and I sat back in surprise. "What? What's wrong?"

"Sandy came to me in a dream. She told me you're thinking about leaving, just leaving me behind. Is that true?"

"Tam, when I was in so much pain, all I wanted to do was escape. I considered leaving. You deserve so much better than to have to put up with me and my crazy moods and stupid moves and having to take care of me when I screw up. But I love you. And I know you love me. I'm not going anywhere."

"I watched you talk to Dr. Mason when we met with him together," she said, her eyes flashing. "And I saw how easily you talked him into believing you're okay, that how you've

210

been feeling and what you did was a fluke. And that's how you're talking to me right now."

She was pacing the living room, and I could do nothing but watch her. After a bit, she turned and faced me again, her face full of pain and anger I didn't understand.

"You seriously thought about leaving me? Sandy warned me. Goddamn it, Janice. Do you have any idea how many people you would hurt if you made that decision? Take me out of the equation, and you still have Ocee. Did you think about her? Do you realize how much she has cried since you were admitted to the hospital? Since before that. She already decided you didn't like her anymore since you wouldn't let her come over or take any more piano lessons."

I bowed my head.

"She didn't want a birthday party or a 'gotcha' party because you couldn't be there. She hounded her daddy until he made a trip to your house and planted your gardens, front and back. How hurt would she be if you deserted her and those plants she's taken care of since Duke planted them? Duke or Mae takes her to your house almost every day so she can make sure no one's messed with them and they're growing okay. She loves you with every pore and you would leave her, just up and go? Shame on you, Janice Halston."

She took a deep breath and kept going, not giving me a chance to respond.

"And what about Allison and Beth? Beth used every day of her time off to be with you in the hospital, to make sure you were getting the best treatment possible. If something was off, she made a fuss until it was right. And Allison. Your oldest friend. Goddamn it, Janice. I've never seen someone cry as much as she did when they got to the hospital that night. She was so sure we were going to lose you. But you'd go off and leave her?"

She paused and took another deep breath before pulling a small digital recorder from her pocket and throwing it at me. It bounced on the sofa next to my leg.

"Listen to that," she growled. "Melba tells you in song how much she and Carmen love you and miss being able to perform with you. It's Melba playing the song you wrote me and the song you wrote for yourself, both on the guitar and the keyboard. And it's Ocee, trying so hard to play your song and get all the fancy parts right because she was sure if she could do that, you would be okay. Listen to it, and then tell me you're leaving."

"And none of those things even takes into account how I feel. But why should it? You obviously don't care how I feel, or you wouldn't even be thinking about doing this."

"Tam, listen to me," I begged. "Please believe me. I'm serious. I'm not going anywhere."

She was standing with her back to me, but she whirled to stare at me.

"You said you wouldn't do anything to hurt yourself," she whispered. "And you did. Look at your arm. Look at your legs. If you could see your back, it would make you sick. I had a feeling something was wrong. It's why I came over that night. And now I wonder if it wasn't Sandy who sent me.

"How do I know she's not right this time, too? How do I know that as soon as you're better, you won't pack your new Jeep and disappear from our lives? How do I know?"

"You've already decided it's a done deal, so maybe it is."

I put the digital recorder in my pocket and headed for the door, praying she would stop me. When she didn't, my heart broke into a million little pieces, and my mind started composing a dirge, which took my breath away. I made it to the fire hydrant before I had to stop and rest. Even though I'd been moving around at the hospital, I hadn't walked so far and definitely hadn't done it with as much stress on my shoulders.

After a few deep breaths, I headed off again. Even the sight of my new Jeep in my driveway and the pops of color Ocee had planted along my sidewalk, didn't cheer me up. I collapsed in one of the rocking chairs and winced when my sore back touched the back of the chair. Once I rested a few minutes, I fished my keys out of my pocket and let myself into my house.

It had been weeks since I was home last. I looked around at the cottage I had tried hard for the past year to make home. Everything was as I left it. My paintings hung on the walls, and my keyboard sat waiting for me to make music again while my bookcases held books with my name on the covers, and the awards I'd won in each of the three mediums of art I called mine. But the one thing that hurt me to my core was the painting I did of Ocee when my art came back to me. I loved her and wondered if I would ever see her again.

I stumbled to my bedroom, pulled my T-shirt off, and collapsed on my bed. Pain ruled my body, but I'd left my bag with the pain medicine in it at Tam's. I pulled the recorder Tam had thrown at me out of my pocket and pushed play. The sound of Melba's guitar and her beautiful contra-alto voice didn't soothe me like I thought it would. Instead, it made my spirit and soul hurt worse. And then I heard Ocee's little voice.

"Gah-Gah, I love you and want you to get well again so I can hug you, and you can see Aaron walking, and we can take care of your garden together. I hope this makes you feel better."

The strains of the song I wrote rose in a beautiful spiral from the recorder into my heart. I put it on repeat and laid it next to my head. I fell asleep listening to my granddaughter playing my music better than I ever thought would be possible.

CHAPTER TWENTY-EIGHT

I awoke alone and in pain. I wasn't sure if the pain woke me or something else. As I tried to sit up, I heard low voices and someone puttering around my house. I put my robe on backward so it wouldn't rub on my back and proceeded to see who was doing what.

Ocee had a tissue in her hand and was wiping off every surface she could reach. I watched with tears in my eyes for a few minutes. I was about to announce my presence when the kitchen door swung open, and Mae stood staring at me.

"Hey, Janice," she said in a not very friendly voice. "Mom asked me to bring you your bag and a plate of food and to make sure you were okay. Well, there's your bag, the food is in the kitchen, and I'm not sure if I care if you're okay."

Her eyes were flashing, and she took a deep breath. I stepped back.

"I told you when Mom and you got together, you better not hurt her, and now you've gone and done just that. Why are you even contemplating leaving her? I'm taking her home with me tonight because I don't think she should be alone in the condition you left her in." She turned and held her hand out to Ocee. "Come on. Let's go take care of Grams."

Ocee pushed past her and wrapped her arms around my legs. I rested my hand on her head. I wanted to bend and kiss her, but I was in too much pain.

"Are you going to stop loving me, too?" she asked as she looked up at me.

"Oh, baby. How in the world can I stop loving you?" I cried. "And I love your Grams, regardless of what she says or thinks. Go with your mom and tell Grams I do love her. With all my heart."

Mae took Ocee's hand and practically dragged her to the door as Ocee cried and reached out for me. I closed my eyes so I wouldn't see her anguished face. When they were gone, I locked the door and set the alarm. I dug through my bag and found my pain medication. I sat on the sofa and studied the brown bottle.

Don't even think about it.

The cool breeze swirled around me. It circled my head, whipped around my arms, and skimmed my sore back. I sprawled on my belly on the couch and sobbed. I heard Allison's ringtone on my phone, but I couldn't answer it through my grief. It stopped ringing and almost immediately started again. And then it was Beth's ringtone. And then Allison's again. But it was like I'd forgotten how to use the phone. I ignored it and continued to sob until I ran dry.

Even though I was no longer crying, I didn't move off the sofa. It was easier to stay where I was, except the pain was becoming unbearable. I sat up and looked around for the bottle of medicine, but it was nowhere to be seen.

"Sandy, what the fuck did you do with it?"

But there was no answer; no cool breeze; only painful silence. Until my doorbell started ringing, and someone was pounding on my door. Without even checking the security app, I stumbled to the door and opened it before returning to the sofa and lying back down. I didn't care who was there.

"Why didn't you answer your phone?" Allison gently touched the back of my head. "Don't you know how worried we are and how much we love you?"

I didn't say anything as I trembled in pain. Someone put their fingers on my neck, and I knew Beth was taking my pulse.

"Your heart is racing, Janny," she said. "Let me take your blood pressure."

I shook my head, but she was stronger than I was, and it was only a moment before she was pumping the blood pressure cuff.

"Damn. Your blood pressure is off the charts. I had a feeling they released you too soon. What is your pain level?"

"Two-thousand and twenty-two," I said into the pillow.

"Have you taken your medicine?" Beth's voice was gentle, but I could hear the heightened concern in it.

"Sandy hid it."

"Ooo-kay."

I sensed Beth pulling out her phone, and I raised my head.

"If you're calling someone to take me to the loony bin, it will be the last thing you ever do for me," I warned. "I put the bottle on the table, and when I reached for it, the damn thing was gone. Sandy's spirit was here, and I think she thought I planned to do something stupid because I don't know where she put the fucking bottle."

"It's under the sofa," Allison said. "I'll go get the broom and get it out."

I put my face back in the pillow and wished they would leave, but I knew they weren't going to, just as they didn't that night so long ago when they found me drunk off my ass and two more bottles of liquor on the table.

"Why do you think Sandy thought you were going to hurt yourself?"

I shrugged and wished I hadn't. The pain in my back ramped up, and I found I was holding my breath against it. Beth peeked under my bandage.

"Let me help you sit up so you can take this pill," she said.

With her help, I sat up long enough to accept the pill and glass of water from Allison. Once I'd taken it, the two of them helped me back to the bedroom. Allison pulled the covers back, and Beth arranged the pillows behind me so I could sleep on my side. Allison kicked off her shoes and stretched out beside me. She laid her hand on the side of my face.

"I don't know what happened between you and Tam. But I know she loves you with all her heart, and I know you love her."

CHAPTER TWENTY-NINE

"Why are you doing this?" Allison asked, her voice shrill. "You can't just run away."

Six weeks had passed since Tam and I last spoke. She didn't trust me, and I was damned if I was going to be in a relationship where someone questioned my every thought and motive. My body had healed, but my soul had not. I put the clippers and basket I had taken from the Jeep on its hood before turning and taking Allison by the arms.

"I'm not running away. You and Beth know where I'm going. But you have to stick to your word and not tell anyone. Any. One. No one. Please."

Allison leaned her head against my chest.

"Promise you won't do something stupid. Too many people love you."

I lifted her chin with my finger and kissed her forehead.

"You can trust me when I say I won't hurt myself or try to commit suicide." I looked her in the eye and hoped she believed me. My promise was sincere, but if death came looking for me, I would take its hand and go with it.

I let go of her and looked at my little house, the house I hoped would be my home until death came. But there in the middle of the yard, in full view of anyone who drove by, was a For Sale sign. I would come back to the area but not to this neighborhood. It was too full of memories, too full of what I couldn't have.

I went to the flower beds Ocee had so lovingly tended for me while I couldn't and filled my basket. Since either Mae or Duke kept a close watch on her, I hadn't been able to hug or acknowledge Ocee, even though I watched her through my doorbell cam.

I put the flowers on the front seat and turned to Allison again.

"I love you, Allie. Thank you for taking such good care of me all these years." I reached for her, but she stepped back.

"That sounds like a 'goodbye' instead of a 'see you later.'" Her arms were tight across her chest.

"It is a 'see you later.'" I reached for her again, and this time she let me hug her. "You know my phone number. You know where I'm going. I promise to stay in touch, and I'll let you know when I'm ready to come back. It'll probably be when they complete the community in Hillsborough. That's a nice area to live."

"And it might as well be on Mars," Allison said into my chest. "What about the one in Rocky Mount instead?"

I laughed as I let her go and climbed into the Jeep.

"It's almost as far, silly. I need to hit the road. Please be careful going home and give Beth a hug for me."

I watched her in my rearview mirror as I drove away. Allison stood on the curb watching me, hugging herself. I hoped she would keep her promise and not tell anyone where I was going.

When I reached the cemetery, I parked in my usual spot and looked around as I climbed out of the Jeep. This quiet, serene place had almost become like a second home in the eight years Sandy had rested here. I wondered when I would see it again.

I had to smile as I approached Sandy's resting spot. Someone had been there before me. Fresh flowers lay at the base of the stone, leaving the vase for the flowers I brought. An unopened can of Dr. Pepper, Sandy's favorite drink, sat with the flowers. Stones and coins that Sandy's visitors left covered the top of her marker. After I arranged the flowers in the vase, I squatted in front of the gravestone and traced Sandy's name.

"I love you, and I always have, and I always will." I stopped and sighed. "Sweets, I don't know how long I'm going to be gone, but you'll always be in my heart. I miss you visiting me. Please come back."

I sat in silence for a long time, leaning my forehead against the cold marble. Finally, I kissed it and returned to my Jeep. A pink carnation sat on the front seat. I hadn't dropped it because there weren't any pink flowers in the bunch of flowers I took to the gravesite. But I had to grin. Neither Sandy nor I were fond of the color pink. Over our years together, we teased each other about it by buying something pink to give to each other. My pink elephant, one of the last things she gave me before she got sick, rode safely in my duffel bag. But it had been quite a while since she last left me anything pink.

I picked up the flower and looked around. There was no one in sight.

"I love you, too, Sandy." I climbed in the Jeep and laid the flower on the dashboard.

I arrived at the little cottage near the ocean a few hours later. Before I unpacked the Jeep, I walked around to the back and climbed the steps to the deck. I could hear the ocean from where I stood, but I couldn't see it for the protective dunes. A boardwalk stretched from the deck over the dunes to a gazebo and steps down to the beach.

"It's perfect," I said to the salt air. "Perfect."

After I unpacked, I decided to explore a bit. I changed into my swim shoes, which were going to be beach shoes while I was there, grabbed a bucket from the stack the hostess had next to the back door, and headed for the beach. There weren't nearly as many people on it as I expected there would be. I was relieved since I had no desire to deal with people any more than humanly necessary.

I smiled when I saw the washes of seashells spread at the tide line. To my surprise, a cool breeze blew across and around my hand, which held the bucket.

"I'm going to find you a special shell while I'm out here," I whispered as I headed out to do so.

CHAPTER THIRTY

The first evening was not a harbinger for the following days and weeks. The peace and happiness I experienced that day was gone, and everything I lost took center stage as I sank further into my dark tunnel.

"Oh, Tam. Why?" I cried as I hugged a pillow. "Why couldn't you believe me, trust me? I wanted to stay with you. You're my life."

I barely got out of bed the first week I was in the little cottage. Even though I knew Tam would want me to eat, the thought of putting food in my undeserving body sickened me. But I tried anyway. I kept praying Allison or Beth would call me and tell me Tam was begging me to come home, but my phone stayed silent. Maybe it had been a mistake to get a new phone and share the number only with them.

One sunny day, I dragged my butt out on the deck and collapsed in a chaise lounge. Almost immediately, several laughing gulls were floating over me, calling for me to throw them a morsel of food. I tried to wave them away, but they seemed to think it was a game, and more joined them, even though I had nothing to share. I sat and watched as they swooped and cawed, and soon I was laughing along with them.

The laughter opened my heart for a few hours, but as the sun set behind me, my mood sank, too. This was the time of day when Tam and I would spend on either her patio or mine cuddled in one chair, talking and kissing until the mosquitos ran us inside.

My cellphone rang, and I rushed inside to grab it off the table. The caller ID read Allison, and I almost threw it across the room before I remembered once again Tam didn't have this number.

"You okay?" Allison asked when I answered the call in a less than friendly manner.

"Yes. No. Who cares?" I paced the family room. "I shouldn't have come. I shouldn't have sold my house. I shouldn't, I shouldn't, I shouldn't. Goddamn it, Allison. Why didn't you stop me?"

"I'm coming to get you. It's dangerous for you to be alone when you're like this. You're scaring me."

"Damn you! You don't trust me any more than she does," I screamed at her. "I promised you I wouldn't do anything stupid. Why doesn't anyone believe me? I won't hurt myself. I won't do that to you."

I collapsed into a puddle in the middle of the floor, a sixty-two-year-old big baby.

"Janice, you need to pull yourself together." Beth's stern voice broke through my near hysteria. "You're scaring both me and Allison. If you can't get it together and convince me you're okay, we're going to be on our way as soon as we can get out the door."

"Fuck you, Bethany," I growled. "My heart was torn from my chest and cremated eight years ago and buried in the cemetery. I never thought I'd love again, and now I do, but she reached down my throat, pulled the rest of my heart out, and threw it at me. It doesn't matter where I am or whether or not you're with me; I'm alone. She threw me out like a piece of fucking garbage."

"You're not garbage, Janice." Beth's voice was soft. "Allie and I love you more than you know. We can't take Sandy's or Tam's place, but I wish we were worth living for. And Ocee. Hon, you know she doesn't understand what is happening, but she still loves you. Please, babe. You're making yourself sick like you were the night you burned yourself."

"I'm not going to be that stupid again," I said as my tears and hysteria began to subside. "I'm not going to hurt myself, intentionally or unintentionally. All I want is to have my lady back. Beth, how do I do that?"

"I don't know. Have you tried to call her?"

"I'm scared to. What if I call and she doesn't answer? Or if she answers and hangs up on me? Or tells me to get lost, out of her life? My heart can't handle it."

"Give me the phone," I heard Allison say. Beth and Allison spoke to each other for a moment in voices too low for me to decipher. "You still there?"

"Yes. I'm sorry I screamed at you. I love you."

"I love you, too, Janny. Are you eating? Please tell me you're eating, but tell me the truth."

"I have food in the house," I said.

"That's not the same thing." I could almost see Allison shaking her head. "Janice Kirsten, you have to eat. At least open a can of something, anything. You don't even have to heat it. Just eat something. Please. We love you too much for you not to."

"I promise I'll eat something as soon as we hang up."

"Unh uh. You go in the kitchen right now while I'm still on the line. Next time I'm video calling you so I can watch you eat."

I pushed myself up off the floor and went to the kitchen. I set the phone on the counter and found a can of chili. I pulled the top off and got a spoon out of the drawer before putting the phone on speaker.

"I'm eating a can of chili," I said around the spoon in my mouth. "Are you happy now?"

"Thank you," Allison said. "I love you. I'm going to call you again tomorrow and the next day and the next day until you either come home, we come out there, or you're better."

CHAPTER THIRTY-ONE

Allison kept her promise and called me every day, sometimes two or three times. And most of the time, it was a video call. Each time, she wouldn't disconnect until she physically saw me eat at least part of a meal. Because of her sisterly love for me and Beth's care and support, the darkness receded even if it didn't completely disappear. After a while, my friends' calls lessened to two or three times a week, and Sandy's breeze returned to visit me.

As I started feeling better, I spent almost every morning with a cup of coffee in the gazebo. One morning, as I watched the sun rise over the ocean and the little sanderlings chase the waves, I got the itch to paint. I hadn't painted since before I burned myself and almost hadn't brought my easel or canvases or any of my painting supplies. But Beth bypassed me when I tried to put them in the storage unit I had rented to store my household goods in until I found a new place to live. She put everything back in the Jeep and made sure my keyboard was there as well, and it all came with me to the beach.

I barely ate as I painted seascape after seascape. I photographed the pelicans as they skimmed the waves and was lucky enough to capture a dolphin as it leaped from the waves one turbulent morning, and I used those photographs as inspiration for my paintings. By the time the itch was relieved, I had half a dozen canvases leaning against the furniture in the living room, each in various stages of drying. I continued to paint but not in the marathon painting session I had at first.

As the days passed by, I took the keyboard out on the deck and played for the seagulls that liked to hover over me. I played every piece of music I knew except for the song I wrote for Tam and the song that turned out to be Ocee's introduction to advanced piano techniques. Those songs were no longer mine, and I refused to think about them. A new song didn't come to me until Sandy's and my anniversary in September.

I missed going to visit her like I usually did on that day. It didn't help that it was a miserable, wet, windy day as a tropical storm edged its way along the coast. I pulled a chair from the family room over to the slider so I could curl up in it and watch as the waves of rain pushed over my deck. As I watched, a melody began to play in my head. I listened to it for a while before moving to my keyboard, pulling the notes from my brain, and letting my fingers find them on the keys. I continued to hum as I stood up to go find my notebook and a pen and transpose what I heard to paper.

"Sandy, my love, this one's for you," I said as I wrote the last note on the paper. I put the notebook on the music holder and played the song, occasionally making slight corrections on the page. I only stopped to switch on some more lights as the already dim day darkened into night. My growling stomach finally reminded me I needed at least a little bit of sustenance.

You need to eat. I could hear Tam's voice in my heart and head as I studied the slim pickings in my refrigerator and pantry. I missed the fresh vegetables I had feasted on this time last year. Finally, I settled for opening a can of mixed vegetables, which I ate along with my last piece of ham and the few stale saltines I found hiding behind the cans.

I hated the idea of having to drive into Beaufort to go grocery shopping, but it was obvious I had no choice. I ripped a page from my notebook and started making a list. As I did, I noticed there was no sound of rain hitting the sides of the house. Even though it was dark, I decided to take a short walk on the beach. I put on my swim shoes and grabbed a flashlight.

The sky was still cloudy, but the moon was trying its best to find a hole to shine through. I followed the flashlight beam out the dock to the steps to the beach. I stood at the top of them and swung the beam up the beach and back again. There was a lot of debris washed along the tide line, and I hoped it included some awesome shells. That search would have to wait until daylight.

I descended the steps, holding tight to the banister as the stairs were more slippery than I expected. At the third step, my foot slid out from under me and, try as I might, I could not stop my fall. Somehow, my left foot wedged between the steps while the rest of me headed for the beach. I heard the snap and felt the pain simultaneously. I screamed and passed out. When I came to, someone was shining a light on my face.

"Are you okay, lady?"

I recognized the voice of the young man who came around and took care of the yard every week.

"Do you need some help?"

"My ankle is broken," I said through gritted teeth. "I can't get up. Will you please call an ambulance for me?"

"Oh, fuck," the kid said. "I'm going to go get my dad and call nine-one-one. I don't have any reception out here. What can I do for you right now?"

"Go get me some help, please."

I pulled my now useless foot off the steps and down to the same level as the rest of my body, but the pain was intense, and I thought I was going to vomit. It seemed like an eternity before the young man returned with a man, a woman, and another boy.

The woman kneeled beside me and handed me a bottle of water. I took a long swig.

"What's your name, honey?" the woman asked as the man examined my ankle by the light of the flashlights the two boys held. I winced when he touched it, and he grimaced along with me.

"Janice Halston," I whispered. "Goddamn, it hurts. How much longer before someone gets here?"

"They're on the way, but there's a lot of debris on the road, and they're having to go slower than normal," the man said. "We brought a couple of icepacks and ace bandages, and I'm going to wrap your foot and ankle. Hopefully that will keep you from swelling more than you already have. But, Miss Janice, it's going to hurt like hell. You can scream and cuss all you want and none of us will judge you for it."

I wanted to laugh at his permission for me to react to the pain, but then he placed an icepack on each side of my ankle and the scream that escaped me as he wrapped the bandage around it sounded as if it belonged to another person. The woman took the bottle of water from me and put some in her hand and bathed my face. I was close to passing out again when a truck with red flashing lights appeared down the beach from us. I tried to sigh with relief, but it was ragged. My throat was raw from screaming.

Late the next afternoon, the hospital in Morehead City released me with my left leg encased in a hulking big cast from my toes to my knee and a pair of crutches, which had a learning curve I wasn't sure I could surmount. Mrs. Lambert, the angel from the night before, helped me hop from the wheelchair to the front seat of her car.

"Did they feed you?" she asked. "We can stop at El's for a hamburger if you want."

The mention of food made me groan. I remembered I had no groceries in the house.

"No thank you. Do any of the supermarkets in Beaufort deliver out to my house? I had planned on going grocery shopping today, and it's obvious I'm not going to get it done."

Mrs. Lambert shook her head.

"Oh, honey. You're in the boonies now. No place here goes out there. Tell you what, though. I'll make a quick stop at the supermarket and grab some things for you while you wait in the car. There's a pad and a pen there in the glove compartment. Just write down what you need."

"But I don't have any cash on me," I said, wondering how I would pay if I was waiting in the car.

"You don't worry about it." She reached over and patted my hand. "I'll spring for it this time, and you can pay me

231

back when we get to the house. You lean back and relax, and let me worry about it."

"Thank you."

The nurse at the hospital had made me take a pain pill before they released me, and it was starting to affect me. I reclined the passenger seat a little, so that I was more comfortable. My next memory was of the passenger door opening and Mr. Lambert looming over me.

"Miss Janice, let me help you out," he said as he bent over. "You lean on me, and we'll get you inside and comfy on your sofa. Good thing this house is all on one level."

He was good to his word as he practically carried me inside and set me on the sofa while the boys followed with my few bags of groceries. Mrs. Lambert put my foot up on a stack of sofa pillows.

"Well, I was going to bring you a glass of tea, but you weren't kidding when you said you had nothing in the house. You relax right there while I brew some for you and make you a sandwich."

"Mrs. Lambert, you don't need to do all this. I have to figure out how to do it myself anyway. I might as well start now."

She put both of her hands on her hips.

"Young lady, my Bible teaches me I'm supposed to help those in need, and right now, you're the one in need, and I'm going to help you. I promise not to hover, but at least let me take care of you right now."

Her calling me *young lady* made me laugh. I was sure I was old enough to be her mother. But I let her wait on me until it was time for her to go home to take care of her own family. She gave me her phone number and Mr. Lambert's.

"Now, Miss Janice," she said. "Don't hesitate to call us if you need help. That's what neighbors are for, after all. I'll check on you later this evening, but for now, you try to get some rest."

As soon as she was gone, I took my phone from my pocket and speed dialed Allison.

"Hey, friend," she said when she answered. "Did you survive the storm?"

"I did, but my ankle didn't." I winced as I tried to sit up straighter. The damn cast was heavy.

"What do you mean?" The tone in Allison's voice changed from jovial to worried in an instant.

"What's wrong?" Beth asked in the background.

"I fell down the beach steps and broke my ankle." Allison's screech caused me to pull the phone away from my ear.

"You did what? How in the hell did you fall down the steps? And if you landed in the sand, why is your ankle broken? What really happened?"

My hackles rose when she asked the last question.

"I don't think I want to talk to you. You obviously don't trust me to tell you the truth."

"I'm sorry, Janny." There were tears in Allison's voice. "I shouldn't have said that. But, hon, we're worried about you being out there alone, and this is a good reason why. None of us are spring chickens anymore, and we need people to lean on."

"Don't get maudlin." I wondered why I put myself in a position to have conversations like this. "It happened exactly like I said. I was going down the steps, and I lost my footing. My left foot got stuck between the steps while the rest of me kept going. Fortunately, one of my neighbors' sons saw me, and his family came to my rescue. They stayed with me until beach rescue got here, and Mrs. Lambert insisted on staying with me at the hospital and feeding me when she brought me home."

"Give me the phone," I heard Beth say. "You can't talk when you're crying so hard. Go get a drink and wash your face."

Allison said something I couldn't make out.

"I know, babe. I'll tell her. Now go on."

"Is she okay?" I asked, concerned about my friend and wondering if I shouldn't have called.

"She's having a hard time with you gone. She's become a recluse. I picked her up from work a couple of weeks after you left, and Danny beat her out to the car. He asked me if she's sick and told me she won't talk to anyone and keeps to herself."

"Why is she doing that?" I was almost in tears. "Is she sick?"

"Not physically." Beth sighed. "I dragged her to see the doctor a couple of weeks later. They took a shitload of blood, and there's nothing new there. I threatened to call our therapist if she didn't tell me what was wrong. Janice, it's because you asked her not to tell anyone where you are. She figures the best way to keep her word is if she stays away from everyone and doesn't give anyone a chance to ask her any questions."

"Shit." I swiped at the tears rolling down my face and looked around for the box of tissues. They were, of course, on a table on the other side of the living room. I used the tail of my shirt to wipe my face. "Double damn shit. I'm sorry, Beth. Maybe I shouldn't have even told y'all where I was going. Why are you just now telling me this? Especially since I can't do anything about it with this fucking foot."

"She'd be in a padded room if you hadn't told us where you were going. Janice, I didn't tell you because of your state of mind. I'm not sure why I'm telling you now. I probably shouldn't have. But you need to tell me what happened to your foot."

I took a couple of deep breaths and repeated my story. After commiserating with me for a few minutes, Beth took a deep breath and was quiet a moment too long.

"What?" I asked. "Why does it feel as though you need to tell me something you don't want to tell me?"

Something occurred to me, and I gulped.

"Is Tam okay? Ocee? Are they okay?"

"As far as we know. Tam won't have anything to do with us. Our calls go to voicemail, and she doesn't answer our emails. But Allison saw her the other day when she drove over to take the picture of the Sold sign for you. Allison didn't talk to her, but she said Tam was standing in the driveway with her hands in her pockets, staring at the sign. Allison parked the car, but Tam shook her head and turned and left."

"Oh," was all I could think to say.

"Janny, we're as worried about her as we are about you. Won't you at least consider calling or writing her?"

"No. She believed a spirit in a dream instead of the human standing in front of her." I wanted to pace, and it was impossible, which was driving me nuts. "Even after I confessed the idea had crossed my mind, but I couldn't imagine leaving her, she doubted me. She let me walk out of her house, Bethany. I was crushed. There I was in pain because of my own stupidity, and she let me leave. Now I have to go. I can't talk about this anymore. Hug Allie for me."

It took everything in me to keep from throwing the phone across the room. I put my feet on the floor and tried to figure out how to stand up. Finally, I fell to the floor and crawled to the bathroom, dragging my left foot.

CHAPTER THIRTY-TWO

I learned to navigate my house and deck on crutches. The muses slammed the door on my creativity, and I reverted to sitting around with too much time to think, but this time, unable to escape to the beach and the calming sound of the waves washing ashore. Tam and Ocee were heavy on my heart, but I didn't know what to do about it. I couldn't be in a relationship with someone who didn't trust me, and Tam had made it clear she trusted Sandy's spirit over me. If she didn't trust me about that, what else didn't she trust? But without a relationship with Tam, there was no relationship with Ocee.

I wondered if Ocee was still playing her piano or if Mae and Duke had put it away now that I was out of their lives. I hoped she was still playing, still practicing, still trying to learn the crossovers in the music I wrote.

I wondered if the community had ripped out my garden and all my flowers when they prepared the house for its new occupants. Having my hands in the soil was so therapeutic, and I thought about asking my landlady if I could put some potted plants on the deck come spring. But I didn't know if I would still be there or if I would return to the Triangle as I'd promised Allison and Beth.

Cabin fever finally got the best of me, and it coincided with the day I had my second appointment with the orthopedist in Beaufort.

"I can take myself," I told Mrs. Lambert for the umpteenth time. "I can drive okay, and I want to spend some time looking around after my appointment. Can I bring anything back for you?"

Mrs. Lambert's eyes lit up.

"Oh, if you can get me some saltwater taffy, I'll love you forever."

I laughed and hugged her before she started the trek back to her house. The Lamberts proved to be a godsend. Wyatt continued to take care of the yard while his brother, Hayden, did the chores around the house that I couldn't, such as sweeping and mopping my floors. I wanted to pay them, but they wouldn't let me. I hoped to find them a gift while I was in town.

The appointment with the doctor went well. He cut off the cast and x-rayed my ankle.

"The break is healing nicely," he said. "I'm going to put you in a walking boot. I still want you to use one crutch as support, but you can start putting weight on your foot, as much as you are able."

It was such a relief to have the heavy monstrosity off my foot. They bandaged my foot and ankle so that they were immobile, but the walking boot made maneuvering much easier.

The doctor's office was in a historic building in downtown Beaufort, close to the tourist area. I left the Jeep in their parking lot while I hobbled on my crutch to a building close by which housed several tourist trap shops. One of them probably sold the saltwater taffy Mrs. Lambert asked for.

There were two choices to get to the elevated front porch where the shops were located—either by a fairly steep set of steps or a long wheelchair ramp which doubled back on itself. The stairs made me shudder, and I chose the ramp. The trek to the top was longer and more difficult than I expected it to be. Using the one crutch and the handrail, I made the slow journey upward.

"Janice!"

I stopped for a moment. Even though the voice sounded familiar, I reminded myself that I had a common name and continued up the ramp. I jumped when someone took my elbow. I almost fell over when I turned and looked into Charles' face. It took everything in me not to burst into tears. I hadn't realized how homesick I was until that moment.

"Hi," he said. "Let's get you to the porch so you can sit down before you fall down."

He took my crutch and put his arm around my waist. We moved at my speed until we were on a level surface. I turned and pulled him into the tightest hug I'd probably ever given him.

"What are you doing here? How did you find me? Y'all didn't finally break Allison, did you?"

"One question at a time," he said with a laugh. "Let's sit over here and talk."

We made our way along the porch to find some chairs away from the hubbub of the entryway.

"First, what happened to you?" He pointed to my foot. "Finally get mad enough to kick someone?"

I laughed.

"No. I fell down the beach stairs after the last tropical storm came through. It's a clean break, so no surgery or anything."

"Kinda puts a crimp on being at the beach, doesn't it?" He reached over and patted my hand before taking it in his and studying the scars on my arm, which were fading. He ran his free hand over them. "How are you doing? I was sorry to hear you and Tam split up."

"Thank you. Me, too. I thought I had found my life mate in her, but I can't deal with her lack of trust in me." I closed my eyes to the memory of that day. "Otherwise, I'm doing okay. You haven't answered my question. What are you doing here? And where's Danny?"

I looked around, but the younger man was nowhere to be seen.

"Y'all are still together, aren't you?" I asked, now worried about my friends.

Charles smiled and lifted his left hand to reveal a simple gold band on his third finger.

"We're engaged and plan to get married next spring. We'll let you know the details when it gets closer."

I squeezed his hand.

"Congratulations. I'm so happy for you. So, what are you doing here, and where is Danny? It feels like you're avoiding answering my questions."

He looked away and stayed quiet for a long moment before scooting forward in his chair and turning to look at me.

"We have a friend who is having a hard time, and we brought her here to try to cheer her up. We didn't know this is where you're hiding."

My heart clenched, and a lump formed in my throat. I struggled to get to my feet, but he stopped me with a hand on my shoulder.

"Janny, please don't do this. Y'all need to at least talk and see if you can find some common ground so you can both stop being miserable. And don't tell me you aren't. I can see it in your eyes. Don't forget, I've known you this side of forever."

"I'm not the one with trust issues," I whispered, so I wouldn't scream. "Please let me up."

But it was too late.

"Janice? Oh, my God." Danny was bending over me before I could react to the sound of his voice. He squatted beside my chair and took me into a gentle embrace before kissing me on the side of the head. "We miss you, lady."

"I miss you, too." I watched Tam backing down the porch toward the steps. I wasn't sure if I was talking to her or Danny. Charles hurried to her, took her by the elbow, and walked her to the other end, talking the whole way.

Danny sat back on his haunches and studied me for a long moment.

"You look tired." He put a light hand on my boot. "You just can't stop hurting yourself, can you?"

I laughed a forced laugh.

"The beach steps decided I was their mortal enemy and fought back. They won the battle, but not the war."

I hadn't taken my eyes off Tam as we spoke. Danny looked over his shoulder.

"She loves you, you know," he said in a quiet, gentle voice. "And she misses you. She's devastated you sold your house. Are you moving here permanently?"

"I have a one-year rental on my cottage with an option to rent for another year, but everyone I love is in Raleigh, so I'll probably come back at some point."

"Where will you live?"

I shrugged. "The community has built several other neighborhoods in the area. I considered Hillsborough, but Allison pitched a fit. I might look at Rocky Mount or Smithfield instead."

He nodded, and I watched a tear escape from one of his eyes. I dried it with my thumb pad.

"Why are you crying?"

He stood up and looked down the porch again before sitting in the chair Charles had vacated.

"Do you plan on trying to reconcile with her at all? That's my mom for all practical purposes, and I hate seeing her in so much pain. And, damn it all, Janice, Ocee is a shell of the child she was."

My heart dropped to my stomach, and I couldn't have said anything if I'd known what to say. He pulled out his phone, tapped it a couple of times, and handed it to me. My beautiful Ocee sat at a baby grand piano dressed in a red tuxedo with a pale pink blouse and a red bow in her dark hair. She gave a half-smile toward the audience and started playing. My heart and soul sang as she did the crossovers perfectly and brought the song I'd written to life. I had tears flowing down my face, but I didn't try to stop them.

After Ocee played the last note, she held her fingers over the keys for a moment before proceeding to play *Twinkle Little Star* with one finger. The audience was quiet, so quiet, before they erupted in applause, and calls of "Bravo." Ocee slid off the stool and bowed, but there was no smile on her face even after someone laid a bouquet of roses in her arms.

I sat with my hand at my throat, staring at the now quiet phone. My girl, my song. I was so proud of her, but my heart broke that I hadn't been there for such a perfect moment.

"Masters School of Music accepted her."

Tam stood a few feet away, still wringing her hands. I offered her my hand, and she stared at it for a long time before stepping forward and taking it. When I gave her a little tug, she stepped closer, bent over, and hugged me.

"Why don't y'all go back to the bed-and-breakfast to talk so you can have some privacy?" Charles put one hand on my shoulder and the other on Tam's back. "Danny's gone to get the car so you don't have to walk over."

Tam stood up and wiped her face with the back of her hands. She looked at me with her unreadable face.

"Are you willing?" she asked. "I'd like to try to explain. I should have tried the night this fell apart. Please."

I nodded. Charles held out his hands and helped me to my feet. He kept his hands on my elbows until I was steady before handing me my crutch.

But instead of going to the B-and-B, I asked them to take me to my Jeep.

"Tam and I can go talk, and you guys can keep sightseeing." I pulled out my wallet and handed a twenty-dollar bill to Charles. "Would you buy as much saltwater taffy as that will get? I promised my neighbor who is helping me that I would bring her some."

"You need help getting in your car?" Danny asked.

I gave him a playful scowl.

"It is not a car, it is a Jeep, a Jeep Rubicon."

243

"You got ducked." Tam laughed as she plucked the small bright yellow rubber duck from between the side mirror and the side of the Jeep.

"Cool. It's my first duck," I said as she handed it to me.

"Okay. At some point, you'll need to explain that to us." Charles became serious. "I love you two. Please be kind to each other and call us if you need to."

Tam hugged him and Danny before Danny followed me to the driver's door. He held my crutch as I hefted myself into the driver's seat. He put the crutch behind me and then kissed me on the cheek before closing my door. I watched them drive away and then looked at Tam. Her hair was longer than it used to be, and her eyes were not as bright.

When we arrived at the bed-and-breakfast, she came around the Jeep and stood ready to help me if I needed it. Once I had my crutch, she led me along a deeply shaded driveway to a gorgeous garden with burbling fountains and intimate settings of tables and chairs.

"Let me go ask Lola if they have a cushion to put on a chair so you can prop your foot up," she said after we found chairs at the back of the garden, away from the main traffic area.

Tam came back carrying a couple of pillows, followed by a short, round woman carrying a tray of glasses of iced tea and some dainty pastries. She set them on the round table between the two chairs and scurried to bring an extra chair over for me to prop my foot on.

"Thank you," I said as she fluffed the cushions around my ankle.

"You need to be taken care of." She waved over her shoulder on her way back to the house.

"She's cute," I said after Tam handed me a glass of tea and settled into the other chair.

"Lola's a dream. I don't know how Charles and Danny find these places, but they're always greeted as though they're old friends."

"Have you gone on many trips with them?" I watched her out of the corner of my eye.

"This is my third one since you left. The other two were close to the Triangle, but they were nice and peaceful and out of the way."

She rubbed her face before looking over at me.

"I'm sorry, Janice," she said with a catch in her voice. "Where am I supposed to start except there? This was never meant to happen."

I was unsure of how to respond, so I waited to see if she would say anything else. She walked around for a couple of minutes before pulling her chair so it was facing me and as close as she could get with my leg stretched out in front of me.

"I was scared. I'd never seen you like you were both before your accident and after. You were so distant, so. . .so away from everyone and everything else, even though you were right there. And you were so adamant about getting Ocee into Masters, you couldn't listen to reason no matter what I said or did. And then, oh, God, Janice. When I saw your poor back and legs and arm…"

She looked at the scars on my arm and ran her hand over them. She glanced at my legs. My shorts had ridden up some, and the scars on my thighs were barely visible. I resisted the temptation to tug on the legs of my shorts.

"Janny, I was afraid you were trying to kill yourself. I thought you were trying to get away from me by dying. I couldn't go through losing someone again."

She rose and turned her back on me. I knew she was crying, but there was nothing I could do for her. Using both hands to lift my foot off the chair, I tried to reach my crutch. She turned back around.

"Oh, Janice. Please don't leave." She hurried to my side. "Not yet, anyway. Please."

I sank back in my chair.

"Tam, I wasn't leaving. I wanted to come to you, but I can't move as fast as I could before I broke this damn ankle. I'm sorry I gave you the wrong impression."

She helped me get my foot back in the chair before returning to her own seat.

"When you were in the hospital, there were so many times it seemed you were giving up. Sometimes, I wondered if you even wanted to be alive. And you kept calling for Sandy. I never heard you call for me, and I wondered if you truly loved me."

My tears were flowing freely, but I didn't interrupt her.

"About a week before they discharged you, Sandy visited me in a dream. It was as real as you and I are right now. She told me you were going to run away. I told her to stop you, and she said she couldn't. You had to make your own decisions unhindered by her. But she told me I could, and should, stop you.

"Janny, I had the same dream two more times, including the night before you came home. It had me so rattled, so angry, that I lashed out at you instead of trying to talk to you and hear what you had to say. My only excuse is that I was exhausted. I barely slept the whole time you were in the hospital. Seeing and hearing you in so much pain tore me up. When I did sleep, I had those dreams. And I was scared shitless I was going to lose you, either through death or your leaving me."

She put her face in her hands and doubled over so her hands and face were on her knees. After a few minutes, she looked up at me through her tear-streaked face.

"And I did lose you. Lock, stock, and barrel. Seeing the *For Sale* sign in your yard as I drove along your street is a memory I wish I could forget. I almost drove off the road, and then I barely made it to my bathroom before I got sick. I slept on the bathroom floor that night, and that's where Mae found me the next day. She was all for hunting you down and skinning you alive after calling you every name in the book in as many languages as she could think of. And I hate to admit it, but at first, I was all for it.

"I called Allison and asked where you were, but she wouldn't tell me. All she would say was you were safe and trying to get healthy. I asked her if you were coming back, and she wouldn't answer me. I haven't spoken to her or anyone except Charles and Danny since.

"Janice, I never stopped loving you. When I saw you sitting on the porch talking to Charles, I wanted to run to you and kiss you and hug you and hold you. But I didn't know if you wanted me to. I couldn't bring myself to go near you until I saw you watching the video of Ocee playing your song. Even then, I wasn't sure if I should. Did you move out here permanently?"

I desperately wanted to pace.

"No. Allison needs me, and I miss the rest of my friends. I'll eventually move back to the Triangle or close by."

I took a ragged breath and looked at Tam.

"I sold my house and came out here because I love you so much. Being around the corner from you and knowing you don't trust me preyed on the little mental health I had left. And watching Ocee take care of my flowers. I wanted to go out to hug her every time she came, but Mae stood at the end of the sidewalk, scowling at the house like she knew I was watching, and I didn't have the courage. I couldn't stand it anymore.

"But not being able to be with you was my catalyst for leaving. It seemed we had a rare thing going, and then you trusted a spirit in a dream more than the person standing in front of you. You didn't even give me a chance to explain how I felt or what I was going through. You trusted... Oh, Goddamn it, Tam. I can't enter into a commitment with someone who doesn't trust me—me! Implicitly. You didn't even try to stop me from leaving your house. That's when I knew. That's when I knew."

"Oh Lord, Janice," Tam said, her voice hoarse. "I do trust you, and I always have. I was confused that night. It was a mistake on my part not to go over to your house that evening with Allison and Beth. They told me how sick you still were and how you thought Sandy hid your pills from you."

"She thought I was going to take them all," I whispered.

"Were you thinking about it, Janny?"

I closed my eyes as I nodded.

"I couldn't imagine my life without you, but I can't stand being with someone who is going to question everything I do, everything I consider doing. The pain from that is more intense than the burns, which were more painful than anything I've ever experienced, including this broken ankle." I gestured at my foot. "And I still had that horrible empty, nothing feeling I couldn't shake. It's still with me, but it's not as bad. I was painting and composing again when I broke this fucking ankle. And now it's all gone. I've had a hell of a lot of time to think, and I'm getting used to the idea of being alone forever. I'm alone. I obviously will be the rest of my life."

Tam began to pace again. She stopped and looked at me.

"You don't have to be alone, Janice. I do trust you. I wish you could trust that. How can we fix this? Is it fixable? Do you want to fix it?"

Her eyes were wide, almost wild, and bright with tears. I put my foot on the ground and pushed myself to my feet.

"Do you want to fix it?"

She nodded. "But how? Will you ever be able to look at me without wondering if I trust you?"

"Will you ever be able to look at me without wondering if I'm finally losing the little sanity I have left? Or if I'm telling you the truth? Or without questioning my motives? And even if you will, you have a family to consider. Will Mae and Duke ever forgive me, ever let me be Gah-Gah again?"

I hid my face in my hands as I sat back down. The thought of never seeing Ocee again broke every part of my being. Tam squatted beside me and rubbed my back, but I twisted away from her.

"When Mae brought my bag to me, Ocee asked me if I was going to stop loving her like I stopped loving you. I told her I would always love her and that I love you. I guess she doesn't believe me now, and I've probably lost her trust, too."

"Ocee told me you said you love me," Tam said. We were both quiet. "I want us back. I love you. And I do trust you."

I bowed my head and sighed.

"I don't believe we're ready. Like you always say, I think we've got some thinking to do. I'm tired, and I'm hurting. I need to get back to the cottage so I can take a pain pill."

"Let me drive you, Janice. Let me take care of you."

I shook my head.

"Thank you. But not yet."

"Then when?" Her tears flowed again.

"I don't know yet. I'll call you in a few days or a week or sometime, and we can go from there."

"How will I know it's you if you won't let me have your phone number?"

I heard a touch of ire in her voice, and I looked at her.

"I guess you'll just have to trust that I'll keep my word and call. You'll have to answer your phone and see if it's me." I grabbed my crutch and struggled to my feet. She didn't move to help me. The crushed, lost feeling of the night in April flooded over me. Without another word, I hobbled to my Jeep and headed back to my self-imposed isolation, forgetting about the salt-water taffy I had asked Charles to buy.

CHAPTER THIRTY-THREE

"Danny called me," were the first words out of Allison's mouth when she called that night. "Are you okay?"

"No. I don't think I ever will be again," I said.

There were no tears left in me. I was out of everything. I wanted to go sit in the ocean and let the waves take me. While I wouldn't, the idea was there.

"We're on our way, and we're not taking no for an answer."

"Okay." I closed my eyes and put my free arm over my eyes. "But stay in town. This place is too small for me to have company."

"Bullshit. We've stayed there, remember? It's how you found it in the first place. Put fresh linens on the bed in the spare bedroom. No, don't worry about it. We can do that when we get there. Do we need to buy groceries?"

"I don't know. Probably." I couldn't find any enthusiasm for anything.

"Danny asked me again for your phone number." Allison was quiet for a long moment. "Is it okay if I give it to him?"

"I don't care. They know where I am now anyway."

"You're fucking scaring me. Was your talk with Tam so bad? Do I need to put my mother bear apron on and go have a talk with her?"

"No. I probably ended any chance of us getting back together. I told her we need to think. She was ready to forgive, forget, and move on, try to get back together. She wanted to drive me back out here and take care of me. I said no, and I told her I'll call her in a few days or a few weeks or sometime, and she got mad because she doesn't have my number. I told her I guess she'll have to trust me and answer her phone, and I left."

"Why, Janny? Why were you so mean to her?"

"I don't know."

"I thought you wanted to get back with her."

"Can we do this when y'all get here? I'm tired. I took a pain pill, and now I feel sick."

"Did you take it with food?"

"I'm hanging up now, mother," I said and did.

Leaning off the sofa, I quickly grabbed the trash can I had placed nearby. I retched and dry heaved, but I had already emptied my stomach of everything I had eaten earlier in the day. Using the water from the bottle I earlier put on the coffee table, I rinsed my mouth and spat it into the trash can. I was supposed to take my medicine with food, but I hadn't bothered to fix anything. And now I was paying for it. I lay back down and tried to feel anything except the pain in my stomach and foot. But my heart and soul were empty, my future bleak and empty.

I was almost asleep when someone knocking on the door woke me up. I groaned. Dealing with people, even people as sweet and kind as the Lamberts, was the last thing I wanted to do.

"Just a minute," I yelled as I swung my foot off the sofa and used my crutch and the coffee table to push myself up. I hopped to the front door and threw it open. But it wasn't any of the Lambert family standing there. "Charles, how the hell did you find me? Did Allison call and ask you to do a welfare check?"

I unlatched the storm door and turned to go back to the sofa.

"Do you need a welfare check?" He put his arm around my waist to help me.

"Probably." I hefted my foot back on the couch and fell back against the pillows. "If that's not what you're doing here, why are you here and how did you find me?"

"You forgot these." He held up three boxes of saltwater taffy. "You were speeding away as we got back. I wanted to follow you, but Danny insisted I stop so we could check on Tam."

I glanced over at him as he set the boxes on the coffee table.

"Is she okay?" I whispered.

He shrugged as he flopped into one of the side chairs.

"I don't understand you," he said. "I only remember one time you and Sandy had a real out-and-out fight. Do you remember what it was about?"

"What does this have to do with Tam?" I looked away from him.

"Bear with me. I asked you a question. Do you remember the fight you had with Sandy, the one that almost led to your separation?"

I shook my head even though I did.

"Well, I remember it, and I'd warrant a bet anyone around at the time remembers it, too. I don't remember what happened, but Sandy gave you the third degree about something and didn't like the answers she was getting. And you, in your infinite wisdom, decided she didn't trust you. You called Allison and asked if you could stay with her until you found your own place to live. She and Roberta were still together, and Roberta said no sofa surfers. So you called Melba, who had just moved in with Carmen. Stupid move, Janice. I mean, really? They were still in their honeymoon phase, but you were going to crash on them because you thought Sandy didn't trust you."

I struggled to sit up and glare at him.

"She didn't fucking trust me," I growled. "She made it quite clear when she kept asking me the same questions over and over, only phrased differently. It was like she was trying to catch me in a lie I wasn't telling. What was I supposed to do? Stay with a person I knew would trust nothing I said about anything?"

"Yeah." Charles leaned forward, his elbows on his knees. "You were supposed to talk to her, find out why she doubted you, work together to get back on track. It's what finally happened simply because you couldn't find any place to stay.

"Janice, you could have fixed things with Tam back in April if your pride hadn't gotten the best of you again. You were in a lot of pain for a lot of reasons, not the least of which were the burns you got because you were upset about something else—"

"And acted stupid." I finished his sentence for him.

"Yeah. Did something stupid. None of us understands how or why you did that to yourself. Beth thinks it was a cry for help, but when you had an opportunity to get some help, you turned your back on it. We all know you knew the right things to say to get out of the hospital when you should have stayed and let the fucking doctors help you."

I sat back, my mouth hanging open. I couldn't remember the last time I heard Charles curse about anything.

"The fact you turned on Tam when she had a legitimate concern showed all of us you weren't okay. Yeah, she didn't approach the subject as diplomatically as she should, but she had a right to be worried and scared and concerned. And, since you ran away from everything and tried to fall off the side of the earth, you proved Sandy's spirit right."

He stopped and rubbed his face.

"I know she comes to you." He glanced over at me. "You've talked about it before, about the cool breeze of her spirit, and how comforting it is to you. When's the last time she was with you?"

I knew if I spoke, I would blow up.

"Been a while?" Charles moved over to sit beside me on the sofa and put an arm around my waist. "Why do you think she's staying away? Could it be because of how you've been acting? You didn't have to run away. You sure as hell didn't have to sell the house you loved. What's the real reason you ended your relationship with Tam?"

"I didn't end it," I yelled, wishing I could stomp away. "She did by not trusting me."

"You are so damn stubborn." He put his hands on my shoulders and turned me toward him. "Yes, she trusted you. At least until you walked away from her today. I don't know

if there's anything left to rescue. You had a golden
opportunity today, and you threw it away like you have so
many other things in your life. Why, Janice Halston? Why?"
  I leaned forward and put my head on his chest. I couldn't
cry, even though his words hurt my heart and soul to their
core. He wrapped his arms around me and leaned us both
back. He kissed me on the forehead, and we sat in silence.
  "You didn't tell me how you found me," I said.
  "I knew you were staying in a cottage away from
Beaufort, and I figured it had to be on the water. So, I just
started driving. I figured if I got to the end of Harker's Island
before I saw your Jeep, I would have twenty dollars' worth
of saltwater taffy for myself. About the time I was ready to
give up, I finally saw the Jeep. And here I am."
  "To ream me." I put my head against his shoulder.
  "Partly," he admitted. "And also to tell you we love you.
All of us do. We can't figure you out, and I'm not sure we've
ever been able to. Sandy kept you grounded most of the time,
and since we lost her, you've been like a ping-pong ball. I
hate to admit it, but we weren't particularly surprised when
all hell broke out at the school because of that woman. We
wondered when the earthquake would hit, and when it did,
we almost lost you, at least the you we love. Physically, you
were still walking the earth, but you were emotionally and
mentally absent. You met Tam and started coming back to
us. But babe, we see you leaving us again. You have to get
some help and not just a pill to take. None of us like seeing
you like this."
  He turned so we were face to face.
  "Tam loves you, but you've broken her heart twice now.
And to be honest, we love her too much to let you do that
again. Once we got Tam calm enough to take a nap, Danny

and I had a long talk. We don't want you to contact her until you get some help. Or either of us. We want you at our wedding in May, but only if you're healthy, or at least healthier, up here."

He tapped my forehead before standing, leaning over, and kissing my cheek.

"You know our phone numbers. Let us know once you've gotten some help and are on the road to healthy. We love you."

I sat in total shock as I watched him walk out the door, locking and closing it as he left.

CHAPTER THIRTY-FOUR

The next morning, as I was stripping the trash bag off my foot after my shower, the doorbell rang.

"Good effing grief. It's not even seven-thirty yet."

I put on my T-shirt and my gym shorts. Using my crutch and holding my boot, I hopped to the front door. I peeked through the peephole and shook my head. Once I opened the doors, Allison came in and wrapped me in her arms. I put my forehead on her shoulder and tried to keep the tears at bay.

"Y'all take this inside." Beth pushed past us carrying several bags of groceries, careful not to jostle me.

Allison supported me and helped me hop to the sofa. She picked my foot up and put it on the coffee table. She took the boot from me and gently eased it over the bandages. She put a finger under my chin and turned my face to hers. I squirmed under her scrutiny.

"When's the last time you had a good night's sleep?" She lightly traced the bags under my eyes.

"I don't know. The last night I slept in Tam's arms, I guess. March, maybe?"

"It's almost the end of September, Janny. You have to get some rest. And you're so skinny. We bought groceries. I'm going to fix you a good breakfast, and you're going to eat. Okay? Please?"

"For you, I'll eat," I said as I hugged her.

"I talked to Danny last night." Beth joined us. She leaned over and pecked me on the cheek.

"We talked to him," Allison said. "The only time I've heard him this sad was the day he told you about Aaron. He's worried about you. Him and Charles both."

"I know." I put my hands over my face. "Charles found me last night, and we talked for almost two hours. When he left, he told me not to contact Tam or them until I get some mental health help. Everything he said made sense. He reminded me of the fight Sandy and I had, about three lifetimes back when I thought she didn't trust me."

"Oh, damn," Allison said. "God, you were horrible—no offense. We were glad when you and Sandy figured things out because you were making everyone's life hell."

"I'm sorry." I rubbed my face. "To be honest, I had no idea I was so awful. Charles said I'm doing the same thing to Tam. Am I really so unforgiving and horrible?"

Allison leaned back beside me, slipped her arm around me, and pulled me close.

"You have a tendency to be, love. I've watched you try to change, but you trade being hateful to someone else for being hateful to yourself. I think that's why you decided to take a scalding shower and hurt yourself."

"So, you agree with Charles about me needing help?"

Allison nodded and held me tighter. I put my head on her shoulder and let the tears of regret and fear flow. Beth got up and came back with a cool cloth and bathed my face. Once I settled down, Allison headed to the kitchen to fix the breakfast I promised I would eat.

"I'll get you a list of good therapists when I go back to work next week," Beth said.

"Female therapists. I don't want to tell a man what I'm going through."

"Have you forgotten the bitch you talked to after Sandy died?" Beth asked, a hard edge in her voice. "I tried to get her license revoked, but all she got was a slap on the wrist."

"I'd still rather have a woman therapist."

"Okay. I'll see what I can do." Beth paused for a moment. "Sweetie, I think you ought to consider in-house treatment."

"You mean go to a loony bin?" I tried to move away from her. "Why the fuck do you think that?"

"Because you'll get more intensive therapy, and you'll be in a safe place, and you won't be alone. Someone will be available twenty-four seven in case you have problems in the middle of the night or after office hours. Janny, every time you've hurt yourself or gone off the deep end, it's been in the evening or at night. The hospital isn't a prison. You can leave anytime you want, as long as the doctors don't believe you're suicidal."

"No." I was restless and felt as though I was held prisoner by my own body.

"Shh. Settle down," Beth said. "We'll help you find a good therapist, and we'll help you however we can to get you healthy."

"I don't have a fucking place to live because I'm a fucking, goddamned idiot. I sold my fucking house, and I don't know where I want to live and—"

Beth pulled me to her and rubbed my back. Allison had come back from the kitchen, and now I felt her arms around me from the other side.

"Beth and I've been talking about that, Janny," she said. "We want you to stay with us until you're on a stable plane. I want to make sure you're okay, and that's the best way for me to do that. We have room. You know that. And you've told me a million times our bonus room would be a great place to paint."

"I don't know. I'll be too much of a burden. My heart is broken in a million pieces, and each piece weighs a million tons. I don't want y'all to have to deal with it."

Allison turned me to face her. Her face was wet with tears.

"You and I have known each other since first grade. We were each other's only family for a long time after our families threw us away. We've supported each other, held each other, laughed and cried, and screamed obscenities at each other ever since we were freshmen in college. You and Sandy are the only reasons I survived those years until Beth and I got together. Let us help you. Please."

"My lease here is through next April," I said, desperately looking for excuses.

"Pfft." Allison blew a raspberry. "You're renting. Helen will understand and let you out of your agreement."

"I already paid, though."

"So tell her you want to come back at some point in the future to cover whatever time is left that you paid for when you aren't here."

"Come again?" Beth said. "I dare you to say that again and make it make sense."

"Y'all come to the family room and keep me company while I'm in the kitchen," Allison said. "After we eat, I want to go to the beach."

"I can't get to the beach," I protested as they helped me to my feet.

"You can sit in the gazebo and watch while we do." Allison grinned at me.

"Wow. That sounds like loads of fun," I said, sticking my tongue out at her.

CHAPTER THIRTY-FIVE

I moved in with Allison and Beth the week before Thanksgiving. They gave me the mother-in-law suite over the garage so I could come and go without going through the house, although I spent a lot of time with them. Beth helped me interview therapists before I chose Dr. Bryant to work with. She was empathetic, sympathetic, and gentle, and I felt safe with her.

But she asked a lot of hard questions and forced me to face my demons head on.

"What made you think they don't trust you?" she asked one day. "And don't tell me because of what they said. Dig deep, Janice. What happened to you in the past that put the fear in you of not being trusted by someone you love?"

I stared at her from where I had stopped pacing her spacious office.

"How the hell am I supposed to know that?"

263

"You do know," she said in a soft voice. "Your heart knows. It just hasn't told your brain yet. Ask it to reveal its secrets."

The timer on her desk beeped, and she stood up and came to stand in front of me. She gave me a light shake.

"That's your homework, dear. Write in your journal and ask why you're scared people won't or don't trust you. Ask who hurt you when you were a child and why. Write whatever comes to your mind, and don't worry about how it sounds. Just write. By hand. And we'll talk about it some more at our next appointment."

I was exhausted as I left her office. Beth was curled on one of the sofas in the waiting room, supposedly reading, but I could see she had dozed off. I touched her shoulder, and she jumped.

"You're already done? Didn't you just now go in there?"

The receptionist laughed. "Beth, you've been snoring for forty-five minutes."

Beth blushed. "I'm sorry. Why didn't you wake me?"

"I was laying bets with myself about how long it would take before you fell off the sofa. Unfortunately, I lost all of them, and now I owe myself several hundred dollars." Carla grinned at us. "See y'all next week."

†

Over the course of the next four months, I filled many spiral notebooks with stream of consciousness writing, trying to learn more about me: what I'd experienced and lived with and through for the past forty-two years of my so-called adulthood, and the repercussions my childhood had on me as an adult. Some things I learned filled me with horror and sympathy for the people who had to live through it with me. But other things filled me with pride when I realized what I had given and had to give to the people in my life.

Slowly, I began to like myself, to trust myself, to learn to put my trust in others, and not to question if others trusted me.

I visited Sandy often, not only on my birthday, her birthday, and the anniversary of her death. I read from my journals to her and wrote in them as I leaned back on her headstone. But she stayed absent, and I grieved her absence even as I learned to live without her.

One night, alone in the garage apartment, I heard a melody echoing off my soul. I hadn't composed any music since the day I broke my ankle. After almost six months, I switched on my keyboard and closed my eyes as my fingers found the keys, and the notes rose and swirled around my head. My eyes popped open as I realized the music was mixed with a cool breeze that danced around the room.

"Hi, Sandy," I said through my tears. "Thank you for bringing my music back to me."

I felt rather than heard her spirit speak to me.

Call Tam, was the message. *Play her this song.*

I hesitated a long time, but the cool breeze continued to swirl around me and urge me to make the phone call.

"She won't know it's me." I tried to reason, but Sandy's breeze was adamant.

The phone on the other end of the call rang and rang. As I was about to disconnect, I heard a hesitant voice.

"Hello? Who is this?"

I caught my breath at the sound of the woman I loved speaking to me.

"It's Janice." My voice cracked around the words. "I have something I want you to hear."

Without waiting for her reply, I set the phone on the keyboard and played the little bit of the song I had composed. When I finished, I looked at the phone, fully expecting to see that she had disconnected the call. But she was still there. I lifted my phone and listened.

"Janice, it's beautiful." I could tell Tam was crying. "But you need to hear something, too."

I heard her talking to someone, and my heart stopped in fear that she had fallen in love with someone else. Then I heard a little voice.

"Does she want me to play it for her?" Ocee asked.

"Yes, baby, she does," Tam said.

After a moment, the strains of a song made their way through the phone, and my mouth fell open. Except for a couple of slight variations, it was the music I had just played.

"Oh, my God," I said over and over.

"Janice, are you still there?"

"I'm here. Where did she learn that song? And when?"

"She told me she dreamed it during her nap this afternoon. She's been working on it all evening."

"Sandy gave it to her," I whispered. "And she gave it to me, too."

"Janice, how are you doing?" The wistfulness in Tam's voice almost broke my heart.

"Is Ocee staying with you tonight?" I asked. "Or can you get away? I'd like to meet you somewhere so we can talk. If not tonight, maybe tomorrow?"

"I can be at the All-Nighter in twenty minutes," Tam said.

Twenty minutes later, I stood in the postage-stamp-sized yard of the diner, nervous as a cat. I didn't know what I planned to say to her. I didn't even know why I invited her to meet me. A teal-colored Jeep Wrangler pulled into the parking lot, and, to my surprise, Tam climbed out. She smiled at me, and I could see she was as nervous as I was. Before I walked over to meet her, I retrieved one of the ducks off the dashboard of my Rubicon. I held it out to her as she walked toward me. She took it with a grin.

"My first duck," she said. "Thank you."

I looked at her and was relieved to see she looked healthier and more rested than when I saw her in Beaufort. Her hair was as thick and beautiful as ever, and her blue eyes pierced my soul. I opened my arms, and, to my relief, she stepped into them. I hugged her, a genuine hug in which I hoped she could sense my love.

"I don't really want to talk here," I said. "But I don't know where we can go where we will have a bit more privacy."

"The tennis courts over at the park near the University had their lights on when I drove past," she said. "There's a little pavilion there."

It didn't take too long before we parked side by side at the little park. Two couples were playing tennis but didn't pay us any mind when we sat at the picnic table near the parking lot.

"You look good," I said.

"So do you. You've put on some weight, and you look rested." She cocked her head at me. "Are you in town for a few days?"

I shook my head.

"Right now, I'm living with Allison and Beth. I've been back in town since right before Thanksgiving."

"Why are you just now calling me?" Tam's face looked hurt.

"Because I needed to do some work on myself before I got back in touch with you. I've been in intensive therapy, sometimes doing three sessions a week, since the week after Thanksgiving. And I spent four days in the hospital being treated for emotional and mental exhaustion in January."

I looked away before looking into her beautiful face.

"Even though I'm not an alcoholic, I'm using the twelve-step program to try to rebuild my life. It's been an ordeal, and I've filled close to a hundred notebooks with my journaling. And so much of it's about you and how abysmally I treated you. Oh, Tam."

I covered my face with my hands. She touched me on the shoulder, and I peeked at her from between my fingers. Taking a deep breath, I covered her hand with one of mine.

"I'm so sorry, Tam. I put you through so much. You deserved so much better. I understand now it wasn't that you didn't trust me. It was me transferring the trauma of my youth and some things that happened to me onto you. I did the same thing to Sandy and nearly lost her. My therapist and I have spent hours and hours talking about this and what I need to do to change. And I'm working on it, Tam."

"Why did you call me tonight?" She reached out and dried my tears with the pads of her thumbs.

"Sandy told me to." I took a deep breath. "The song I played for you started swirling around in my head, and while I was playing it, a cool breeze started swirling around my face and hands. She hasn't been with me for months. That's when I knew the song was special. When I finished playing,

Sandy told me to call you and play it for you. At first, I wasn't willing. I was afraid you wouldn't want anything to do with me after what happened in Beaufort."

I leaned into the hand she laid on my cheek.

"How is Ocee? I'm so glad she didn't stop playing her music."

"She tried to." Tam shook her head. "But the therapist Mae and Duke took her to encouraged her to keep at it, and she has. But tonight was the first time she played something original."

She paused.

"We were afraid she was sick," she said. "She hasn't voluntarily taken a nap since she was three, but this afternoon she announced she was tired and wanted to go to sleep in my bed instead of hers. When I checked on her about an hour later, she was still asleep, but she was curled up hugging the picture I have of you on my bedside table."

"You have a picture of me by your bed?" I whispered.

Tam nodded.

"Some nights I can only go to sleep after I've had a long chat with you."

I looked down and fought back the tears.

"Tell me more about Ocee."

"After I checked on her, I had to go in the bathroom and cry. I've been missing you a lot lately."

She gave me a strange look.

"You didn't go see Sandy on her birthday," she said. "Ocee and I waited almost all day for you, and you never came."

My mouth fell open.

"Uhm, well, I visited the next day. I had an appointment with my therapist on the morning of her birthday, and I was exhausted and drained, so I went home and went to bed. I'm sorry I missed you."

"Ocee took her some flowers from her little garden and told her she was sure you still loved her even though you weren't there."

"I saw the flowers but thought Allison had left them. Please tell Ocee I said thank you."

Tam cocked her head at me.

"Why don't you come over tomorrow and tell her yourself?" she said. "We're celebrating Aaron's birthday a little late since he was sick on the actual day. Charles and Danny will be there, too."

"How will Mae and Duke feel, though? I know Mae hated me after the way I treated you."

"Janice, it wasn't one-sided. I treated you pretty bad, too."

"Yes, but you apologized to me in Beaufort, and I was too stupid to accept the apology. And that's something else I need to apologize for."

Tam put two fingers over my mouth.

"Stop. No more apologizing." She was quiet for a moment. "What we need to talk about is where are we going from here? Are we going our separate ways again to live our own lives without each other?"

"Is that what you want?" I held my breath while I waited for an answer.

Shaking her head, she leaned towards me.

"I want to jump your bones so bad, right here and right now," she whispered.

She leaned back and grinned when I blushed. With a gentle touch, she kissed my knuckles.

"I love you, Janice Kirsten Halston. I never stopped loving you, and I never could make myself believe our relationship was over. As far as my heart is concerned, you've been on a long journey. I hope you're back now. Or at least in the process of returning."

We stared at each other a moment and then jumped when the lights at the tennis courts turned off, sinking us into darkness. Tam still held my hand, and I drew her close and kissed her. And she kissed me back, a kiss full of promise, of hope, and of need.

"Come back to the house," she said, her voice hoarse. "I want to show you how much I love you now and how much I've always loved you."

I put her hand to my cheek and sighed.

"Tam, I'd love to do that, but I have to move slow. Not to make sure I still love you because I know I do, but I need to be as healthy as I can get before we get intimate. And I still have work to do. Will you wait for me? Will you let me court you, take you on dates, bring you flowers, help you around the house? Can we stay platonic for now, knowing someday it will change?"

She placed her hand behind my head and pulled me to her for another kiss.

"As long as we can do that," she said.

CHAPTER THIRTY-SIX

"Are you sure this is a good idea?" Allison said as she stood at the driver's door of the Rubicon. "I mean, I'm proud of you for getting back in touch with her, but are you ready to face what might be a rather uncomfortable situation with her daughter and son-in-law?"

"I don't know, Allie," I said, "but if I don't face it now, I'll have to face it some other time."

I paused as the face of a beautiful child flitted through my mind.

"And I want to see Ocee. I'm more worried about her than I am about her parents. What if she hates me now?"

"I don't think that will be the case." Allison leaned forward and planted a kiss on my cheek. "Be kind to yourself, Janny. If it gets too hard, excuse yourself and come home."

"Thank you. I love you."

I shuddered when I saw the plastic flowers stuck in the ground around the tree I had so lovingly planted in front of my old house. I wondered if I would ever forgive myself for selling it. Tam's family was already at her house when I arrived. I'd hoped to have her to myself for a bit before I had to face everyone. Once I parked, I sat in the Jeep trying to build enough courage to go to the door. I jumped when someone knocked on the window but smiled when I opened my eyes and saw Charles standing there.

"Hi," I said as I got out of the Jeep.

"Hi, yourself. It's good to see you back on your feet." He raised his eyebrows at me. "How are you?"

"A lot healthier than the last time we saw each other," I assured him. "I've been working hard since Thanksgiving."

"Tam told me you're living at Allison's and Beth's. They're getting pretty good at keeping your secrets."

"It wasn't a secret." I struggled not to get defensive, something else Dr. Bryant and I were working hard on. "I kept to myself because I wanted to concentrate on the work I needed to do. I don't know why they didn't tell anyone."

He rested his hand on my arm.

"I'm sorry. I shouldn't have said that."

"I deserved it," I said with a grin.

He clasped my hand and led me to the house.

"I'm proud of you, Janice," he said before opening the front door for me.

I looked around when I entered the house. Little had changed since I was there last, except there were more photos on the wall, some of them of me, and the pile of toys under the front window was larger. But the room was empty.

"Where is everyone?"

"Out back. Duke is putting burgers on the grill. It's too pretty to be inside."

The two of us headed through the kitchen, and a flood of memories washed over me, and I had to swallow hard.

"You okay?" Charles put a hand on my back.

I nodded, but before I could say anything, the slider opened, and a child who looked a lot like Ocee but was far too grown up stood there, staring at me. I opened my arms and waited. She stared for another moment before she burst into tears and ran to me. Charles put a chair behind me, and I sat down and pulled Ocee onto my lap. I buried my face in her thick black hair and held her as tight as I could. My own tears wet my face. After a moment, Ocee leaned back and placed a hand on each of my cheeks.

"Gah-Gah, are you really here, or am I having a dream?"

"Oh, baby girl." I leaned my forehead against hers. "It's really me. I've missed you so much. I'm sorry I had to stay away for so long."

"Grams said you were sick and trying to get well. Are you well now?"

"I'm getting there. But I'm well enough to come back to you now. We have a lot to catch up on, don't we?"

Ocee grinned and enthusiastically nodded her head. She slid off my lap, grabbed my hand, and pulled me toward the backyard. I stepped out onto the patio and into Danny's arms.

"You look good," he said. "I'm glad you're back."

I kissed him on the cheek before looking around. Mae and Duke stood beside the cooker with their arms around each other. I couldn't read their faces, but at least they didn't look like they wanted to skin me alive and throw me on the grill. Little Aaron was standing behind his mother, peeking around at me. I waved at him, and he grinned before burying his face in the side of Mae's leg. The one person I wanted to see more than anything was nowhere in sight, but before I could ask where she was, arms encircled my waist from behind. I turned so that I could hug her. She gave me a gentle kiss on the lips, and it felt like I was home.

"Hi," she said. "I'm glad you could make it."

"Don't hog her, Grams." Ocee wrapped her arms around my legs. "May I bring my keyboard out here, please?"

"Let's eat first," Duke said. "The burgers are ready if y'all want to help yourselves."

Charles picked Aaron up and brought him to me.

"Aaron, this is Gah-Gah," he said. "Can you say hello?"

Aaron shook his head and buried his face in Charles' shoulder.

"You're being silly." Charles shrugged at me. "He's not usually this bashful. I'd bet anything he'll be on your lap soon."

"Come on, Gah-Gah," Ocee said, taking my hand. "You have to eat something."

I glanced at Tam, and she grinned.

"I can't imagine where she heard those words," I said.

After we ate, Danny and Ocee went inside and came back with the keyboard and Ocee's stool. Danny plugged the keyboard in as Ocee arranged the stool just so before smiling at me and running through the scales before she turned it on. Everyone laughed when she picked *Twinkle Little Star* out with one finger. She put both hands on the keyboard and began playing Pachelbel's *Canon in D*. She played it flawlessly and segued into *Für Elise*. I sat with my mouth open, tears stinging my eyes.

275

Ocee stopped playing for a moment and looked at me without saying anything. She looked at Tam, who gave a small nod. Ocee closed her eyes and put her fingers back to the keys, and the strains of the song I gave her over a year ago, the song she played at the recital I missed, floated into the air. She did the crossovers as though they were the most natural thing in the world. When she finished, she bowed her head, waited a moment, and played the bit of melody from the day before. I couldn't control my tears. Tam came and sat on the arm of my chair and rubbed my back. Ocee moved into my arms, and I rocked her back and forth.

When I could finally stop the tears, I looked over at Mae and Duke. Duke was holding Aaron, who had his head on his dad's shoulder. Mae's face was wet with tears, and I held my hand out to her. She joined her mother and daughter at my chair, taking my hand, leaning over, and kissing my cheek.

"Does this mean I'm forgiven?" I asked her.

She laughed through her tears.

"This time," she said.

CHAPTER THIRTY-SEVEN

The healthier I got, the more my friends and I came together once again. Melba brought her guitar over, and we started making music together, but she didn't ask me to perform with her, and I was glad. It was one of the few places in my life where I still had a lot of anxiety. Dr. Bryant and I were puzzling that out.

Tam and I started dating as though we were just getting to know each other. And in some ways, we were. I was more relaxed, which made her relax, and I rediscovered what a wonderful sense of humor she had. Plus, she was respectful of my request to refrain from getting sexually intimate. We kissed and on more than one occasion, we lightly necked. But we did not take our touching below the waist.

"I guess I should start looking for a place to live," I said one afternoon as Allison, Beth, and I lounged on their patio nursing iced tea. The weather was warm, but it wasn't yet oppressive.

"Why?" Beth asked from the chaise she and Allison shared.

I shrugged. "It seems like it's time I grow up and leave home, fly the coop, let y'all have your lives back."

Allison frowned.

"We have our lives," she said. "You don't crimp our style. Much."

I laughed as Beth made a face at her.

"Besides, you haven't painted anything in all the time you've been here," Allison said. "I won't believe you're healthy enough to move on until you do. And what about your writing? Have you done any except in your journals? At least you're making your music again, and for that, I'm eternally grateful."

Reflecting on my painting, I scrunched my face. I didn't know why the painting muse was staying away. The Lamberts and my landlady received all but one painting I did at the coast. I kept the one I did of the dolphin leaping from the waves into a glorious sunrise, all the yellows and pinks and purples of the sky reflecting in the water and off the dolphin's back. It was the best painting I'd done in years. But nothing since.

"I can't just start painting. My heart and soul have to welcome my muse, and she hasn't been around since I broke my ankle. Same with my writing. I can't just do it. It has to come to me. I'm happy to be blessed with my music, especially since Ocee and I are collaborating on some pieces. She's my musical muse."

"I will say this," Beth said, glancing at me. "You're happier than I've ever seen you in the almost forty years we've known each other."

I frowned at her.

"Forty years? Is that all? It seems you've been hounding me for a lot longer than that."

She chucked a cushion at me, and I ducked.

"I am happier," I said.

It was impossible for me not to smile when I thought about the main reason why. I looked over at my friends when I heard them chuckle.

"And the expression on your face tells us who is making you so happy," Allison said.

I grinned at her.

"Speaking of, I have a date in a couple of hours. I'm going to go shower and get ready. She's picking me up, and she won't tell me where we're going."

†

"Oooo-kay," I said when Tam parked the Wrangler in front of Charles' and Danny's house. "Why are we here?"

"I don't know. They asked me to stop by before we get our evening started. They promised it won't be for more than a few minutes."

She came around the Jeep and met me on the sidewalk. Danny threw open the front door before we were on the porch.

"Here are our ladies," he called back into the house as he hugged each of us. "Y'all come on in."

"Would someone like to fill us in on why we're here?" I asked as I looked at the coffee table loaded with a meat and cheese tray, a fruit and vegetable tray, and crackers and dip as well as four glasses of iced tea. I glanced at Tam. "It doesn't look like we're only going to be here for a few minutes."

"Oh, quit your bellyachin' and sit down," Charles said with a laugh as he joined us. After we sat down, he looked at me and Tam with a serious expression. "We have something important, at least it's important to us, to discuss with you."

Danny reached over and took his hand, and they shared such a sweet smile. Danny looked at Tam with a look of true love and devotion. He held his other hand out to her.

"Momma Tam, would you do me the honor of not only walking me down the aisle to marry this man, but also to stand with me as my witness?"

Tam nodded as she jumped to her feet and hugged Danny. They rocked so hard that I was afraid they were going to fall. After a moment, Danny urged Tam back to her seat next to me. I leaned over and kissed her on the cheek. Charles smiled at me, and I couldn't help but wonder what he was planning.

"Janice, will you do me the honor of being my witness?"

My mouth fell open.

"Why me?" My voice cracked in surprise. "That sounded rude, but, uhm, why me?"

Charles and Danny laughed. Charles reached over and patted me on the knee.

"Janice, you and I have been friends since college. I've watched you go through hell and high water, and here you are better than ever. I'm proud of you, and I'm proud to call you 'friend.' And I want the world to know that. That's why."

"Oh." I stared at him. After a moment, he started laughing.

"Should I take that as a yes or a no?"

I nodded. For some reason, I was tongue-tied. He grabbed my hands.

"That doesn't tell me anything, silly. Yes? Or no?"

"Yes, you weirdo," I said as a grin crept across my face. He stood up and pulled me up and into a hug.

"You're weirder than I am," he said.

"I'll take that as a compliment." I kissed him on the cheek. "Okay, now, what's with all the food? Is this our dinner?"

"We want your opinion. What do y'all think of doing something like this on each table instead of a sit-down dinner or a buffet?" Danny asked.

"Why are you asking us?" Tam said, a hard note in her voice that surprised me. "Darla and I got married, but it was a quicky just over the Canadian border, and we never had a reception."

She looked at me with an odd look on her face.

"You and Sandy didn't get married, did you?"

She had become agitated and anxious, and it was making me nervous, so I sat back and watched and listened.

"Calm down, Tam," Charles said. "You're about to blow a gasket. We want your opinion. You planned a wedding for Mae. Or at least I assume you did. Unless they eloped."

Tam sat back and crossed her arms, and I wondered why she was upset. I put my hand on her knee and smiled at her when she glanced at me. She drew in a long breath and took my hand.

"Mae was still grieving for Aaron when Duke proposed. She was uncomfortable having a big wedding, so they got married on Leona's deck with a few members of Duke's family and me there. One of Leona's brothers brought some buckets of chicken, and that was the reception. They wouldn't even let me bake them a wedding cake. I was so disappointed."

"Oh Momma." Danny gave her a hug. "I'm sorry. I didn't know that."

"It's okay," she said. "Just when I think I'm over it, I discover I'm not. This idea is good. It'll keep everything from being too formal."

"Thank you." Charles circled the table and hugged her. "I'm sorry we upset you. Will you consider baking our wedding cake?"

The smile gracing her face illuminated the room.

"Of course I will," she said. "Right now, Janice and I are on our way to dinner. Thank you for honoring us by asking us to be your witnesses. I love you both."

The Wrangler was quiet as Tam drove us to a local sushi restaurant. When she parked, she made no move to get out. I reached across the console, took her hand, and waited for her.

"I'm sorry," she finally said with a sniffle. "I was looking forward to eating here tonight, but now I'm feeling down in the dumps. Do you mind if I take you home?"

Leaning over, I gave her a kiss on the cheek.

"I'm sorry. If you want to talk about it, I'm a much better listener now than I used to be."

She nodded but didn't say anything.

"Do you want me to drive?" I asked.

She leaned her head back.

"I'm in a murderous mood," she said. "It might be a good idea if you drive. But I'll still have to drive home from your house."

"I'll take you home and call a rideshare."

Tam looked at me, and I could see her eyes were bright with tears.

"Will you stay with me until I'm asleep? For some reason, I'm feeling so alone and insecure."

"Let's get you home, babe."

I jumped out of the Jeep and rushed around to help her out and back to the passenger seat. I stood on the sidestep and buckled her in. She reclined the seat and closed her eyes. The drive back to her house was quiet except for an occasional sniffle on her part. We pulled into her driveway just as she fell asleep. I sat and looked at her for a few minutes before going around to her door. I was worried because this was so unusual for her. I hoped she wasn't getting sick.

"Come on, sweetie," I said as I unbuckled her seatbelt. "Let's get you inside."

She nodded and turned to slide out of the Jeep. She held me close and kissed me. I put my arm around her waist and led her to the door and then to her bedroom. I urged her to sit on the bed and slipped her shoes off.

"Lay down, love." I helped her slide into the bed and put her head on her pillow. I spread the light blanket from the end of the bed over her and kissed her on the cheek. She was asleep before I turned off the light.

I was reluctant to leave her alone when she was feeling so fragile, so I didn't call a rideshare.

"Now what do I do?" I said as I looked around the living room.

Since starting therapy, I had become used to eating three meals a day, and I was hungry. I went to the kitchen to scavenge some food. I found sliced roast beef, a container marked horse radish, some fresh lettuce in the refrigerator, and homemade bread in Tam's bread drawer. My mouth was watering as I prepared myself a sandwich and cut it on the diagonal, but I wondered if I should make her one, too.

I tiptoed back to the bedroom to check on her. She'd flopped over on her back and lay spreadeagle across the bed. I caught my breath at the sight. I closed my eyes for a moment before returning to the kitchen, but now I had an appetite for something other than a sandwich. After I ate and cleaned the kitchen, I lay on the sofa with the TV remote control but dozed off as I looked for something to catch my attention.

"Mmmm." I woke to kisses all over my face and a hand making its way up my shirt. My eyes popped open as the hand cupped my breast through my bra.

"Did you have a good nap?" Tam continued to caress me and kiss my face.

"Tam. Uhm, babe," I said, as my body responded to her touch.

I grabbed her, pulled her down on top of me, and kissed her properly.

"Oh, God, Janice." She laid her head on my chest. "I'm sorry. I know I told you I would wait. Let me call you a rideshare, and I'll talk to you tomorrow."

She started to stand up, but I stopped her and kissed her again. She leaned into the kiss and accepted my tongue into her mouth. I slid my hand into her shirt and unhooked her bra. She sighed as she slid off and urged me to turn on my side so that we both fit on the sofa. But first, she pulled her shirt over her head and her bra off. My breath caught as she turned to face me. I leaned forward and kissed her chest between her breasts, using my hands to push her breasts together so I could bury my face between them.

I wrapped my arms around her, pulled her to me, slid my hands into her pants, and cupped her butt cheeks.

"Let's go to the bedroom," she said, breathless. She stood up and offered me her hand. I accepted it and let her lead me to the bedroom, where she unbuttoned my shirt and pushed it off my shoulders before unhooking my bra and sending it to join the shirt.

"You are so beautiful," she said as she cupped my breasts and ran her thumbs over my nipples.

I shuddered with desire. She slid her hands down my sides and pushed my pants over my hips. I returned the favor, and we stood nude, facing each other for the first time in over a year. Tam kissed me and guided me back until I was lying on the bed with her on top of me. She kissed along my body. I cried out as she brought me to an intense climax.

We spent the rest of the night renewing our familiarity with each other's body. We finally fell asleep in each other's arms as the sky outside her windows was lightening. When I woke up, the clock read almost ten o'clock. I seldom slept past seven, and I panicked as I wondered if I'd had an appointment that day. But then I looked at the bed, and nothing else mattered. I loved the woman lying there in all her glory. And I knew I never wanted to be apart from her again.

I slid back in bed beside her and kissed her on the shoulder and near her ear, and I kept kissing her until she stirred and turned over. I pulled her to me before raising up on an elbow and looking at her through my tears.

"Tam Murphy, I love you with all my heart. My life feels complete again. Let's try to never be apart again. Please."

"Oh, my dear lovely lady. I love you, too." She pulled me down and kissed me long and deep. "You are my heart. I had

285

such special plans last night, but I allowed myself to get upset, and I ruined everything."

"You didn't ruin anything."

"Can we get dressed and go fix some breakfast?" she asked. "I'll be able to think more clearly once I have some coffee in me."

Within a few minutes, we had easily fallen back into our roles in the kitchen as she stood at the stove scrambling eggs, and I buttered the toast as it came out of the toaster. I set the table and poured each of us a mug of freshly brewed coffee. We ate in silence, smiling at each other over our coffee. When we finished eating, she leaned over and took my hands as she kissed me.

"I had big plans on how I wanted to do this, but you know what they say about well-laid plans." I wondered what she was talking about. She kneeled beside me and placed her hand on my cheek. "Janice Kirsten Halston, I love you. We've already been through the wringer and to hell and back, and we've survived. Janny, will you marry me? Will you be my wife? Will you move in here with me and play house with me? Will you be Ocee's and Aaron's Gah-Gah forever?"

I slid off the chair to kneel in front of her and take her in my arms. The kiss we shared was gentle and full of passion all at once.

"Yes. Yes. Yes, and yes," I said. "I love you more than I know how to express. I'll be proud to be your wife. In fact, let's go get our marriage license today."

"And get married today?" she asked, a grin on her face.

I laughed.

"If that's possible, if there's not a waiting period, yes, married today."

She pulled me to her, and we kissed again.

"I almost forgot." She reached into her pants pocket.

She grinned at me as she turned to me and showed me a blue velvet box. Inside was a dainty gold band with a single diamond shimmering from it. She took the ring out of the box and held out her hand. I put my left hand in her hand, and she slipped the ring on my fourth finger. I burst into tears, grabbed her, and held on for dear life.

When I calmed down, I kissed her, a gentle peck on the lips.

"Can we wait to get married until I've bought you a ring, too?" I asked. "And if we wait, you can plan us the wedding you didn't get to plan for Mae, and our friends will have time to buy us elaborate gifts we'll never use."

Tam laughed, took my face in her hands, and kissed me again.

"You and your wise words," she said, standing up and offering me her hand.

CHAPTER THIRTY-EIGHT

Three months seemed like an eternity, but Tam's and my wedding date finally arrived. A couple of weeks after her proposal, I had presented her with an engagement ring, a braided band with a small diamond twinkling between Ocee's and Aaron's birthstones.

And now, now I stood in a small room off the main chapel at a small wedding venue in a small town outside of Raleigh. Beth straightened my tie once again and smacked my hand when it strayed back to the knot.

"You should have eloped. Trying to keep you neat and clean is close to impossible. Stand still and don't move. No, do not put your hands in your pockets. You'll wrinkle your slacks."

Duke laughed as he stuck his head in the door.

"Sounds like what Pops said to me while we waited before my wedding. The officiant is ready when y'all are."

He offered me his elbow, and I took it with a sigh of relief. I hadn't seen Tam for over twenty-four hours, and I missed my lady. I wanted to hug her, touch her hand, look in her eyes, and kiss her.

Duke led me to stand in front of Della, the owner of the venue and the officiant for the day. Allison was already there, and Beth followed me. They stood at my side while I bounced on the balls of my feet, looking down the aisle for Tam. Beth placed her hands on both of my shoulders and tried to hold me still. On the other side of the officiant, Mae and Duke smiled over at me.

The strains of *How Long Will I Love You* rose into the air as our beautiful Ocee, looking radiant, played the piano and Melba played the guitar. They played the introduction, and Melba began to sing the lyrics. The doors at the back of the chapel opened, and Carmen entered, holding Aaron by the hand. He walked with her down the aisle, grinning, before he saw me and ran pell-mell into my legs, almost knocking me over. Everyone laughed as Charles grabbed him and carried him back to his chair.

And there she was, standing in the doorway, holding Danny's elbow, her eyes meeting mine. The smile on her face lit the room, banishing any cloud that might have dared gather. The teal blouse she wore with her ivory pants suit made the blue in her eyes sparkle, and it was all I could do not to run to her.

When they finally reached the altar, I grabbed her hand and kissed it.

"Don't jump the gun," Della said with a grin. After the laughter settled down, she led us through our vows, which, although simple, brought tears to my eyes. "Now, if you would like to seal these vows with a kiss, you may do so."

Tam and I stepped closer to each other. She wrapped her arms around my neck, and I wrapped mine around her waist, and we kissed, a kiss that brought hoots and hollers from our friends and family.

The venue hosted the reception in a room behind the chapel. We had hoped to have it outdoors in one of the venue's pavilions, but the weather had turned wet and blustery. The decibel levels were higher than either of us usually liked, but I, for once, didn't care. All I wanted to do was look at my wife and hold her hand.

"If I can have everyone's attention?"

My head jerked around. Even though we had agreed with our friends there would be no toasts, Allison stood holding the DJ's microphone and grinning at us.

"I'm breaking a promise, and I'll hear about it later." She grinned as everyone laughed. "But I have to say something, or I'm going to pop. Janny, Tam, y'all are so special in so many ways. Few couples have had as many obstacles as you two had to get to this point, and I am so proud of you for making it. Y'all are perfect together. And you deserve each other."

Tam looked at me and squeezed my hand. I could barely see her through the tears in my eyes.

"I love you, and so do all these people." Beth, Charles and Danny, Melba and Carmen, Mae and Duke, who carried Aaron and Ocee, joined Allison. "And one of them has composed a song for you."

The DJ pushed a keyboard out from behind his stand, and Ocee grinned at him and hugged him.

"Grams and Gah-Gah," she said as she played an intro on the keyboard. "This is for your first dance."

Tam offered me her hand, and we headed around the table to the dance floor. But before we danced, we hugged and kissed these people who made our lives so special. I stepped to the keyboard and bumped Ocee out of the way.

"Hey," she said, grinning at me.

I pulled her back in front of me and took her hand so that one of her forefingers was extended. I used it to play, one key at a time, *Twinkle Little Star.* She turned and threw her arms around me, and I once again had to fight back the tears.

"Go dance," she said as she pulled my arm so that I bent down and she could kiss me on the cheek.

While Ocee played the introduction to her song, I rejoined Tam on the dance floor. I almost forgot to start dancing as the beauty of the music enveloped us, but Tam pulled me to her and put her forehead against mine.

"I love you, Mrs. Halston-Murphy," she said.

"And I love you," I said as I put my cheek next to hers.

ABOUT THE AUTHOR

GLENDA POULTER

Glenda Poulter has been writing poetry, short stories, and novels since she was ten years old, well over a half century. Slice-of-life novels with women who love women as her main characters are her specialty. Strong women with human weaknesses and foibles populate her stories along with their sometimes-quirky friends. Her past published work includes *Welcome Home* and *Out of the Past.*

Glenda lives in central North Carolina with her long-time partner, Lisa, and the felines that rule their lives. She is the proud mother of a daughter and son and doting grandmother of two. Other interests include collecting seashells, the fiber arts (crochet, knitting, quilting), reading, and photography. Glenda seldom meets a stranger, and she strives to leave everyone she encounters with a smile. Glenda has an affinity with the ocean, and she is sure she was a mermaid in a previous life. The gift of seashells calls her name on a regular basis.

OTHER BOOKS FROM AFFINITY

Nothing But Net by Ali Spooner

Hunter James, a rising star in college basketball, has her career and life sidelined after experiencing a family tragedy.

An opportunity for a fresh start opens the door to return to what she loves most: playing basketball. Hunter rushes through that door to make the most of her second chance.

Back in the basketball arena, doing what she loves, will she open herself and her heart to another chance to forgive herself and fall in love?

The Kitten Trap by Annette Mori

Inspired by the classic movie, *The Parent Trap*, two adorable black kittens, Midnight and Onyx, play matchmakers for their human mothers, Mac and Carmen. Struggling with the complexities of farm life, Mac can barely believe her beautiful girlfriend, Carmen, has agreed to move to the drafty old farmhouse to live with her and her beloved

Pops. When Carmen is forced to leave the farm to care for her ailing mother, Midnight and Onyx as well as Mac and Carmen must struggle with the difficult separation. Just when it appears Carmen and Onyx may come back home to the farm, cruel fate raises a further challenge, one that will need the help of two mischievous kittens to overcome.

To Autumn by Katie M Hall
Sixteen-year-old Robyn Gale, along with her younger sister Anne, is sent away for the summer holidays of 1997 to stay with her grandmother at a caravan park in Devon. Robyn's had a tough few months: trying to cope with the fallout of their mother's attempted suicide, messing up her GCSEs, and finding herself attracted to girls. Perhaps getting away from her real life is just what she needs…she can focus on finding a boyfriend, watching *Neighbours,* and swimming. A solid plan, until she meets charismatic Australian lifeguard, Autumn, and her life is turned even more down under.

Fairytail Farm by Ali Spooner
Dr. Hill McCall and her wife Alice dreamed of developing a sanctuary for unwanted cats and dogs to live out their lives as a retirement project. Hill has secretly worked on the project for months when a wealthy benefactor surprises her with a large donation, allowing Hill to be more aggressive with the project's opening. A group home operator approaches Hill about summer volunteer positions

for four girls as Fairytail Farm becomes more than just a sanctuary for the animals. It creates an environment of love and kindness for the animals and all that support the project. Several love stories develop from first love to mature couples who have found their forever person. Fairytail Farm is more than a dream come true. It is a home for happily ever afters.

The Love Demand by Annette Mori

In the dazzling realm of reality television, where love and drama entwine in a complicated dance as old as time, a groundbreaking series emerges that transcends the ordinary. *The Love Demand* is not your typical reality show. Lacey Fellows isn't sure she wants to subject herself to further humiliation, however, on the off chance her girlfriend may agree to accept a second marriage proposal, Lacey reluctantly consents to participating in the new reality show. What she doesn't count on is meeting a kindred spirit—one she can't seem to shake from her thoughts. Jaimie would do almost anything for her girlfriend, including following her to the ends of the earth and participating in a conniving television show that puts her in front of a camera, which happens to be her least favorite place. Her girlfriend, Sabina, hasn't met a camera she doesn't like. They couldn't be more opposite, but Jaimie still hopes Sabina will want marriage, kids, and the whole shebang. The last thing she expects is to fall in love with someone else. Let the games begin.

Sullivan's Trace by Ali Spooner

Micah "Sully" Sullivan has settled into a solitary life at the family horse ranch after her father's death. When her long-term vet, Doc Barton, plans to retire, his granddaughter, Bryn, arrives to take over his practice. An attack on one of Sully's prized horses throws Sully and Bryn into a whirlwind as they fight to save the young animal. Just as Sully is becoming comfortable with her growing attraction to Bryn, tragedy occurs, and her brother and his wife are killed in an accident. Sully's solitary life drastically changes when a family of three is born.

Love Sins by Annette Mori

Jessica Green's life is predictable and boring. As the chief engineer for Solar Flair, her career is right on track. Her love life, not so much. The last thing she expects is a call from her estranged father's attorney. Too curious to ignore the message, she can't resist meeting with him and discovering more about specific instructions related to his estate, as well as the letter her father left for her. Rattled by what she finds at her father's home, she promptly dials 911.

Special Agent Amanda Forrester is perplexed by a call to join a homicide investigation until she arrives at the scene and learns the victim is not only a serial killer but an elite assassin the authorities have been after for years. To Amanda's increasing irritation, the daughter recognizes a picture of the last target and insinuates herself into the investigation. As the case takes a surprising turn, Amanda

296

finds she has landed smack dab in the middle of a complicated and dangerous situation. The facts lead her to a puzzle weaving together the recent suicide of a wealthy businessman with the activities of several prominent politicians. Amanda must join forces with a mysterious organization and the persistent woman she finds increasingly hard to resist. Her instinct to protect the alluring and vulnerable Jessica Green kicks into high gear, taking the reader on a roller-coaster journey for the last book in *The Next Generation* series.

A Wild Moon Rises by Jen Silver

Successful author, Malory G Holmes, has had a rough year. Wounded by an emotional breakup and writer's block she returns home after eight months travelling to discover the startling results of a DNA test. Apparently, through her mother's side, she is related to a baronet with an estate in Briarbay, Northumberland. She decides to visit the place to find out more about this unknown side of her family.

Selene Wylde is content with life, running a bookshop in the small hamlet of Briarbay. She also looks after her father, Reginald, who is grieving over the recent death of his husband, Sir Alan Guyatt. Reginald is worrying about his claim to stay at Briarbay Hall as the Will of Sir Alan has not yet been found.

With the arrival in her shop of a very attractive, well-known writer, Selene's world begins to tilt alarmingly. Malory and Selene become entangled in a web of secrets and deceptions with the added complication of a rapidly growing attraction.

The Wolf and The Unicorn by Ali Spooner (Erotica)

Ready to explore a steamy, passionate, and tantalizing erotica romance....

Keagan and Celeste have built a solid relationship on trust and independence. A successful surgeon, Keagan understands Celeste's supercharged libido and her desire to experience a variety of sexual encounters. Everything changes when Sky, a new doctor, arrives at the hospital, and Celeste is immediately drawn to the younger woman. Keagan is surprised when she is also attracted to Sky, who shares common interests with Celeste and her. When more than a physical attraction develops, the three women discover a loving relationship beyond the bedroom.

The Blank White Page by Ali Spooner

Tatum Chastain, Corporate Officer of Chastain International, her family's real estate empire, accepts the challenge her father, Charles, has set forth. Charles has tasked Tatum and her brother, Charlie, to survive in the wilderness for six months to prove their skills in taking over the family business once he retires. Charles fails to realize that Tatum would fall in love with the southeastern Alaska cabin he has chosen for her to test her resilience and creativity. Tatum prepares for life in the bush, and shortly after she arrives, Poe, a beautiful raven, becomes her companion and guardian. When River Foster, a designated hunter for her village, crosses Tatum's path, she finds a different kind of love awaits her.

Love Hacks by Annette Mori

Joy Stiles is adrift. Having finally finished her graduate degree at the National Defense University, the only thing keeping her interest is an ongoing feud with a fellow hacker to gain access to sensitive information. Against all odds, the person snuck their way into her tech and kept leaving taunting messages. It's driving Joy crazy. She doesn't have time for this. Operation Elephant Bites isn't working as The Organization thought it would when they started down that path two years ago. Now they have a new worry. Someone is desperately trying to find out more about The Organization, believing they are behind the attacks on the mines. Whoever that person is has not only ties to the Chinese and Russian governments but also members of the US Government. Top secret files at the NSA call their unknown group The Crusaders. Joy's efforts to uncover the identity of the enemy lead The Organization to a lot more than evil plans, and it's up to The Next Generation, with support from senior members of The Organization, to thwart the inevitable trajectory, perhaps with the assistance of Joy's irritating foe.

Affinity
Rainbow Publications

eBooks, Print, Free eBooks

Visit our website for more publications available online.

https://affinityebooks.com/

Published by Affinity Rainbow Publications
A Division of Affinity eBook Press NZ LTD
Canterbury, New Zealand

Registered Company 2517228

www.ingramcontent.com/pod-product-compliance
Lightning Source LLC
Chambersburg PA
CBHW051519260626
47170CB00003B/690